Mark Hurst

# Your Secret

*Can things ever be the same again?*

***Wooded Hill Books Limited***

**www.woodedhillbooks.com**

This is a work of fiction. Names, characters, businesses, places, events, locales, and incidents are either the products of the author's imagination or used in a fictitious manner. Any resemblance to actual persons' living or dead, or actual events is entirely coincidental.

# Prologue

It started out as a bit of fun, but now that I know the truth, there are days when I wish it hadn't started at all.

Secrets are sometimes best left as secrets, never to be told or unearthed. Do I wish this secret had remained buried? Yes. But then…

Before daring to ask the question, a person should appreciate the consequences of the answer; the person needs to first be sure they can live with the answer, whatever it will be, and wherever it will take them.

Benjamin Franklin once famously wrote, "*Three can keep a secret, if two of them are dead,*" which reinforces what I now believe, the fewer who know about it, the easier it will remain a secret, and a secret known to only one person, must go with that person to the grave, to ensure it remains a secret forever.

# 1

## Police Constable Addleshaw

## Wendcaster Canal

It's the first time I've witnessed a body being pulled from a canal. I've already seen a few dead bodies, but generally in town or at roadside accidents. Standing on the small, stone arch bridge, looking down at the body only a few feet below me, the peaceful surroundings are interrupted by the blue flashing lights and people starting to linger around on either side of the cordoned-off towpath below and on the bridge. The deceased, face down in the water, partially covered in water weeds, seems well-nourished and fully dressed in what looks like designer clothes.

I jot down some notes in my pocketbook before crossing the bridge and heading down the side of the bridge abutment to join the water recovery team on the towpath.

In a low enough voice for the officers in the water to hear me but not the public onlookers standing about a hundred or so feet away, I ask, 'What do you reckon, suicide?'

The officer in a police dry suit standing in the waist-deep water looks up to me. 'Nice spot for it but suicide in this depth of water? Nah, it's not the most certain of ways to check out.'

'How do you mean?'

'Look at me; I'm standing on the canal bottom; one would have to be really determined to commit suicide in water that you can quickly stand up in to save yourself. The natural urge to breathe oxygen again would kick in.'

'Good point.'

'We'll bring the body ashore in a second. Just need to check if there is anything around the body that could be of interest to us.'

I nod and continue to watch as the two officers in the water check around and beneath the body. The hands are pale and shrivelled, grey in colour, the energy of life long since departed, slowly bobbing on the small waves created by the officers moving about their business. I notice at least three rings on different fingers; married.

After a few minutes, the two water recovery officers start to pull the body towards the low stone wall lining of the canal side, where two more officers step forward to help lift the body up onto the towpath, placing it down on a rolled-out plastic sheet.

As they turn the body over and lay it face up, it quickly becomes apparent this is no suicide. The deep gash across the right-hand side of the head with discolouration of the skin indicates significant head trauma.

As the lead officer climbs out of the canal using the small temporary ladder, he looks at the body and across at me, 'I doubt this person even drowned; probably already dead before hitting the water.'

Pointing towards the head wound with my pen, 'Could that be an injury from a passing boat?'

'No, I don't think so; I've seen enough to be confident that's not a boat or propeller. Looks like we have a potential murder victim.'

'Ah, OK; I'd best call it in then.'

# 2

## Four Months Earlier

## Kate - The Wedding Vows

‘If there is any person here present who knows of any lawful impediment to this marriage, then they should declare it now.’

Save for a guest coughing to clear their throat at the rear of the room, followed by a gentle titter of humour from the guests and witnesses; no one speaks up. This is a major relief; I thought she would take this opportunity to say something, something to spoil our day, my perfect day. For sure, she has tried all kinds to destabilise us since they split and went through the divorce, but Paul is mine now; he is no longer hers. I do not wish her any malice, but time has moved on, and her time with Paul has slipped backwards to history, relegated to memories past. Paul and I look forward to our time together, creating memories now for our future.

The Registrar looks at us, smiling, and in my excitement, my mind only picks up on certain key sentences. We look at each other, and Paul speaks.

‘I, Paul, take you, Kate, to be my wedded wife. I promise to be loving, faithful and loyal to you for the rest of our lives together.’

And then the Registrar looks to me.

'I, Kate, take you, Paul, to be my wedded husband. I promise to be loving, faithful and loyal to you for the rest of our lives together.'

The Registrar continues, and with what seems like seconds whirling past, the Registrar concludes the ceremony.

'Paul and Kate, you have now both made the declarations required by law and have made a solemn and binding contract with each other in the presence of your witnesses, guests and the registrar of marriages. It, therefore, gives me great pleasure to pronounce you are now husband and wife. Congratulations! Mr and Mrs Hunter, you may now kiss.'

The room erupts with applause as we embrace and kiss. We turn and look at the guests and see the joy on their faces and the warm, celebratory body language of most of them, but there are a couple of exceptions. Paul's son and daughter, both invited to our wedding by their father and attending to please him, are not really joining in with the celebration, with Ruth overtly displeased at our marriage and no doubt, they both blame it all on me. His son, Ben, is only a few months younger than me, and Ruth, his daughter, is just two years younger than me; we are the same generation, and this has brought its own uniqueness to our relationship. They both struggle with me being their new step mum, no doubt a struggle compounded by me being the other woman and me being a good friend of Ruth before I met her father, Paul, my new husband.

Mum walks up to me, all smiles under a large brim ornate hat and hugs me, then kisses Paul on his cheek. Mum likes Paul, and yes, she had her reservations when we started seeing each other, more so when he asked me to marry him, and I said yes, but she really wants the best for me, which is my happiness. Although it is a struggle for them to refer to each other as son-in-law and mother-in-law, seeing as there is just over twelve years difference in their respective ages. Paul is forty-six years old, and I'm twenty-three. Mum and Dad had me later; I was their precious little miracle baby.

Dad struggled with our age difference more than Mum, but he has come to terms with it, especially when he sees how happy I am with Paul and knows full well how successful Paul's business is and how stable our financial future will be together. Gosh, it sounds a little medieval, but I am Daddy's little princess and will always be; he just wants the best for me.

As we leave the wedding room, walking down the aisle between family and friends, followed by my bridesmaids and Paul's Best Man, Graeme, we are wished well from both sides of the makeshift aisle. Soft classical string music is being played by three musicians as we enter the large central hall of the Manor House and turn towards the open doors, out on the terrace overlooking the perfectly manicured lawns at the rear of the property. It's a beautiful day for precious memory photographs outside. My bridesmaids distract me for a few seconds, asking if I'm going to throw my bouquet after the photos, and when I turn back to Paul, I see him and Graeme hugging each other like the wonderful, great friends they are. They separate and shake hands, with Graeme then turning to me, complimenting me on my dress, saying how beautiful I look and how genuinely pleased he is to see Paul so excited for our future together.

Following the photographer's directions, we all pose for photographs, but when it comes to the Groom's family shot, Ben and Ruth are nowhere to be seen, and Paul is turning his head, looking around for them, clearly frustrated. Graeme sees this and walks away in search of them.

I squeeze Paul's hand, lean into him and whisper, 'Paul, it doesn't matter; honestly, it doesn't.'

'It does to me. I am their father, and they should be a part of our day.'

'They are Paul, they're here. We're fortunate they turned up today, given all the ill feeling that has gone on. It's tough for them; leave them be. It's been a big change in their lives, but they made the ceremony; let's accept that.' I lean in and kiss him on the cheek. 'Come on, we have your other family members here.'

'You're right, as always. That is what I love about you: your compassion and generosity. I know I am a very fortunate man to have a woman such as you for my new wife.'

He tips his head and kisses me fully on the lips, followed quickly by one of his uncles commenting, 'Now, Paul, save it for later; I don't want you giving your Aunt Rita here any ideas,' which brings a little laughter and helps diffuse the situation with Paul.

Looking into Paul's eyes and grabbing both his hands, I quietly say, 'Come on, let's enjoy our special day.' Smiling at each other, we turn and head towards the photographer.

# 3

## Lauren – At Home

I'm not happy both Ben and Ruth went to the wedding, and they know it, but Ben made me appreciate the difficult position he and Ruth are in with Paul being their father, who they do love dearly, despite everything that has happened. Even though he has hurt me and the pair of them with his decision to be with her, he is still their father who raised them, cherished them and was always there for them, and hopefully will remain so. I know they are upset as well, but Ben and Ruth have a little more pragmatism in their DNA than me; well, Ben has. I can still hear Ben telling me that life goes on and things change and that we must learn to adapt to this changing journey we're all on.

When I found out about their affair, I was willing to put it behind us, to work at staying together, but he decided he didn't want that, that he didn't want to spend the rest of his life with me and for that, I will never forgive him, or her. I mean, she's young enough to be his bloody daughter, for god's sake. I can't get past this as easily as others, and I don't think I ever will. I've tried counselling, which did help take the edge off my anger, but at times like these, when I'm alone, and they are all together, that overpowering feeling of being abandoned comes flooding back. Discarded. Yes, that's how it feels; I feel discarded, used, and put to one side after over twenty years of married life together. The highs, the lows, the joys and tears, with the four of us bonding in our family unit against the world; that was until she came along.

She. Kate Leyden. She's half his age, one of Ruth's former work friends.

I know it happens; ageing film stars with younger women, powerful businessmen with socialites and models, these hit the news and social media all the time, but I never expected it to happen to us. Paul is none of these; well, I know he is successful in his business ventures, but it hasn't made him a media mogul or business tycoon, and he's far from being a famous actor or rock star.

I should have listened to my friends when they said I should have planned to do something today, to go away somewhere, have a distraction, but I didn't; deep down, I know it wouldn't have changed what was happening today, and I know it would have still preyed on my mind wherever I was and whatever I was doing. I've just got to bear it and try to put it out of my mind, but it keeps coming back to me, like the sun setting before the imminent darkness of nightfall, it just does, and similarly, I can't stop it.

My mobile phone rings and looking at the screen, I see it's Ben calling. I snatch it up and press the answer button, 'Hi Ben, is everything alright? Are you OK? Is Ruth OK?'

'Hi Mum, yes, we're both OK. Stop fussing. I, we, wanted to check in with you, see how you are doing?'

'I'm fine darling, truly I am.' I know I'm not, but I won't push my feelings and anxiety onto my children. 'I presume the wedding is over now, is it?'

'Yes, it's done. What are you up to?'

Bless him, instantly trying to change the subject without the deftness of age and experience. ‘I went shopping this morning, then I’ve been clearing out the spare room, tidying away some stuff, throwing out unwanted things, keeping busy, you know.’

‘Ah, good. Ruth and I are thinking of calling around later to see you. Will you be in this evening? We could bring some food with us, watch a late movie or something?’

He knows I’ll be home, more likely than not, alone, and given I rarely venture out at night anymore since he left. Bless them; their hearts are in the right place; they’re only thinking of me on this ridiculous day, but it does make me feel as though I’m a bit of a charity case or someone who needs to be checked on. ‘No, don’t be silly, I’m fine. Your Aunt Milly is coming over, and I’ve treated us to some lovely Scottish salmon and a bottle of wine. I’m fine, really, I am.’ Why did I just say that? Milly isn’t coming over; I’d better ring her now, as no doubt Ben will mention it to her at some point. I just want to be on my own.

‘Ah, that’s good, say hi from Ruth and me. We’re still OK for lunch tomorrow, the three of us, my treat? Ruth is joining us before heading back south on the train.’

‘Yes, oh good, I’m glad Ruth will be with us; I’ve not seen much of her on this latest trip home. Will you pick me up, or shall I meet you there?’

‘The reservation is for one-thirty. We’ll pick you up at one o’clock if that’s OK?’

‘Yes, that’s fine, I’ll see you then.’

‘Love you, Mum.’

‘Love you too, sweetheart. See you tomorrow,’ and he ends the call.

Of all the things Paul and I did, the one thing we got right was our two children. They're kind, thoughtful and loving. They are both well-balanced, hardworking, and charitable with their time, following different pursuits in their spare time to help different causes that mean something to them. I worried when the news of the affair grew into a decision, a decision that Paul broke to them in private. Through the door, my heart broke when I heard Ruth burst into tears and Ben shouting at Paul, and Paul took it; in the eyes of his children, he knew he was the villain, and he took what was coming to him; he deserved it, of course.

The three of us sat down over the following weeks and discussed Paul's decision, and it was Ben who first started to show signs of coming to terms with it, realising his mum and dad were splitting up and that his dad wanted a different future with a different woman, a new wife. I don't know if it was because Ben, being a male, aligned more readily with Paul in this decision or whether it was Ben's general practicality of life, his philosophical acceptance that we are all adults and there was no real way to change this or return to how things were; still, he did come to terms with it well before Ruth and I did.

Ruth took it badly. At first, Paul wouldn't say who the other woman was, but a few days later, when Ruth heard rumours from her friends, he eventually confirmed She was one of Ruth's work colleagues, and that was an added issue that pushed Ruth into isolation mode, not wanting anything to do with her father and completely taking a side with me against him. It was an ugly time, fraught with angry exchanges and snipe comments; we fired each other up, and poor Ben, stuck in the middle of all this, stayed calm and eventually took on the role of a practical mediator. Ben found a path for us all to get through the divorce sensibly, and he managed to broker a good divorce settlement with Paul, probably after playing the guilt card on his dad, leveraging more emotional tactics than practical legal ones.

I was surprised, though, when Ben convinced Ruth to attend the wedding today. Up until a few days ago, she was dead set against it. I don't know what Ben, and possibly Paul, said to convince her, but even though I could never forgive Paul for what he did to me, I can see the sense in why, in the end, Ruth went to the wedding: after all, She, who's name I cannot utter, is now Ruth's new stepmother; and one day, Ben and Ruth may even have a half-sibling or two. My word, that's a thought; I wonder if Paul has thought about the prospect of starting a family again.

# 4

## Paul – Morning after the Wedding

I should feel like the luckiest man alive this morning. I have a beautiful new wife who loves me dearly, and we're about to set off on our new life together, but the weight and enormity of what evolved before our wedding still bears heavily on me. I didn't want to hurt Lauren; God knows I didn't, but it couldn't be avoided; we wanted different things in life, and time moves on.

We weren't in the best of places or the worst when I met Kate. I suppose I was just in a vulnerable place. Is vulnerable the right word? No, not really; I was in a place where if a certain distraction came along, one which showed me a path to a more rewarding future, then, with my guard lowered, I was going to be more receptive in entertaining it. Again, I'm struggling to find the right way of describing how I was back then. I certainly wasn't actively out there looking for an affair or a new wife; I was, I suppose, at best, confused. I had no one I could talk to who would understand my state of mind. I tried to talk with my best friend Graeme, but he couldn't understand what my problem was or why I wasn't settled. I was married to a beautiful, devoted wife with whom we had two grown, well-adjusted children well on with their respective paths in life; my business ventures were profitable, and we had no money or longer-term security concerns to worry about, so he couldn't understand why I had this in-built feeling that something was missing, that I felt a void. For a few years, I had an inner personal thought in my head that I was missing something, and I couldn't nail what it was in a few words for anyone to appreciate. I struggle now to describe it, but when Kate came along, it was like the proverbial epiphany; there was no longer any void as we were destined to be together.

At first, I thought it was nonsense, the stuff of classic drama: the older man swayed and tempted by an attractive younger woman, whirlwind romance and sex life, drawn in by attention and wanting, both physical and mental, to the extent the siren drew me to my doom. But no, it wasn't a classical marital failure; this was profound love, a serious relationship for the both of us; it was as if we had a past life together and our reincarnated persons had reconnected, and heaven knows, Kate is the better of the two of us; she didn't want anyone to get hurt by this, especially Ruth and Ben; but there was no other way for us to be together, I had to leave Lauren to be with Kate.

I suffered the comments of friends and family at the beginning, 'he's having a mid-life crisis', 'why not just go and buy a sports car instead', all that shit, but they couldn't see what I saw in Kate, her compassion, her love, her utter commitment to our relationship. There is not a spiteful bone or nerve in Kate's body, and if it could have been any other way we would have taken it. I risked it all to be with Kate, and now we are one.

Looking at her sleeping softly beside me, I know our future is set; we are fully together now.

Her eyes open slowly, and she sees me looking at her, 'I love how you do that,' she says softly.

'Do what?'

'Look at me in the morning like it's the first time you've seen me.'

'I can't help it. I fell from the earth toward the heavens the first time I saw you, and I've not stopped falling since.'

She reaches out under the sheets and tickles me, jabbing me a little in the ribs, 'Stop it, don't you go all mushy on me now; the wedding is over, I'm all yours now.'

As I move closer to her, I whisper, 'Ever since we met, I've been mushy on you.' We kiss and hold each other closely.

# 5

## Ruth – Sunday Lunch

‘I don’t care what you think, Ben, it is still wrong; Dad should not have married that woman.’

‘Ruth, not here, not now, OK? Mum will be back any second.’

‘And how do you think Mum took it? I mean, us both going to the wedding and her at home alone, fretting, frustrated, angry; it wouldn’t have been a good day for Mum.’

‘Look, I didn’t enjoy it either, but he is our dad, and he always will be; we have to make some adjustments, some compromises at least, or we’ll all suffer even more in the long run, we’ll lose touch with Dad.’

I sigh deeply and look away from him, towards Mum talking with a friend across the restaurant. ‘Look, it happens, I know, parents get divorced and one, or both, remarry. But she’s practically the same age as me, it’s… it’s disgusting.’

‘No. You cannot think of it like that. She makes Dad happy and…’

‘And Mum miserable,’ I end his sentence for him.

‘Well, she doesn’t look that miserable at the moment.’

I turn back to him, ‘I can’t believe you just said that.’

'Look, I'm sorry, I shouldn't have. I know how upset Mum is with all of this, but life goes on; we must come to terms with things that we can't alter.'

'I shouldn't have let you talk me into going yesterday. When I saw her in her wedding dress at the front, I could have scratched her eyes out!'

'Ruth! Enough! You have to stop thinking like that. We weren't raised as animals in the jungle; we have some decency and respect. Dad knows what this has cost him, us, and most of all, Mum, but he fell out of love with Mum and into love with Kate. It happened. He still loves Mum, but as a friend now, that's what has changed.'

'You know as well as I do Mum won't treat him as a friend. He betrayed her, their vows, and us.'

Ben lifts his glass and takes a long drink, I presume to help him calm down. As he places the glass back down on the table, he nods in Mum's direction, and I see her saying goodbye to her friend and start crossing the restaurant to join us again.

'Mum's coming over, don't bring this up again. OK?'

'What do you take me for? For god's sake, Ben, I'm not a kid.'

Mum pulls out her chair and talks as she sits down. 'Sorry about that. An old friend who had heard about the wedding yesterday wanted to know if I was alright.'

I reply quickly before Ben has a chance to speak, 'And are you, Mum?'

'Yes, I think so, darling, it is what it is. I have to move on; there's no way of changing what's happened. How about you two?'

'I shouldn't have gone yesterday, Mum, I'm sorry.'

Ben tutted as Mum replies to me, 'No, it's fine, dear, truly it is. He is still your father, and I want you to maintain a relationship with him; I do, honestly.'

Ben cuts in, 'Thank you, Mum.'

Mum continues, 'How else better to discover the latest gossip? Now, what do you fancy for dessert? I think I'll have tiramisu.'

'Mother; gossip?' Ben asks.

'You know what I mean. I still have feelings for your father and wouldn't want any harm to come to him.'

'After all that he's done, I can't believe you are letting him off so lightly.' I had to say it; it's not a surprise how I feel about it all.

'Ruth. Please?' Ben says, trying to contain the situation.

Mum takes my hand and holds it with a firm but confident squeeze. 'Try to let it go, Ruth; it'll only eat away at you. Best to put it behind you and move on.'

'Thank you, Mum, that's what I've been saying for some time.'

Mum looks at Ben as she gently raises and lowers my hand just above the table, instilling a gesture of care whilst nodding to Ben. 'Now, are we sharing dessert, or are we being a little piggish and going for one each? The latter, I think,' as she smiles and winks at us both.

Mum gives off a persona of being such a strong character, but I can't help thinking this is all a front, that she is crumbling from the inside out. I think she's like this when Ben is around, playing the neutral card to indicate he did the right thing in maintaining a relationship with Dad and helping sort out the divorce, but I know it to be different.

‘By the way, Aunt Milly sends her love to you both,’ Mum says with a smile as she picks up the dessert menu again.

# 6

## Kate – Ally's Apartment

As Ally opened the door to her apartment, she wasted no time. 'So, how was the honeymoon? Did he manage to entertain you into the evening?'

'As a matter of fact, he did thank you.'

'Oo, so there is life in the old dog then.'

'Ally! That's between me and the old dog, thank you. Are you ready?'

'Ah, one second, before we go, I have a little treat for us; come in,' as she turns and walks towards the living room. 'I'll be with you in one second, make yourself comfy, I'll just pop in here…,' as she ducks into the bathroom, 'I have a little something for us.'

'Oh, intriguing.' I enter her apartment, close the front door and head into the living room, walking up to the open sliding glass doors and out onto the balcony. 'It always gets me this view, it's fabulous.'

'Now. Here we go,' Ally says from behind me.

As she walks into the living room area, she is holding two boxes, offering one out to me. 'I ordered these for the Hen Party, but there was a delay due to short stock availability, and they were only delivered after your wedding. A bit annoying, but then I thought we could do them anyway when you came back from your honeymoon for a bit of a laugh.'

'What are they?'

'DNA testing kits. I've wanted to do one for ages to see where my ancestry lies and where I come from. I thought we could do one together; it'll be a blast.'

'Really? You never mentioned you wanted to know; I'm not so sure if I want to know about my past or not?'

'Oh, come on, a simple little spit test into a tube, post it off, and then they let us know where we come from. A work colleague did one some time ago, and it turns out she is forty-five percent Scandinavian, fifteen percent Irish heritage with the remainder a smattering of northern Britain background, you know, Celtic; she thinks she's the product of Viking raiders or something. The thing is, she had no idea; she thought her family background was mainly from the Preston area, with a bit of Irish and a bit of Scottish. I want something exotic or find out I'm from a title or something.'

'What are you like? I don't think either of us will be from royal blood, do you?'

'We'll never know unless we try it. Here.' Ally hands me a box, and we open them at the same time.

'I wanted to do these with us and the bridesmaids before the wedding so that we had the results to share at your wedding, like a reveal party, and we could have all had a giggle.'

'Well, I must admit, it's an unusual gift from a Chief Bridesmaid. Are you still doing it with the others?'

'No, I cancelled theirs when I knew they wouldn't reach us in time, but I thought we could still do them, if you're up for it, that is?'

'Oh, OK, let's do it, this should be interesting.'

'Yes!'

Ally seems quite keen on this, and it'll be fun to see where my ancestors are from. We have never really talked of our family further back than my great-grandparents; I just assumed most of the information had been lost in time. There was some talk of a family rogue in the late eighteen hundreds on Dad's side, something to do with a business fraud and an insurance claim; I think he ended up spending some time in prison. Mum and Dad will be interested in this and, to be honest, now that I'm thinking about it, I would like to know more about our family. Paul has mentioned it now and again as he watches a television series researching where people are from, usually famous people though, not the likes of us.

We unscrew the lids from our test tubes, spit into the bottles, which is not the politest of samples to do, and then re-fasten the lids tightly. We each complete the information and declarations and seal the packages for return to the testing company.

'Great. I'll send these off; it'll be a few weeks before we get anything back. Now, do you fancy a quick drink here, or do you want to go straight to the wine bar and meet the girls now?'

'We'll head off now if that's alright with you. I don't want to be out too late tonight; after all, I am a happily married woman now,' I say with a cheeky smile and a wink.

'Haha, OK then, I'll just grab my jacket.'

# 7

## Paul – Sunday Breakfast

The lads down at the Cricket Club were up for a full session last night, wanting to sample all the real ales at the annual Beer Festival. I can still match them, drink for drink, but uncharacteristically, I didn't want to. They were happily pulling my leg about my being a newly married man again, with a new younger wife to please, wanting to go home early, being under the thumb again, the usual banter, but it didn't bother me; I just wanted to get home at a decent time and make sure Kate got home safely also. That said, I did manage to sample quite a few beers, and my head is a little thick as a result this morning.

Walking into the kitchen, Kate is at the worktop island preparing breakfast, gently humming along to a tune on the radio. I stop and look at her, admiring her relaxed, happy demeanour and, of course, at how wonderful she looks in her thin, silky nightdress. I know I'm a fortunate man to have such a young and attractive wife who loves me dearly, who was willing to put up with the pressures and aggravation during my divorce from Lauren and stand with me through the pains still to come with Ben and Ruth. Ruth has been particularly hard on the pair of us; on me, I understand, being her dad and all, but more so it seems on Kate, probably for her age and their being friends, and perhaps that it was her that inadvertently brought the two of us together; there is deep buried regret there within Ruth.

I quietly sneak up behind Kate and put my arms around her waist, pulling her in tightly to me. 'Good morning, Mrs Hunter, you know how best to rescue me from a silly hangover.'

'Yes, I do, a full breakfast complete with a little secret hangover cure my dad swears by.' As she spins in my arms to face me, she raises a glass containing a concoction of green juice with bits and puts it to my lips. 'Down the hatch in one go, doctor's orders.'

'Really? No kiss first? Mrs Hunter, you are so cruel.'

'Definitely no kiss with that breath, Mr Hunter. Now open wide.'

I release my hold on Kate and step backwards as the glass in her hand follows me. I over-exaggerate a gulp, and she smiles, 'Honestly, it'll work a treat.'

'Are you trying to convince me or you?' and seeing her raise her eyebrows, 'OK, OK, I'll try it.'

'All down in one, no pausing,' she adds as I take the glass from her.

I take a deep breath and down the contents in one go. As I take the final swallow, something spicy in the bottom of the glass hits me, and I pout my lips, letting out a blow of spice-laden air. 'My word. What the hell was that?'

Placing her hands on her hips and tipping her head to one side, 'Well, if I tell you, it wouldn't be a secret hangover cure, would it?'

With eyes slightly watering from the spice, I suddenly feel brighter. 'Well, it's certainly doing something, something is stirring down there.'

Shaking her index finger at me, she says, 'Ah, ah, stand down. Breakfast is next. Go sit down, and I'll bring it over in a minute,' as she nods toward the table.

'Yes, Miss. Oo, I do like it when you're all dominant with me.'

'Really? We'll see about that later,' she says with a cheeky wink.

As we tuck into our hearty breakfast, I ask about her night with Ally and friends. 'It was nice, really good to catch up after the wedding and honeymoon. It seems our wedding has set off a chain reaction as two of the girls have got engaged to be married; can you believe it?'

'You're kidding, right?

'No, I'm not, and now Ally is getting a little worried that her boyfriend will ask her next.'

'Haha, and if he did, would she say yes?'

'To be honest, I'm not sure.'

I bite into toast with marmalade, and Kate continues, 'Funny thing though, Ally had a couple of DNA testing kits for just the two of us. Apparently, she was going to get the girls to do it at the Hen Party, but the kits didn't arrive in time, so just the two of us did them last night. One of her work colleagues did the test and was surprised by her ancestry roots.'

'Really, so you've done it, the test?'

'Yes, well, the sample, and I'm excited for the results now; they should be with us in a few weeks.'

'Umm, sounds good; it's something I've seen advertised a couple of times and thought of doing myself.'

'Oh, I didn't know you were interested in doing it too; shall I pick up a kit for you?'

'Nah, let's see what your results are like first, see if it's worth the money.'

'OK.'

As I finish my toast, Kate picks up the near-empty cafetière, asking, 'Would you like some fresh coffee, darling?'

'Yes, that'll be great, thanks.'

While Kate makes more coffee, we continue talking about our respective nights out and the latest news with friends. Comparing the news topics and discussion subject matter, it's clear that there is an obvious generational gap between our respective friends; something else we'll need to work at, although I think I'll find it harder to get in tune with Kate's younger friends than Kate will with my older group.

Returning to the kitchen table, Kate drops a little bombshell on me. 'With all this talk of ancestors and family roots, it's raised a question I've wanted to ask: have you thought about the two of us starting a family?'

I expected this conversation to crop up one day, but not so soon after the wedding. I need to tread carefully here as we never really discussed this before the wedding; we should have broached such sensitive topics before we married.

'I hadn't really, have you?'

'I have, a couple of times, but I didn't want to open Pandora's Box in case it became an issue between us.'

'Firstly, never be afraid to ask me anything, no matter how hard or difficult the topic may seem. We need to be open and honest with each other for our marriage to work. Promise?'

'Yes, I promise. I'm not suggesting we start a family now; far from it. I want you all to myself for a bit yet, but I'm conscious you'll be an older father when we start; is that going to be a problem for you?'

Wow, I didn't expect such a heavy topic of discussion this morning. The thing is, I've done it once, the whole family thing, and my children are all grown up, but I knew what I was signing up for with Kate; Kate is a young woman, and naturally, if she wants children then I'll need to step up to the plate once more and become a father again.

'I hadn't really thought about my age,' and with that response, I lied to her for the first time since we've been together, even though I just made her promise to be open and honest.

'You'll have a few years on our baby darling; if we started now, you'll have already walked through the door of sixty before baby turns sixteen.'

'Jeez, when you put it like that, it's quite daunting. If we are thinking of starting a family, it seems like sooner rather than later would be preferable.' I would rather do it younger when I have some energy. The thought of teenagers around the house when I'm in my late fifties and early sixties is scary.

'It feels like we need to find a compromise somewhere; I'm still young and want to travel a bit and enjoy time with you before we have a little one, or ones, to occupy our time.'

'Erm, well, yes.' I don't really know how else to respond right now; this could be more than one child. 'Let's think about it a little more and discuss it when I'm not recovering from a night out with the boys. Is that OK?'

'Yes, that's fine, but let's make sure we talk about it soon.' She leans across the table and plants a long kiss on my lips, one which I am slow to respond to. She pulls back from me.

'Is everything alright?'

'Yes, sorry, I was just thinking over what you said about me being in my sixties; it just, well, it just…'

'Don't worry, I'll still love you when you're old and grey and walking with a cane. Very distinguished you'll be too.'

She blows me a kiss and collects the plates from the table, returning to the kitchen area to load the dishwasher and tidy up. Starting a family again, and soon. What will Ben and Ruth think about having a half-sibling so young? And poor Lauren, how will she take this news?

And how will I handle it? The sleepless nights and illnesses, school runs, sports days and exams, all things from a life already lived and passed. Easy; I'll handle it with all the gusto I can muster. Kate is the woman I want to spend the rest of my life with, and if she wants to start a family, I'm with her, and I'll be fully supportive.

# 8

## Ally – Test Results

Opening the letter, my results are ready to be viewed. I log into my account at NeuvaGen, insert the code reference provided, and click on the origins button. I read through the results, and well, I never expected that! My ethnic origins are thirty-four percent Mediterranean, with a strong bias towards the Italian mainland, thirty percent European, twenty-nine percent to English and Scottish located communities and seven percent Oriental, primarily centring in and around the Hong Kong region. Wow. But now, thinking about it, my dad, my grandfather, and I think at least one of my great-grandfathers were all either Navy or merchant sailors, and some of my female relatives travelled with them; I know my great-grandmother lived in Hong Kong years ago. I've got to phone Kate to tell her my news and find out what her results are.

I dial her mobile number, and she picks up on the third ring and speaks immediately, 'Hi Ally, how are you?'

'Yeh, I'm all good; you?'

'Same. Sorry, I'm just about to go into a meeting. Can I call you back later?'

'Yeah, sure, I just wanted to let you know the test results are back, and I've seen my ancestor origins; it's really amazing.'

'Oh, cool. Did they email you the results?'

'No, I received a letter. You should have received a letter through the post that will give you a log-in reference on their web page. Have a look when you get home later and give me a call. It's exciting stuff.'

'Yes, will do. Sorry, I have to dash; chat later. Love you.'

'Love you too; later.'

I wonder what other information is on here? I click into other areas on the web page and find I can share and search for others with matching DNA, people with DNA results that link to mine, and other relatives. I didn't realise I could do that. Should I? I'm not sure.

Given the sailing background and the old adage that a sailor has a woman in every port, I don't know if I want to know; I could be opening up a real can of worms. My fingers hover over the keys while I mentally flip over the things that I could uncover and what they could mean to my family. The adage 'once you know, you cannot unknow' flashes through my mind, so I decide to wait for now, log out and close my laptop. Something to discuss further with Kate; I'll see what she is going to do when she gets her results before I decide.

Crikey. I could have so many relations out there that I don't even know about.

# 9

## Kate – Test Results

It has taken a week longer for my letter to arrive from the testing company; I'm not sure why, although their web page does say results for samples sent in the same package can be tested at different times, so I suppose it's nothing unusual. Ally told me about her results and inner concerns, given the history of her direct-line male relatives and some of their wives sailing around the world. I must admit, I share her reservations, and I told her I didn't agree to do the test with the intention of finding long-lost relatives or family members; I just wanted to know about my origins. Ally has decided not to click and share her DNA results, and I can see the sense in her decision; all manner of things can evolve from sharing personal information, especially on the internet.

Paul is away on business again in London, staying in the apartment he has in Southwark, and when we spoke earlier, I didn't mention that I had received my results letter. I don't know why; it's not that I purposefully kept it from him; we just chatted about our day and plans for our trip at the weekend.

So, with my laptop open and a glass of wine at hand, I log into the web page, enter my user reference code, and open my results. My origins aren't that revelatory; in fact, the opposite, quite boring really and a bit of a let-down, especially when compared to Ally's results. I sip my wine and top up my glass whilst looking at the DNA share button. Can I click on this to see what matches I may have without sharing my results with the world? Reading through the guide notes, unfortunately not, if I click to review matches, my results are also shared. No, I'm not doing that; Paul sometimes refers to the World Wide Web as the Weird Wild Web; maybe it's a generational thing.

I close the lid of my laptop, wander over to the record turntable on the shelving system, and flick through Paul's album collection. He has a great mix of music genres and styles, and I opt for a collection of love songs, placing the album on the turntable. Turning the volume up a little, I sway to the music as I cross the floor again to recharge my glass. The laptop is sitting there, menacing me to reopen it and look at my DNA results; I turn away from it and carry on gently dancing in rhythm with the track playing, eyes closed, breathing gently, and relaxing.

The words to the next song begin to strike a chord within me as I dance; "if I never asked, I would never have met you, our relationship would never have been". As the track finishes, I turn back to the desk and look at my laptop. The guide article said I can control what level of information I share, so I must be able to lock it down again later. Should I do it? If I do, I won't tell Ally.

Go on, let's do it. The mood and the wine have got the better of me.

I pull out my chair, sit at the desk, open the laptop, and log back into the web page. I re-enter my secure reference number and move the cursor to hover over the share button. I take a long drink of wine and refill my glass, count down from five to zero then click the button.

My mobile phone rings within five seconds of clicking the button, and the screen shows the number is withheld. No! No one can be calling me about this already; besides, I haven't shared my mobile number. I press answer, 'Hello.'

Silence. There is someone there, I can hear light breathing, but they're not speaking. 'Hello? Who is it? Who's calling?'

Still no reply. 'I think you may have dialled the wrong number. Who is this?' The call ends without a word from the caller. That was strange. Placing my mobile back on the desktop, I look back at the screen, and that's when I notice it; I have matches, matches with others, people I share DNA with. What? Really?

Staring at the screen, I can't quite believe what I am looking at; I have two matches, each with a twenty-five percent shared match; what does this mean?

I search within the web page for answers when a ping alerts me to a message against one of the matches, a message from someone called Oscar. Who the hell is Oscar? And as I look at his icon and his waiting message, another message pings in, from the other match, Sarah. What the hell is going on? I slam the lid down without thinking.

What have I started? What have I walked into? Who are Oscar and Sarah?

# 10

## Kate – Late Evening

Reading more of the supporting information on the web page, a match of circa twenty-five percent is highly likely to be a half-sibling. A half-sibling! Wait, so I have two then, two half-siblings. That can't be right. I search deeper into the information provided, and the accuracy percentages stated convince me that the results are correct. This means, out there, somewhere, I have a half-brother and a half-sister. But how can that be?

For this to be correct, either Mum or Dad had two children before they married each other, or Dad could have had an affair with another woman or women whilst married to Mum? My mind is spinning, playing with the scenarios. If it's the former, is Mum or Dad aware that the other had children before they met and if it's the latter, Mum may not even know about Dad's infidelity and him fathering two children with another woman or women. How the hell am I going to find out the truth without letting on that I know and upsetting my family?

I can't believe this. Why did I share my results?

No, it could still be an error; it's got to be.

I can't risk discussing this with Mum or Dad and letting them know some news that one of them may be oblivious to; it could ruin their relationship and nearly thirty-year marriage.

But I can't simply ignore it either. I now have some knowledge, some pieces of a jigsaw that I need to complete. Who are Oscar and Sarah? How do they fit in with my parents and with me?

Looking at the computer screen and the blinking cursor over the message from Oscar, I'll need to click on the message icon to read the content. Will Oscar know I've read his message?

No, I can't do this; I have to bury this information and learn to live with it. I reach for my wine glass and drink the contents, refill my glass, emptying the bottle.

Ironically, I'm now living the dilemma that Ally was worried about and I empathised with.

But I want to know. I need to know. However, these are two complete strangers to me, obviously looking for matches and relatives, maybe to fill in some blanks in their own lives to give them some closure or wider belonging.

It's times like these I wish I had a brother or sister; we could share this information and discuss what to do. I have no one I can speak to about this save for Paul, my new anchor.

I pick up my mobile and call him. As he answers it, I hear him faintly saying, "*Two minutes, just need to take this call*".

'Hi Kate, is everything OK?'

'Hi, yes, I'm sorry, are you out to dinner with colleagues?'

'Don't worry, it's not a problem, they'll be fine. What's up?'

That's when it dawns on me: it's not an emergency or anything; I need to apply some perspective here. 'Oh no, it's nothing. I'm sorry; it's just me being a bit silly. It can wait until you get home.'

'Are you sure? You sound a little flustered.'

'It can wait. It's just a bit of family news, nothing urgent.' I flip the conversation slightly with a change of subject, 'How is work going? Did you manage to sign the deal?'

'Yes, about an hour or so ago. We're just off to celebrate now. We'll have exclusive rights to market the product globally.'

'That's great news, well done, darling. Of course, it's a cause for celebration; go on, join your colleagues.'

'Are you sure it can wait?'

'Yes, absolutely. Enjoy your evening. I love you.'

'I love you too. I'll be back home by late morning on Friday; what do you think about lunch together, say, Vincenzo's? I'll call and reserve a table.'

'That'll be wonderful, thank you. Good night, darling.'

'Good night. I'll see you soon. You must call me if you need me for anything, day or night.'

'I know, thank you. Good night,' and I air blow a kiss to Paul into my mobile, and the line cuts.

Placing my mobile phone down, I lift my glass and take a sip of wine. Dad always tells me not to worry about something until it is something real that I need to worry about, and then focus on it and work it to a solution. He's right, but I do still worry over minor things, things that often don't come to fruition. I'll struggle to sleep tonight, not knowing about these messages from my potential half-siblings; they're preying on me now and I'm not even trying to sleep yet. I need to open them.

Lifting the laptop lid again, I sign in, navigate to the web page again, log in, and move to the message section.

Whose message do I open first, Oscar's or Sarah's?

As it was Oscar who messaged first, I click on his message, and it opens.

"*Hello. We have matching DNA. The match indicates we are potentially half-siblings. Firstly, I apologise if this news comes as a shock to you; it did to me when I first heard from my half-sibling, Sarah. Sarah and I became aware of each other through this process, and we have since met in person and do so regularly now. It is a wonderful thing to find out you're not an only child anymore and that you have a sibling, especially one that has gone through similar experiences to you and can relate to how you feel.*

*Sarah may reach out to you when she becomes aware of the match news. I will drop her a message after this. I would dearly love to meet up with you, and I'm sure Sarah will want the same. You may wish to take some time with this before replying, and of course, we will not put you under any pressure to meet with us; the decision is entirely yours.*

*If you would like to hear more about Sarah and me, this process, or exchange comments, please feel free to do so via this message board, and if you would like to meet up thereafter, we would be pleased to meet with you at a neutral venue near you.*

*Kind regards, Oscar.*"

Wow. Oscar and Sarah already know each other and have met, and from the message, they were not knowingly brother or sister before doing these DNA tests. So, they are from different families of different parents, one of which is common, and who, it seems, is also one of my parents. This is surreal.

I lean back in the chair, staring at the message on my screen. What does this all mean? Has Mum had three children with three different men, two before meeting Dad? Or was it Dad sleeping around?

Sitting up straight again, I close Oscar's message and open Sarah's:

"*Hi, I'm Sarah and we have matching DNA making us half-siblings! This is great news! I know my half-brother, Oscar, has already messaged you and it would be fabulous to meet up and discuss our news and share our stories. Meeting up with Oscar was the best thing to come out of this whole process to date, that is until I found out I have a sister!* ☺

*I hope this was what you were also looking for, and you are equally pleased to have found out you have siblings.*

*Please message back.*

*Love Sarah xx.*"

Sarah's message is more direct than Oscar's, and she clearly wants or expects us to meet up. But this was not what I was looking for; I didn't expect to find out one of my parents is not my biological parent. Shit. I shouldn't have done this test, and I'm now wondering if sharing my match information was a good thing or not.

But now I need to know what this means, how we share DNA, how we fit together. An hour or so ago, it was Mum, Dad and me in our tight family unit; now I have a sister and a brother and, no doubt, aunts and uncles, and possibly wider.

I need to find out what Oscar and Sarah know and see if we can piece all this together before I say something to Mum and Dad if, indeed, I decide to do so. It'll all depend on what I can find out.

I exit the web page and close my laptop. I need to think about this and decide what I'm going to do next. I can try to elicit information via chat messages or actually meet up with them both, the latter being the quickest way to find out what they both know.

But do I really want to know?

# 11

## Alex – The Care Home

I've watched her from a distance, and luckily, so far, I've not had to provide any care for her, as that is the last thing I want to be giving her. She doesn't know me, no one here does, but I know her, and that's why I'm working in this place. I've earned the trust of my work colleagues here at the Home, kept my nose clean for nearly three months, and done whatever tasks they've asked of me, and now I've decided tonight is the night. I managed to pick up a short notice cover for the late-night shift that starts in an hour, so I'll be the last person to see her alive.

Since I submitted my resignation notice two weeks ago, indicating I'm moving back to my hometown as my mother is ill and in need of my support, I've put in a further seven shifts, all quite innocent and regular, and if I do this right, I shouldn't be considered a suspect in her death should anyone think her death is in any way suspicious. But it won't be, I'm sure of that.

She's had this coming to her all my life. Finding her and making her pay for what she did to me has been my primary driver in getting my head sorted out and hunting her down, and when I found out she was still alive, I couldn't wait to get near her. I knew I would find her, eventually, but I had expected her to be dead already, so finding her alive is the first time good fortune has favoured me.

Alex, no, it's not my real name; I'd be stupid to use that; anyway, I'm not that sure I know what my name is these days, what with all the moving about I've done over the years and the different identities I've used.

Still, before she takes her last breath, she will know exactly who I am and why I'm the one ending her life.

She will hear every last sordid detail.

# 12

## Kate – Vincenzo's Trattoria

'Holy shit, you're kidding me, right?' his reply being a little louder than the environment expected.

I notice the woman sitting at the table next to us flash a glance at Paul. 'No, Paul, I'm not. Shh, let's keep it to us though, shall we?' as I nod in her direction.

'Sorry,' his reply as he continues in hushed tones, 'Wow. OK, let's look at this logically; could it be a mistake with the testing or reporting? You know, the results got mixed up or something.'

'No, according to the testing company, they don't make such mistakes; if they did, their whole reputation would be in tatters; their business would collapse, and that kind of mistake would have them facing enormous legal claims. No, they don't make mistakes, so I must take the information at face value.' I know he is looking for anything that could explain this before thinking that Mum or Dad have actually done something secret in their past lives, something that others don't know about.

'OK, then, could these two people claiming to be your half-siblings be hackers or charlatans, looking to scam you somehow?

'Again, I don't see how that could happen. It is the testing company that put us together through matching DNA using unique identity referencing codes; no names are used in the process; a person's identity is strictly controlled and governed. Oscar and Sarah don't know my name yet.'

'Well, so, what do you think? What do you want to do?'

'Looking at this logically, it feels to me like it has to be Dad. I can't see mum having two children with another man and giving them both up before meeting Dad and then not mentioning this to anyone, can you?'

'No, I can't, but… she could have done; it could be your mum, although, on balance, I think it's more likely your dad. The old goat.'

'It's not funny, Paul, this is quite serious.'

'I know, I'm sorry. So, are you going to confront your dad with this?'

'Yes, I think so. But if he admits it and the affairs were after Mum and Dad were married, it'll destroy Mum.'

'Only if you tell her; ignorance is bliss and all that. What she doesn't know won't hurt her.'

I've played with this same conundrum for the last day and a half, but Mum is my closest friend. It wouldn't be right to keep such knowledge from her, for her to continue to live her life in a lie with a man who has done this to her behind her back, and for her daughter to know the truth. I couldn't look at her in the eyes again.

The waiter appears beside our table, 'Linguine Pescatore for the signorina and Tagliatelle Manzo Piccante for the signore,' placing the large dishes in front of us. 'Would you care for parmigiano, signorina, signore?' We both reply in the negative, and he nods, adding, 'Buon appetite,' and leaves.

Paul lifts his fork and starts to twirl his tagliatelle using a spoon as an aide. Without looking up, he continues, 'So, when are you thinking of confronting your dad with this information?'

'Maybe next week. I'm going around to see Mum and Dad for lunch next Wednesday; we were planning on discussing where to go for a few days this coming Christmas. I'll find a spot with Dad on his own and ask him outright.'

'You are a braver person than me; I don't think I could have raised a topic like this with my parents.'

'Maybe that's another generational difference we have?' looking at him as he lifts his loaded fork towards his mouth.

'Yep, maybe it is. And what about your newfound siblings; will you message them back?'

I sigh, and he looks at me as he moves his linguine to his mouth. 'I've not decided yet. They may have some more information to narrow this down, something to indicate whether it is Mum or Dad.'

'And if they don't?'

'Then I'll hedge my bets, approach Dad first, and see how he reacts.'

'Umm,' he replies, now invested in his linguine.

As we eat our pasta dishes, Paul talks of his meetings and the new deal he's struck. I hear him, but I'm not genuinely listening to him; my mind is elsewhere, playing scenarios over and over in my head. I can't stop thinking of what happened, when it happened, what Oscar and Sarah are like, and how this will all turn out.

Paul doesn't seem perturbed by it all; it feels like it is just business as usual for Paul. I don't think he understands the impact this will have on Mum, Dad, and me. I'm their only child, and one of them is not my biological parent. Does either of them know the other has a secret past, that one may have cheated on the other?

Even though this is related to past events, the cheating could still be happening today.

I'm starting to lose my appetite and interest in being here now; the enormity this little, tiny piece of DNA-matched information holds has the potential to ruin everything, to shake the very foundations of our family.

There's a tinging of a wine glass, and I notice Paul gently tapping the side of his glass with his fork, 'Hello? Is there anyone there?'

I look up at him, 'Oh, sorry, I… missed that.'

'I think you missed the last few minutes, darling.'

'Sorry. Yes, I think I did. Sorry, I was lost in this DNA thing.' Shaking my head, I continue, 'What is it?'

'It was about the deal and what it will mean to us.'

'Sorry, darling. I know you've been working on this deal for months, and I'm really pleased you've managed to pull it off, but this family thing is a big deal for me right now.'

'I'm looking forward, Kate, forward to our future. You seemed fixed on looking backwards to things you can't change, but if you rake up the past, it could all blow up on you. Why rock the boat now when things are so good for us?'

'This is different, Paul. This is my family; this is about where I'm from, what lies have been told, and what deceptions have been maintained since I was born.'

'But you have a choice; you don't have to say anything. You can maintain the harmony that exists right now by keeping it to yourself.'

'No, I don't think I can stay quiet about this. I know what I know now, and it'll always be there, gnawing away at me, the unknown, the uncertainty, the deceit.'

'It's best to drop it, darling; honestly, I would if I were you. You love both your parents enormously, and they love each other and you, that's clear. So why throw a hand grenade onto the table and risk destroying that?'

'Because, using your analogy, the pin has already been pulled from the hand grenade.'

'But you haven't released the handle yet. You can return the pin and make it safe, then put the grenade away, lock it up, never to be revisited.'

'But it'll always be there, won't it? The menace in the cupboard, waiting for the day the pin is pulled. The thing is, I'll know; we'll know.'

'Well, I can live with the knowledge locked up in the cupboard; why can't you?'

'Because they're not your parents, are they?'

He nods his head gently, 'True.'

Paul has a different perspective on this, well, on life, generally. I admit that this is one of his more redeeming features: his ability to look forward and compartmentalise the past. His past life with Lauren, the divorce, and his past business ventures that failed, he always bounces back with a positive attitude to going forward. Maybe he's right; lock it away in a cupboard and move on. Life is short, I suppose, and no one needs the added complications of revisiting a past indiscretion.

*Or do they?*

# 13

## Paul – Home

In the taxi home, I can sense Kate is still dwelling on this news and what she should do next. Honestly, I think it's best buried and forgotten about; nothing good comes from raking up the past, well, not in my experience. We have our future to think of and plan for, and now, with this deal in the bag, we both need to remain committed to it for the next couple of years before I can package it up and sell it on to reap the real reward.

I reach across the back seat, searching for Kate's hand, and she places her gloved hand in mine. I squeeze tightly and then release the pressure, but maintain a hold; I want her to know I'm here for her and that we are one.

Entering the house, no sooner had I closed the front door and Kate had deactivated the house alarm, she restarts the conversation, before I have had opportunity to remove my coat.

'I've decided; I'll message Oscar and Sarah to see what they know and if they can tell me anything.'

'Why?' as I'm kicking off my shoes.

'It could be Mum; she could have been in a bad place and had to give up two children for some reason, something deep and personal. If it is, I should consider the impact it would have on her and then on Dad, assuming he doesn't know.'

I look at her as she peels off her long coat, 'And, if it's your father?'

'Well, I'll need to keep my mind open to what may have happened.'

'What do you mean?' I note the confused expression on her face; her mind must be running all kinds of permutations, wondering which outcome it could possibly be and then what effect airing the information could have.

'Well, like, does Dad know about Oscar and Sarah? Was it before he met Mum? Was he playing the wild young man about town, stupidly not knowing the effects his promiscuity could have had? I don't know, but I suppose there could be an innocent side to all of this.'

'And this is why I think it's best left alone. What good can come from this?'

Without responding, Kate slips her shoes off and walks along the hall into the kitchen. By the time I join her, she has poured two glasses of wine and offers one to me.

'That I have a brother and a sister.'

'Sorry?'

'The good that could come from this. You probably won't appreciate this, but being an only child can be quite lonely at times. Growing up, I often thought I'd like a brother or sister, someone to share toys with, play with, chat with, you know, someone on my wavelength as a youngster. I still miss that special sibling relationship, someone I can share things with, to call up and chat about things.'

'But you have me now.'

She's looking at me with her head tipped to one side, 'I said you wouldn't appreciate this. You had your brother with you, and, not to state the obvious, you are a generation older than me.'

'Oo, that hurts,' as I wink at her. 'Now, don't think having a sibling made it wonderful; James and I often squabbled and fought.'

'Yes, but look at you now; you're as thick as thieves, inseparable.'

'Well, maybe that's because we don't live in the same house anymore and only see each other a couple of times a month.'

'But you still have him, and chat with him on the phone and exchange messages. I have no one besides Mum and Dad in my family.'

I suppose I can see why she wants to explore the possibility of a sibling relationship with Oscar and Sarah, but then again, she doesn't know them at all; they could be axe murdering psychopaths for all she knows at this time, and who would want to open the door to that? Should I say this to her, or will it make me look cold again? No, I need to support Kate in whatever course she decides to take, although, to me, it just feels like it could be fraught with all kinds of problems and issues.

'Look, I'll support whatever you decide to do. You know I love your parents; they have supported us when others were sceptical and doubting; well maybe not initially, but they certainly are now.'

'Thank you. I'll sleep on it and decide in the morning.'

'Probably for the best. I'd take your time with it and make sure you've considered all the options before potentially upsetting your mum and dad.'

'I don't want to upset either of them, that's the problem.'

'Then, as I said earlier, the solution is to do nothing.' As I say this, Kate expresses a little grimace across her face; she's not happy at doing nothing. 'Whatever you decide, darling, I'll be with you and support you.'

She places her glass down, walks up to me, putting her arms around my shoulders, and kisses me. 'Thank you. I know you'll always be there for me whatever happens.'

'Without hesitation,' and I kiss her back.

# 14

## Kate – Home

We talked off and on about this all yesterday, and by the time we made it to bed, I still hadn't fully decided what to do. Paul left early this morning, heading to London to meet with his investors to help mobilise his deal. Inaction isn't a position for me; I need to do something with this information, and lying in bed here, looking at the ceiling, I make my decision. Determined to start the ball rolling, I jump out of bed and take a refreshing shower.

*Today, I'll kickstart my own private investigation.*

Sitting at the desk in our study, I open my laptop and log into the NeuvaGen's web page. Navigating the pages, I revisit the messages from Oscar and Sarah and notice another recent message from Sarah, and I click on it.

*"Hi, it's Sarah again. I just wanted to say I am sorry if I spooked you a little with my message the other day. I met up with Oscar over the weekend, and we had a good chat about you and how this may have come as a shock. I've always known my past, but Oscar didn't know his, and he explained how he felt when I first contacted him out of the blue.*

*I hope you decide to contact us and we can meet up. Oscar and I have information to share which we think you will be interested in.*

*I think it is fabulous that I now have a sister as well. We will answer any question you ask as best we can. Thinking of you,*

*Sarah.*"

OK, so both Oscar and Sarah have discussed me, their anonymous match, and they are still interested in communicating further. Oscar was like me; he didn't know about his past, so he at least will appreciate my hesitancy. Well, here goes; addressing my return message to them both, I start to type:

"*Dear Oscar and Sarah,*

*Thank you for reaching out to me following our matched information. I cannot believe I have half-siblings; news I was not expecting. I only did the DNA sample for fun with a friend to learn more about our origins and distant family roots.*

*To find out I have two half-siblings was a shock. At first, I thought it was a mistake, but after reading about the protocols and procedures used by the testing house, I now know this information cannot be a mistake or falsified.*

*So, hello, brother and sister. My name is Kate.*

*It has taken me a few days to absorb this news, and I apologise for my delay in replying to you.*

*I presume you both live in the UK, although I accept that is merely a wild assumption by me; I realise you could be anywhere in the world. I am still deciding if we should meet or exchange further personal details; I am still coming to terms with this information. I hope you understand and appreciate I am on a path I didn't contemplate even existed for me.*

*Kind regards, Kate.*"

Umm, "*kind regards*", it's like we already know each other, maybe just "*regards*" or leave it blank with just "Kate"; then again, it doesn't matter really. I re-read my message and hover the cursor over the send icon. My sending a reply will indicate my intentions to start the ball rolling, but I deliberate over this again, unsure. I wander off, pour a cup of coffee, return, decide to go into proactive mode, hit enter and the message posts. It's done now; there's no turning back now.

Sipping my coffee, I keep looking at the screen, anticipating a quick reply, and when it doesn't appear, I start to get a little anxious. But the reality is, they may both be at work or doing something else entirely different; for them, whilst it is news, it isn't the shocking news as it was for me, the only child of Julia and Duncan Leyden, Mum and Dad.

*Which one of them is it, Mum, or Dad? Who holds the family secret?*

My laptop pings to a new message, and I see it's from Oscar. I eagerly move to the message and open it.

"*Hi Kate, it's great to chat with you virtually. I presume you have read the message from Sarah. I, too, did not know who my biological father was, and it was a shock when I read the results from my test.*"

So, it's Dad! I thought it would be, but I still can't believe it:

*"It was Sarah who clarified the situation for me, and it was a little wilder than I imagined, so I know what you are going through. We would prefer to meet to share and explain what we know so far, and it's possible you will bring more to our journey. Yes, we both live in the UK; I'm in Oxford, and Sarah lives in Bristol. We are happy to travel to you, and now there am I, also assuming you live in the UK too... do you?*

*We are both free this coming weekend, so if you want to meet on, say, Saturday, we'll let you decide where and when and we'll happily see you there. It will be great to meet you; both Sarah and I are excited to have a new sister, and there is so much we need to catch up on.*

*Regards, Oscar."*

They want to meet up this weekend; argh, that's a little quicker than I expected. Subconsciously I am biting my thumbnail, and when I realise it, I pull my hand away quickly from my mouth; I haven't done that since I was a child. So, it's Dad. It seems Oscar and Sarah know more and are willing to share it with me; no doubt, they'll want to know where I fit in and more of my story.

But I can't wait until Saturday; I can't be around Dad now without saying something. I will have to ask him on Wednesday.

# 15

## Kate – Mum and Dad's House

As I pull into the driveway, Mum is standing in the front bay window, waiting for me. Whenever I arrange to visit, Mum is always waiting for me. God alone knows how many hours she has spent standing, waiting in that bay window over the years. Mum would do the same every afternoon when I returned home from school, opening the front door with open arms to offer a big hug and "How was your day, sweetheart? Fill me in; I have treats in the kitchen."

I am clearly cherished by my mother, at times to the point of suffocation, metaphorically, and I had to say something to her when I went to college as it was a little embarrassing when I would return home with a friend.

As I step out of my car, the front door is already open, and Mum rushes to greet me with arms outstretched, anticipating a big hug.

'Duncan! Kate is here!' Mum calls out, over her shoulder, to my invisible Dad, who almost instantaneously appears from around the side of the house.

'Hello Kate, how was the drive?' Dad is his usual formal self.

'It was fine, Dad, no problems.'

'Jolly good. Mother's been busy preparing lunch, as you'd expect; I hope you're hungry?' smiling as he removes his gardening gloves.

'Yes, I am, actually; I skipped breakfast as I know what Mum is like.'

'Kate, I'm just so pleased to see you; it brightens my day cooking for you. Now come on in and bring us up to date with the latest news.'

If only I could, I think to myself. 'I will, Mum, go ahead; I just want a quick word with Dad on something.'

'Oh, yes, of course, dear; now don't be long, you two.'

'We won't.' I turn to Dad.

'This sounds a little ominous, Kate; is everything alright?'

'I'm not too sure, Dad. I need a one-to-one chat with you after lunch when Mum is clearing up.'

'Now, this does sound ominous; of course, we can. I'll tell Mother we have some bits to sort out with hotel bookings; she'll be more than happy to clear up in the kitchen and avoid this kind of detail. This is the first time you've asked for a chat like this, is it serious?'

'Yes, I think it is.'

'Ahh, OK. We'll have some time on our own then in my den. Now, let's go and devour this magnificent lunch Mother has prepared, shall we?'

Dad was right, the spread that Mum had put out would do for a small wedding party. My favourite sandwiches, perfectly quartered into triangles, with homemade relishes and savoury bites to accompany, and small freshly baked cakes to follow.

'Thank you, Mum, it looks delicious as always.'

'Anytime dear, anytime. How is Paul? I presume he is busy at work; we don't see much of him these days.'

'Yes, it's the same with me; I'm not seeing much of him at the moment either. He is working very hard, and with this new deal he has agreed, he'll no doubt be swamped for the rest of the year. He sends his love to you both.'

'So nice of him. I'll pack him some of my cakes for you to take back.'

As I bite into one of my sandwiches, Dad speaks up, 'Mother, Kate, and I need to check out some hotel and travel arrangements after lunch; we'll disappear into my den so we're not boring you; I'll need my computer to look up the details.'

'Oh, right. Yes, of course, not a problem. I'll tidy up when we finish here, and then maybe we can go for a little walk afterwards?'

'Just the ticket,' Dad replies. 'Now, let's have one of these homemade Scotch Eggs; wonderful they are, just wonderful.'

We talk of general matters over lunch, the latest goings on in the village, Dad's latest ailment, his new lawnmower, Mum's book club and the latest reads, but all the time, I'm internally distracted by what I'm about to ask Dad. It's difficult to exchange pleasantries with a person who, in a few minutes, I may come to despise and with another that I'm about to shatter her perfect world. Perhaps Paul was right; maybe I shouldn't say anything.

As we finish up, Mum is already up on her feet tidying away the remnants of lunch, when Dad speaks, 'OK then princess, shall we go and check out these details?' as he winks at me.

'Er, yes. Are you OK with this, Mum? I hate leaving you to tidy up on your own,' which I realise was me feebly attempting to delay what I'd already started.

Looking at me, totally oblivious to any pending storm, Mum smiles and replies, 'Of course, darling. Run along with Dad and sort out what needs to be done.'

Dad is already leaving the dining room and heading towards his den, the small room at the rear of the house overlooking the garden, his man cave, as Paul refers to it.

I follow him in and close the door behind us. Dad sits in his desk chair and rotates it to face me as I sit on the two-seater leather settee against the opposite wall, 'Now, dear, what is it you want to talk about? Is it something serious for our ears only?'

I look at him, then out through the patio door to the garden. Now that I'm here and have the perfect opportunity to ask him, I'm struggling to find the words to begin.

Dad breaks my hesitant pause, 'Is it Paul?' he asks.

'No. No, it's not Paul, it's about me.'

'Oh my, you're OK, aren't you? There's nothing for us to worry about, is there?'

'Dad,' pausing again, turning to look at him, 'I've recently done a DNA test, and the results seem to indicate you may not be my biological father. Can this be correct?' He visibly turns white in front of me, as though all his energy and drive are being sucked from his very bones. He swallows hard a couple of times and takes in a slow, deep breath, gripping the arms of his chair tightly.

'Oh, I see.' Now he pauses, looking down into his lap; it's as though he has been found out and is unsure of his next comment. Without looking up, he continues, 'Why would you do a DNA test and not say anything to Mum and me?'

'Well, firstly, I didn't think I needed to tell you and secondly, I only did it for fun, to find out about our likely ancestor origins. I certainly did not have any reason to suspect anything else that would give me reason to check my parentage.'

Now he looks at me with a very sombre expression, gently asking, 'So, what do you know?'

It hits me how calm he is and how he is not denying anything. 'That one of my parents is not my biological parent and that I have half siblings out there. And,' swallowing hard, 'I think it may be you.'

'Oh. I see.' He sits back in his chair and continues, 'I said you should have been told years ago, that you had a right to know.'

That surprises me a little, 'Oh my God, it's not Mum, is it?'

'No darling, it's not Mum, it is me. It's all my fault, but I need to bring Mum in on this now.' Placing his arms firmly on the chair armrests, he pushes himself up, rising from his favourite battered chair.

'Wow, wait, Dad, don't bring Mum in just yet, this news would break her in two.'

'No darling, it won't; trust me.' He opens the door and calls to Mum, 'Julia, can you come and join us, please?'

I hear Mum reply but can't make out the words. Dad returns, leaving the door open, and sits again in his chair. Within a few seconds, Mum walks in, drying her hands on a tea towel.

'Is everything alright?'

Dad replies, 'Come in love, take a seat. That day we've talked about so many times has arrived. Kate knows I am not her biological father.'

I see the smile fall instantly from Mum's face, 'Oh, I see. Oh my.' She steps into the room, closing the door behind her. I'm not sure why she closes it; no one else is in the house, and it feels like Mum wishes this information to remain a strict secret. She quietly walks towards me and sits down beside me on the settee.

# 16

## Duncan – In My Den

It's that day. There was always the chance that it would come one day, that Kate would find out, but we both hoped it would never arrive. I wanted to control Kate's finding out by letting her know when she turned thirteen, but Julia didn't want to hurt her. Kate always saw me as her father, loved me as her dad, and I her as my daughter.

I look at Julia to tell her that day has arrived. Her reply is short, 'Oh, I see. Oh my,' so very Julia. Deep down, she knew this day could come and if, or when, it did, that we would need to explain everything to Kate. A long time ago, we agreed on what we would tell her if she became aware I was not her biological father.

Julia sits on the settee beside Kate and takes hold of her left hand in both hers, twisting to look at Kate.

'Mum?' Kate asks, almost in a pleading gesture, concerned that Mum already knows this information. 'Mum? You knew?'

'Kate, darling. Now, whatever happens, Dad is, and always has been your dad, your father. He loves you dearly. Know this is without question.' She looks across to me, and I feel her love and a newfound strength; we nod gently to each other, and I silently mouth 'I love you' to her. Kate's eyes are locked on her mum.

'Mum?'

Mum turns back to Kate. 'After we married, we tried to conceive for many years, all to no avail; we were just unable to get pregnant. After trying for a long time, Dad and I visited the doctor and then a specialist and, in the end, we found out we were unable to have children.'

I chip in at this point as I want Kate to know it wasn't her mum's fault and all this was a shared decision, 'It's me, Kate; I am infertile, my sperm count is practically zero.'

'Er, oh,' is all Kate can say.

I continue, hoping to take some of the pressure off Julia, 'When we became aware what the issue was, and how much Mum and I wanted to have a baby to cherish and raise, we asked what options were open to us. Back then, artificial insemination was not regulated, but it was legal, and a few specialised clinics were practising in this field in the UK. We contacted one, and they helped us get pregnant with you.'

The realisation of what I said dawns on Kate. She looks at her mum, and Julia nods slowly to her. They are locked in a mother-daughter exchange that needs no words. Julia then releases Kate's hand and opens her arms to embrace Kate, but Kate does not move. She sits motionless, breathing slowly but deeply. I can't decide whether it is anger or confusion or that she is just stunned by the enormity of what she has just heard.

'Kate,' Julia said to her, clearly wanting Kate to move into her embrace. But Kate does not move to her mum; she turns to me and quite coldly directs her question to me.

'So, if you are not my biological father, then who is?'

The question cuts into me deeply; I didn't expect her reaction to be like this. I thought it would probably be one of anger for what she would see as a betrayal or a deception, or she would go the other way, with an outpouring of love towards her mum, but this simple yet coldly delivered question hits me.

'I… I…' stuttering, thinking of what to say next.

Julia steps in, 'We don't know his name; it was all done anonymously.'

'What?'

Julia continues, 'The donors were all anonymous; no names or anything to identify the donors was exchanged. We know he was a young, bright medical student in his final year at college and that he was fit and healthy and from a good family background.'

'Really? That's it? So, you know next to nothing of my biological father.'

Kate's tone is changing, and I quickly interrupt to support Julia. 'That is how it works, Kate darling. The donors would not donate if there was a chance that their identity could become known. These kind young men donated for altruistic reasons, and naturally, a medical student would see the benefit his donation could make to a couple struggling to conceive a child. The problem was with me; it's all me, Kate, not Mum; please don't hold it against Mum.'

'Duncan, please, we decided together,' Julia interjected.

'I know we did, but Kate needs to appreciate the predicament I put you in. It was the only option open to us.'

Silence falls between us, and I shift my eyes between the two of them, quietly hoping they will embrace. After a couple of minutes, Kate stands and walks to the patio door and looks outside, standing still, staring into the distance. Julia and I both look at her; she is clearly hurting, as are we. I look at Julia, and just as I open my mouth to break the silence, Kate, without turning around, speaks.

'Why didn't you tell me?'

Julia replies before me, 'Dad wanted to, but I convinced him not to.'

'Why, Mum? Why keep it a secret?'

'It wasn't a secret, darling; we simply kept it to ourselves. We chose not to say anything to anyone at the time, and then, when you came along and we were blessed, it never came up in conversation. Our friends and family were over the moon for us, as were we, and we wanted it to stay like that. Dad wanted to tell you when you could appreciate the predicament we were in, but I stopped him.'

'Why, Mum?'

'I could see how much Dad loved you, and you loved him. I didn't want to risk anything that could harm that.'

'Really?' still looking out of the window.

I chip in, 'Come on, Kate, dear, the situation never arose when we needed to tell you.'

'Needed to tell me? So, if I hadn't found out, you wouldn't have told me? When would the need to tell me arise? If I fell ill or something and needed a transplant?'

Julia's tone switches to pleading, 'Oh, please, Kate, darling, please don't be angry with us. We, I, thought it was for the best.'

I can see Julia getting upset now, and no doubt she'll be worrying about how this will affect their relationship and our relationship with Kate. 'We love you dearly, Kate; nothing can take that away. I will always be your father.'

Her look at me is cold, almost like she is looking straight through me; I have never seen that in her before.

'What was the name of the clinic?'

This was another question I didn't expect but feel I need to challenge, 'Why, what possible difference would that make?'

'So I know it was a proper clinic, and this was all done correctly.'

'What? What are you talking about? We just said it was.' I'm not sure why she is questioning this.

'At the moment, I only know what you have told me. It could have been Mum who had an affair or…'

'Kate! Please! Stop it!' Julia shouts out.

I stand without thinking, squaring up to Kate, a reactive action to anyone who hurts my Julia. 'I can't believe you just said that, Kate. Apologise to your mother right now.'

'I think if there are to be any apologies, they should be coming in my direction. I'm not the one who has sat on a secret for some twenty-three, no twenty-four years, only to find out by accident that I am the product of a different man from the one I thought was my father.'

Julia starts to cry, pulling her hands to her face.

'Now look what you've done. We all need to calm down and talk this through. This affects the three of us and…' but I don't finish before Kate cuts me off.

'No, Dad, no; it affects more than the three of us.'

'I'm pretty sure it won't have much effect on Paul.'

'I'm not thinking of Paul… I'm thinking of my half-siblings.'

'What?' Julia's sobs start to slow as she removes her hands and looks up at Kate, tears clear on her cheeks, 'What on earth are you talking about? What half-siblings?

'I have half-siblings; two at least that I know of. I am no longer an only child.'

Julia turns her head sharply to me. Shit! Of course. We never thought of that situation arising.

# 17

## Kate – In Dad's Den

From the expression on Dad's face, he never contemplated the possibility of my donor being the donor to other women, that my biological father could be the father to other children in different relationships.

I turn to look at Mum and see the surprise on her face, too. Did the clinic never discuss this possibility with them? Surely, they must have.

Whilst I didn't anticipate this being the reason I have two half-siblings, it does explain everything quite neatly; why I didn't have a sister or brother growing up, why Mum and Dad doted on my every wish, why they were both a bit older than the other mums and dads when I was at school. And now I know Dad didn't cheat on Mum and that Mum was in on this knowledge from day one.

I can see that my reactions have hurt them, but they have hurt me, not trusting me with this information earlier.

Dad drops back down into his chair, mumbling, 'Half siblings, ahh'.

Mum speaks, 'Oh my, darling, you have siblings?'

'Yes.'

'How do you know? What happened?'

I decide to sit down next to Mum and look at her, trying to repair some of the damage I've just caused. 'Look, Mum, I'm sorry. I've had this information for some time now, and I have been thinking of all kinds of scenarios, but I never thought you needed a sperm donation.'

Mum nods gently, dabbing the corner of her eyes with the tea towel she brought in with her.

I glance a look over at Dad, and he looks dejected, almost lost.

Mum retakes a hold of my hand. 'I'm sorry, darling, we should have told you and before now. You are right; you had a right to know.'

'Yes, I think I did. But… I'm not sure how I would have handled it; hearing this news at any time will be a big shock to any child.'

'You are right, sweetheart; I am so sorry.'

'The Letona Pro Clinic, in London.' Dad says in a deadpan voice.

I look across again to Dad, 'Sorry?'

'The name of the clinic. The Letona Pro Clinic. The specialist was called Doctor Stevens.'

'Oh, right. Thank you.' My questioning is quite matter of fact at the moment, quite cold; I am aware of that. 'Do you know if it's still there?'

'I've no idea. We lost touch with them after you were born, but it shouldn't be hard to find out. Why, what difference will this make?'

I have my reasons for wanting this information, but I don't want to tell Dad what they are, well, not yet. 'I want to be sure a proper clinic was used.'

'Ah, right, yes, it was the best available back then; it came highly recommended. Mum and I discussed it a lot. It was a big step to take, and we decided to go ahead;

we both desperately wanted a child, and this was the only way your mum could be a mother, to carry a child herself and give birth.'

I turn to Mum and see she is on the verge of tears again. I lean forward and throw my arms around her, and we embrace, both of us crying quietly.

Dad stands up, 'I'll make some tea, shall I?' but leaves the room before either of us replies.

Mum pulls back slightly, extracting a small handkerchief from her apron pocket and dabs at her eyes again. 'You'll have to forgive him, darling; he'll be lost now; this is a big hurdle for Dad. He had his manhood dented heavily back then, but he rose above it and embraced you as his own from the moment you were in his arms, he even cried. I loved him immensely for it, and still do; he gave me the opportunity to experience motherhood and have my own baby. He is a strong and capable man; I don't know what I would do without him.'

'Oh, Mum.' We hug again, the embrace only a mother and daughter can have.

'And,' Mum says as she breaks our embrace, looking directly at me, 'He'll make a fabulous grandfather; he will, I promise.'

'I know, Mum, I know he will.'

'He really did want to tell you years ago; it was me that talked him out of it; I was worried you would reject him when you found out.'

I sigh deeply, contemplating how I may have reacted back then; maybe Mum has a point, I might have rebelled, rejected him. To be honest, I don't know what I would have done.

'There was never really going to be a good time or way to broach this subject, Mum. I would like to think I wouldn't have held it against Dad.'

'Will you forgive us? We did what we thought was best.'

'Of course, Mum. I love you both dearly, and if I could love Dad more after what he did for you and for me, then I do so today. I'm sorry I was abrupt; I didn't anticipate this outcome; it caught me off guard a little.'

Sitting up a little straighter, Mum gently pats my thigh while softly clearing her throat, 'Now, darling, tell me all about your half-siblings and how all this came about.'

# 18

## Kate – At Home

The long drive home gave me plenty of time to think about the conversations this afternoon. By the time I left Mum and Dad's house, we had cleared the air, and, to be fair, I think I am now closer to both of them than I have ever been before. It must have weighed heavily on them that one random day, I could walk in and ask them outright, or that they would have to tell me that Dad could not provide me with a blood transfusion or be considered for organ donation if I needed one. Mum and Dad both said they are relieved this is now out in the open, that I know of my background and their problems to conceive, and how they made a brave decision to use artificial insemination.

Were they hoping to never tell me? I don't know. I suppose telling me after the wedding would have made sense, at a point of significant change in my life, a new start and all that, but they didn't. Anyway, it's known now, and I need to decide what to do next.

I now have a brother and a sister to consider.

After such a filling lunch, I won't need much for supper, and settle for avocado on toasted sourdough bread, accompanied with a glass of light sparkling wine.

Paul messaged earlier and said he would call me about nine o'clock; he'll be wanting an update on how today went and, no doubt, what I'm planning to do next. I know he travels a bit with work, but I didn't expect it to be as often as this. The deal requires his attention and time, I get that, but we are newlyweds, and there is video calling and email available to him to stay in touch; I'll have to mention this next time we are together.

While waiting for Paul to call, I lift my feet onto the settee and get cosy. Opening my laptop, I look to see if any more messages have arrived from Oscar or Sarah, but there's nothing new. As I mull over the day's events and stare at the computer screen, I realise there could be other half-siblings out there. If our donor is common to the three of us and we're all from different families, then conceivably, there could be more half-siblings yet to announce themselves. I flick through some of the social messaging from satisfied participants and read one, which is an eye-opener; finding out he has thirteen half-siblings! Wow! As I read more into these messages, some of the half-siblings want to find out the identity of their biological father, but others don't; the reasons provided are mixed, and I can appreciate the various positions for wanting and not wanting to know him.

It's natural, I suppose, to want to know the identity of your father, but my first thoughts, weirdly, are for the donor, not the child. He donated for his reasons and was promised total anonymity; imagine what it would be like to find out some twenty or thirty years later that you are the father of, say, six or ten or twenty children and they want a relationship with you. Poor man. Did he ever consider that could happen? I guess not.

Do I want to know my biological father's identity? I don't know.

My mobile phone rings; it's Paul. 'Hi, darling, how is the trip going?'

'Hi, Kate. OK, I suppose. It would be far better if you were with me, though; I have the night to myself now.'

'I don't think it'll be very exciting for me, hanging around the apartment, with some sightseeing and some shopping thrown in.'

'I thought you liked doing all that?'

'Um, now you come to mention, maybe I should come down to London on a spa and shopping week, all on your business account, the next time you travel.'

'Ah, well, then again, maybe…'

I laugh, and Paul joins me.

'So, how did it go today with your dad?'

'Well, it wasn't what I was expecting. Dad admitted he isn't my biological father,' and as I say it, it feels strange to say it out loud to another person, almost clinical.

'Oh right, well, that's what you thought, isn't it? Are you OK with that?'

'I wasn't, but I didn't know the background, and after we talked it through, I think I love Dad more than before if ever I could.'

'Really? Wow, what happened?'

'Mum knew everything…' and I fill Paul in with the information I had gleaned.

'Bloody hell! Well, that's good then, I suppose. It's better than you expected, isn't it?'

'Yes, it is, especially after considering all the scenarios that were running through my head. The service provided by the clinic cemented and reinforced the love between Mum and Dad and gave the three of us a future together.'

'That's wonderful, darling, I'm glad it turned out like this. I presume you are all on good terms now?'

'Yes, absolutely.'

'And what… what was the name of the clinic again?'

'I don't think I mentioned it; why do you ask?' my curiosity piqued. Given everything else I've just told him, it's an unusual bit of detail for Paul to ask for.

'Oh, er, well… yeh, there's this chap I was talking to, he and his wife are struggling to conceive a baby, I just thought maybe this clinic could help them, you know.'

'I doubt it; I bet it closed years ago.'

'Still, it's worth a shot… what was it called?'

'The Letona something clinic, Plus or Pro, I think.'

'Oh… right.'

'Why, have you heard of it?'

'Er, no. No, I haven't.'

'I didn't expect you to have. I'll get the full name and address if you want from Dad and send it to you if you like?'

'Er, no, it's fine, honest, it's OK. I'm sure he'll have a clinic in mind. Look, I'll have to dash now; I just remembered I arranged to meet one of the investors in a local wine bar for a nightcap; you know how it is.'

'Oh, right, yes, of course, no problem. Chat tomorrow?'

'Yep, yep, let's chat tomorrow. Got to run.'

'I love you. Paul.'

'Er yeh, you too, see you later,' and the line goes dead.

That was weird; first, he's free for the rest of the night, then he's off for a drink with an investor; that's something that's not easily forgotten. I think the pressure of this deal is getting to him; he's getting forgetful.

With my laptop still open, I pick it up again and place it on the arm of the settee, then type "weekend luxury spa breaks in the Cotswolds" into the search engine and start to scroll through the many hits; a lovely weekend away together, just the two of us, will help him relax.

# 19

## Paul – Apartment, London

I can't believe it.

The Letona Pro Clinic, just off Harley Street.

When she said The Letona, I didn't need any more information, it hit me like a sledgehammer in the side of the head. Of course, I know it or knew it; it's where a man could go, deposit a sample for cash, and remain anonymous. I must have been there, I don't know, a dozen or so times in the four months I was in London back in the late nineties.

Plenty guys were doing it back then. I was on a pittance of a pay packet, and every extra penny helped, especially when needing accommodation and living in London; there was so much to do, the nightlife, the girls, the parties. I was interviewed by Dr Stevens at The Letona, and obviously provided him with the answers he wanted; after that, he was happy for me to make weekly deposits for cash. In fact, I made deposits at two other clinics when I was in London; all three clinics committed to absolute anonymity. I had to prove who I was, and the clinics ran some tests first to make sure I was healthy, no infections in any way, particularly anything sexually transmitted.

It's hard to comprehend that Kate's parents visited the same clinic around the same time as me.

Shit! The same time as me! No!

That could mean…

No. No, it can't be; it won't be. Statistically, it's not possible; it just isn't. No, I'm not having it; I won't believe it.

But…

I access the web on my smartphone, type in "*The Letona Pro Clinic*", and press enter. It's the first hit, a sponsored advertisement; it is still open and running. Oh my god!

Putting my phone down on the desk, I stand and walk to the large floor-to-ceiling window and look out over the rooftops towards the buildings on the other side of the River Thames.

*Why did she have to do that bloody DNA test?*

What does this mean now? My God, this could mean that… I can't even think the words, never mind utter them. The possible outcome just makes my head spin; Kate could be my…

A wave of nausea hits me, giving me the sudden urge to throw up. Covering my mouth, I run for the bathroom, just making the toilet bowl as my body reacts, my stomach emptying in three heaves and wretches. I cough and spit to clear my mouth and flush the toilet. Standing slowly upright and moving across to the sink, I turn the cold water tap and cup my hands to collect water, bringing it up to wash out my mouth and then spitting it back into the sink. Looking up at my reflection in the large mirror, I look grey, ashen. With the tap still running, I throw cold water over my face and then just stare back at myself as water drips slowly from my face.

*What am I going to do?*

I love her. I love her with my life. The love of a partner, not a parent.

I gag again over the sink, but nothing comes out.

Lowering my head again, I splash more cold water over my face before reaching for a towel to cover my face, holding the cloth there for a full minute before dropping it and looking at myself again in the mirror.

If she hadn't done that test, then we wouldn't know anything about this; we would be naïve to the possibility, innocent of this knowledge. So that's what I will do; I won't say anything to her. We have a new life to live now, and no one is going to take that from us. Besides, statistically, her mother would not have received my donation; many men were doing it back then, so the odds are in my favour. That's it; I'm keeping this to myself. I am not her father.

Returning to the living room, I pick up the already visited bottle of whisky, twist the cork stopper from the neck, and, not bothering with a glass, take the first hit straight from the bottle, coughing slightly as it hits the back of my throat after I swallow. The second hit goes in the same direction, with the same speed. The whisky seems to steady me a little, slowing my heart rate from the race it was having in my chest.

The Letona Pro Clinic. Did I ever think those donations would come back to haunt me? No, absolutely not; total anonymity was assured. Who would have thought some twenty-odd years later, you could buy a home test kit for fun, only for it to be a disguised Pandora's Box.

I'm keeping this to myself.

I have to.

# 20

## Kate – The Cotton Mill Wine Bar

It's catch-up time for us girls, and we're back at Ally's favourite cocktail place. The décor is rustic, with all industrial bare bricks, wrought iron beams, and circular support columns; the exposed superstructure of a former cotton mill is now on trend with the latest places to be.

'Same again, please,' Ally says to the waiter who nods slightly and returns to the bar. 'I've got to be sensible this evening; I can't have too many drinks; I have an early start in the morning.'

'It's busy at work then?'

'Yes, when is it not these days? New clients, new accounts, new reports; it's good, I suppose; it pays my wages and lets me have the odd cocktail or two mid-week. What about you, how is the life of a married woman going?'

'It's good, yep, all good.'

'Wow, that's a ringing endorsement for marriage.'

'No, sorry, it's great; it's just that Paul is away quite a bit of the time on business, more so with his deal going through. He's stressed, I think, with the workload and deadline pressures.'

'Oh, right, but he can handle it, can't he?'

'Yes. Yes, he can, but I don't know; he seems distracted lately. Ah, that reminds me, I won't be free next weekend; I've booked a nice little retreat cottage in the Cotswolds for the two of us, one of those romantic little places for lovers: hot tub, sauna, chilled bubbly.'

'Oh, for you and me? I never knew…'

'Me and Paul, silly.'

'I know, just teasing. Does he know that you've planned it?'

'Yes and no; I checked his diary, and it's all clear, so I blocked it out for him and told him I have a surprise planned. The weird thing is, he didn't really quiz me about it or ask any questions, almost dismissing it; he's definitely stressed, so it'll do us both good to be alone again without distractions and spend some quality time together.'

'Umm, very nice, very romantic.'

The waiter returns with our cocktails and places them in front of us. 'Thank you,' Ally replies, winking at him. He smiles and walks away.

'You're an outrageous flirt at times, Ally, you know that?'

'Well, got to keep the spice of life going. Anyway, you can talk, what with all this sex retreat you've booked.'

'It's not a sex retreat,' and as I say it, it clashes with one of those short room silences and the two suited men sitting at the table beside us look over, and I can instantly feel my face blushing.

'That sounds interesting,' the one closest to Ally says.

'Yep, it will be, but there are no spare places left, unfortunately; maybe next time,' Ally replies.

'OK, I'll hold you to that,' he responds and turns back to his colleague, raising his eyebrows slightly, and they continue talking.

'See what I mean, an outrageous flirt.'

Ally smiles, winks, and picks up her cocktail, 'Cheers.'

I respond, and we clink glasses.

As I sip at my drink, Ally raises her right index finger against the side of her glass, 'Ah, I keep meaning to ask you; did you get the results from that DNA test yet? It's been weeks now.'

I thought this might come up; she doesn't forget much. We've been the closest friends since we met on the first day of high school. We've confided in everything to each other, boys, men, highs, lows, supporting each other in times of sadness. Mum and Dad didn't ask me to keep this a close family secret, and I don't see any harm in letting Ally in on my news; in fact, it could be great news, I have a new brother and sister to think about and I could sound this off on Ally, see what she thinks about my meeting them.

As I slowly lead her through what happened, she keeps interrupting me with all the same thoughts I had about how this could have come about, but she, too, never expected to hear that my biological father was a sperm donor and that it was all planned and I am the happy result.

'Well, now that is news. So, why didn't your mum and dad say anything to you before?'

'Mum was concerned it would damage my relationship with Dad, and on balance it may have done. Finding out later, as an adult, was admittedly a shock at first, but I could see it from their perspective. Dad has always been there for me and loved me unconditionally, so I'm kind of glad it was later knowledge and not when I was younger, I probably would have struggled with it growing up.'

'Well, you have a half-brother and half-sister now; do you want to meet them?'

'I haven't quite decided yet. What would you do? Would you want to meet them if you were in my shoes?'

'It's a bit different for me; I've already got two brothers and a sister, so I've had my time of squabbles and fights growing up and adding to my birthday and Christmas present list that I already hate shopping for, might sway my judgement to not want to meet them.'

'Um, yeah, I suppose. I often wished I had a brother or sister growing up, it's something I feel I missed out on.'

'It has its moments, believe me. I don't know about meeting them, though; I'd have to really give it some thought. If you think about it, they're complete strangers; they could be nutters, or worse, they could be accountants.'

'Haha, and what's wrong with accountants?'

'I don't know, it's just something I say. I dated one once. Do you remember him? He was always adding things up, checking the bill, assessing the cost.'

'He was alright; he was a nice guy from memory.'

'Yeh, he was, but I just wanted a little more sparkle, energy, you know?'

'Well then, my half-brother and sister should be OK so long as they don't know the cost of sharpening axes or the cheapest poisons then?' We both laugh a little.

'So, the question still stands: are you going to meet them or not?'

'I think I will.'

'Oh, OK. Do you want me to tag along for support?'

'No, I'll be fine, thanks,' even though the idea of Ally's support would be welcome, I can't go to meet them with a friend in tow; it would look like I'm scared of them or not trusting.

'Is Paul OK with having a new half-brother and half-sister-in-law?'

'I'm not sure, he hasn't said much about it since I told him; I can't see him having a problem with it though, it's not like they'll be dialling into our daily lives or anything; to him, they'll just be some other younger people that I know, I guess.'

# 21

## Kate – En Route to Crickleham

Paul is asleep beside me as I steer our car towards the cottage I've rented for this long weekend. He was hesitant at first, not sure if he wanted to be away this weekend, even more so when I mentioned it includes Friday and Monday; he cited the amount of work he has and the deadline pressures he's under. In the end, I had to concede and let him bring his laptop along, but I'll do my best to keep his mind off work and focused on me.

I spoke with his P.A. and asked her to clear his diary for today and Monday free, and she did a wonderful job of reshuffling his appointments, commenting that she also thinks he's pretty stressed and needs a break, adding it's a great idea. Finding this cottage available at such short notice was lucky, a late cancellation falling in with our dates.

He has no idea where I'm taking him, and I offered to drive to keep the destination secret for a little longer, although I didn't expect him to fall asleep within a quarter of an hour of setting off from home. I suppose he really is tired and exhausted, so this weekend break will do him some good. I plan to speak with him at some point over the weekend about my decision to meet up with Oscar and Sarah, my stranger siblings. I've sent them both a message suggesting we get together next weekend in Cheltenham, and they are happy to meet, I thought this location best meets our needs: a neutral location, reasonably equidistant for both Oscar and Sarah, with good road and rail access for us all.

I wonder what they'll be like. We're all relatively the same age group, so the generational aspect shouldn't be an issue; although they are strangers to me as I am to them, they have the advantage of knowing each other already. I'm a little anxious, I suppose; it is like walking into the unknown, but how can it be any different to meeting someone new in a work setting, on a date, or in a nightclub? Well, for starters, we're related by biology, and some of our makeup is shared, with all three of us coming into being in the same manner. Will we look alike and have similar features? I wonder if we'll have any instinctive mannerisms that have carried over from our biological father. Mum sticks out the tip of her tongue slightly when she's deep in thought or focussing on something, and I do the same; Mum said her mother did it too. Do I do something that my half-siblings both do? I can curl my tongue up to make a tube, but Mum and Dad can't, and I do it while driving just to prove it to myself again.

As for our biological father, who could he be? That is one question I want to ask them: have they tried to locate him? Reading into the background of donation, donors could elect to remain anonymous back in the nineties, and if he wishes to stay anonymous, then I suppose we have to respect his decision; it'll be difficult, if not almost impossible, then, I suspect, to identify him. And, if he wants to remain anonymous, why should we not respect that? After all, he helped do a wonderful thing for my mum and dad and for others, like Oscar and Sarah's parents I presume.

I may even have more half-siblings out there yet to come forward; that's a freaky thought. Various web page sites indicate this is a real possibility, citing some examples of nine or more half-siblings from the same male donor.

In a deep sleep, Paul snores gently beside me, oblivious to my thoughts and concerns and tongue-curling exercises. We do need to discuss this matter this weekend, although a part of me thinks he's not really that interested. For sure, he's shown little interest in it since I told him the news, but I've just put that down to his current work pressures.

'Urgh!' Paul wakes himself with a shudder, which startles me slightly.

'Bad dream, darling?' I ask, flicking a quick glance in his direction.

'Oh, yeah, one of those dreams when you feel like you're falling. Where are we now?' I catch him looking at his wristwatch, 'We've been driving for over an hour now.'

'We're only a few miles away; we'll soon be there, and we can chill as soon as we're unpacked.'

'I have some emails to look at when we get there.'

'Oh Paul, it can wait until later, surely?'

'No, they have to be done today. It's Friday; the banks and suppliers don't stop work on Friday just because I've taken the day off.'

'I suppose not, but you won't be on your laptop for too long, will you?' We should make the most out of the cottage and the facilities while we have them.'

'Um, we'll see. I have lots to do.'

'I know, but don't be a party pooper, Paul; you need a break just as much as any person. Try to relax when we get there, OK?'

'You do realise that I'm up to my neck in it at the moment, don't you?' I thought of anyone you would understand.'

'I do understand, but if you carry on going the way you are, you'll either burn out, make a huge mistake or have a bloody heart attack. You need some switch-off time, darling, time to re-boot yourself.'

'If only.' He sighs, and from the corner of my eye, I see him look away from me and out of the passenger door window.

He is tightly strung and obviously feeling the pressure of his tasks and decision-making; I'll cut him some slack today, but tomorrow, he's all mine.

Paul's mobile phone rings. He fishes it out of his pocket and looks at the screen, 'Oh great, here we go.' He accepts the call and speaks, 'Hello, Paul Hunter speaking.'

# 22

## Paul – The Cottage, Crickleham

I still can't believe she booked this cottage for four days, knowing the amount of work I have to do, but for sure, I need a break, and this hot tub is just the thing I need to slow down and relax. So, I'll be switching off for the rest of today; no laptop, no mobile phone, just bubbles in the tub following those in a glass.

The weather is great, and the views out over the countryside are peaceful and serene; there is no traffic or urban drone, the only noise being nature and a distant farmer's tractor a couple of fields away. Kate has just stepped out of the tub and back into the cottage for more champagne. She's not said much about the DNA testing and finding out Duncan is not her biological father; what little she has mentioned, I've managed to deflect from and onto another subject. I'm sure she'll want to talk about it this weekend, so I had best show some interest this time; it's probably better if I'm proactive and raise the subject first.

But the whole subject is still a potential ticking timebomb for me; for us. I simply can't lock it away as easily as I thought I could; it's always there, like a worm in my skull, and I have no one I can talk to about it, to share my thoughts with. It's probably the loneliest time I have had in a long time.

The patio door opens, and Kate returns with two pastel-coloured flute glasses and a bottle of bubbly. She walks slowly across the patio, looking stunning with her blonde hair tied back, wearing a skimpy bikini top and sarong wrap; she is absolutely gorgeous; it's easy to see why any man would find her attractive. She takes years off me.

'It says we can't use ordinary glass in the hot tub and surrounding area; sensible, I suppose, so forgive the plastic flutes.'

As she leans over the side of the hot tub towards me, I take the two plastic glasses and hold them for Kate to pour the bubbly into, 'It'll be fine, I'm sure.' As she pours, I bite the bullet, 'Look, I've been meaning to ask you about that DNA test and your half-siblings. I'm sorry, I've been distracted a lot lately; I should have asked sooner.'

'I know how busy you are, and I've not wanted to burden you with any of it; I know you don't need the added distraction just yet.'

'How are your mum and dad now they know you know? I suspect it was an issue for Duncan?'

'No, Dad has been fine with it, and Mum is so happy it didn't flare up into something between the three of us.'

'That's great, so all good then.'

Kate removes her sarong and, as she steps back into the hot tub, replies, 'Well, yes, I suppose, but I now have a brother and a sister, and they want to meet up.'

'I thought you weren't going to continue with that.'

'No, all I said was that I wasn't sure, but I've decided that we should meet up, and we have arranged to meet in Cheltenham next weekend.'

'Really? What can be gained from that?'

‘I’m not sure, but they want to meet, and I’ve nothing to lose now, only something to gain, I suppose.’

‘Have you checked them out?’

‘No, why should I? They’re both comfortable meeting me, a complete stranger.’

I wanted this whole thing to go away quietly, to simply fizzle out in a dark corner. If she meets them, they’ll talk about the clinic and their biological father; they may even want to find him.

‘I suppose so, but honestly, do you expect to catch up on lost sibling years or something; what is the long play? What is it that you want?’

‘I want to talk with them to see if there is any kind of bond or relationship between us.’

‘But there isn’t, you just said it yourself, you’re a complete stranger to them.’

‘OK, then I need to explore it and put it to bed once and for all. I’ve never had a wide family, no siblings, so I’m meeting them.’

She is clear on that point; she will meet them regardless of what I say, so it’s not worth me labouring on the subject anymore.

‘If you’re meeting them next Saturday, do you want me to come along with you? We could book a hotel for Saturday night if you like?’

‘No, it’s fine. Ally also offered to tag along and support me, but I’m good. We’re only planning to meet up for a couple or three hours in the afternoon; I’ll get the train back home late in the afternoon.’

‘Oh, so Ally knew about your decision before I did?’

‘Well, Paul, to be fair, you’ve shown little interest until the last few minutes. I was out with Ally a couple of days ago, and we discussed it; that's all; she is my best friend.'

'Sorry, yes, you're right.' I lean across the hot tub and kiss Kate on her cheek; she responds but with hesitancy. I didn't want to upset her, but it feels like I may have; I'm not the best at these kinds of emotional matters; Lauren often said that to me. But I do want this thing to go away and not upset what we have together.

What we have is perfect.

# 23

## Kate – The Cottage, Crickleham

He needs to chill a little more. After an hour or so in the hot tub followed by some sunbathing, we retired to the bedroom, and I thought we would make love, but as I moved closer to him and attempted to initiate sex, he wasn't receptive and only wanted to cuddle. He said his mind was still a hundred miles away on other things, saying he still had an email to reply to, which was frustrating him. I told him to go downstairs and get it done.

I'll wait, and we'll try again later.

I've not seen him like this before; he's more often than not the initiator of sex, so this is new territory for me.

The shower was welcoming, refreshing, and invigorating; I played around with the various settings, from massage to pulse jets to rainforest deluge, finding the rainforest setting my favourite.

Sitting here in front of the open windows and Juliet balcony, looking out over the fields, my thoughts return to next weekend, to meeting Oscar and Sarah for the first time. I've reserved a table at a nice restaurant for lunch and sent them the address and time, which they have both accepted; Oscar kindly offered to pay the bill, which I declined and said I'd pick it up. He seems a genuinely nice man, polite and considerate; I'm looking forward to meeting him. Sarah comes across a little more, I don't know, more brusque, less 'polished', no, that's not the right word, a little less mature maybe, or maybe she's just more to the point. They both seem keen to meet and on balance, I would say, from the content and structure of Sarah's messages, it is Sarah of the two who is the more eager to meet up.

I reach across to the dressing table, pick up my tablet screen, and log into the cottage WiFi for an internet connection. I enter the NeuvaGen website and log into the general chat room messages, slowly re-reading them to see if there is any new or nuanced information I've previously missed, but there's nothing I haven't already seen or understood.

Exploring the web page further, the help and support section catches my eye, and clicking on frequently asked questions, there is one of interest, "Can I find out the identity of my sperm donor". Looking at the question, I cannot decide if I want to do it or not. The following information indicates different responses depending on when the donation was deposited with a licenced clinic; I read the information for the range covering that period using my birth year as a guide. The donor is anonymous and will remain so unless the donor himself wishes to rescind his anonymity and make contact with people who received his DNA, his biological offspring. However, it may be possible that the donor left some background information about himself that may be of interest to anyone seeking more about their donor; although this won't identify him, depending on what information he provides, it could help narrow the field. Such information can include the donor's general physical description such as height, weight, eye and hair colour, occupation, religion, interests, or any other information the donor was prepared to leave for a future request for a person conceived from their donation. It indicates some donors are more sharing or open than others, with some leaving the briefest of information or nothing at all to be shared.

It goes on to say that the donor could themselves apply for information on the number of children born from their donations. So, if we could identify the donor, and the donor was willing, he could at least request the number of conceived children from his donation, that will at least indicate whether it is just the three of us or if there are more out there that we don't yet know of. This will be of interest to Sarah as she has hinted a couple of times in her messages of wanting to know how many half-siblings she may have. I'll ask her if she is aware of this on Saturday.

Paul enters the bedroom and sees me by the open windows wrapped in a white robe. Rather than approach me, he simply says he's going to grab a shower and enters the ensuite bathroom, closing the door behind him. Something is not right, but I can't put my finger on it. He would never let me sit here, naked inside a bathrobe, without making advances on me; he said once it was impossible for him to do so, yet here he is, almost ignoring me.

It can't be another woman, can it? We've not had sex now for a couple of weeks. No, no, it won't be another woman, it'll be work; even his P.A. said he was distracted and under pressure, and she sees more of him than I do these days.

I'll not pressure him. We're going out to a local restaurant for dinner tonight, and when we return, I will suggest we get a good night's sleep; then we can see what tomorrow brings.

# 24

## Paul – The Cottage, Crickleham

I want to make love with her, to have passionate sex. I love her dearly and want to be with her, but I'm frightened of the possible connection we have; even though my head is telling me not to be stupid, statistically, it won't be likely. I know something she doesn't, and if it pans out the wrong way, I could be her biological father. I know I told myself I could live with this unverified knowledge, that I'd be able to park it somewhere deep, as not knowing it, factually, can't be a crime, but my conscience keeps gnawing away at me, eating me from the inside. I felt awful rejecting her last night, but since I heard her say the name of the clinic, I just can't get over the not knowing; but it's getting intensely harder as she doesn't know why I'm being distant, and she can never know. But what if it is so? What if my donation was used to conceive her; is it a crime? I don't know. I suppose it must be, but surely it would be a crime of innocents, two parties not aware or knowing of their biological connection.

But I frustratingly hold the knowledge there is a reasonable possibility it could be so, and my conscience is tearing at me.

This must have happened before, surely. Throughout history, before the advance of modern medical science and innovation, this could have happened. Jeez, it could still happen now; look at us. It's the advance of artificial insemination that has fuelled a situation where two people would not know they are biologically related unless they did a DNA test before getting together, which is just sheer nonsense. It's knowing the truth and then continuing a sexual relationship that would make it a crime, but I don't know the truth yet. And, if it turns out I am her biological father, I still couldn't tell her; the trauma could seriously damage her, especially if others found out, and I don't want to hurt her in any way.

The realisation that I do need to get to the truth is daunting, as it's not knowing that will drive us apart anyway.

But how? How do I do this without anyone knowing?

Explaining why to Kate and the thought of doing the tests will create friction, anxiety, and tension in our relationship, and then, assuming all turns out good, I'll be annoyed with myself for putting Kate through all of that.

I can't simply do a test and then look for matches; the match information is shared on the web page, and any potential matches will see it as soon as I do; this could include Kate if it shows we are matched. I wonder if her results are posted in her maiden name, lessening the chance of our connection, our relationship, becoming front page news? I could only find out by asking her or getting my hands on her results letter.

I need to find a way to resolve this quietly without creating a scene that may well not need creating. It's the answer I need, and if it goes against us and I turn out to be her biological father, I'll need to put a stop to our relationship immediately, separate and divorce without letting anyone know the real reason, especially not Kate. My God, what an outcome if this turns out to be the case.

She wants children with me. That thought alone makes this a hundred times worse. We can't have sex again until I know the truth.

How the hell am I going to pull this off? It took six weeks for Kate's results to come through; we can't wait that long; she'll not wait that long without seriously questioning me. Can I tell her about my concerns? Will she be OK with the information that she could possibly be my daughter? What am I thinking? Of course, she won't be OK with it.

And if it turns out that she is my biological daughter, then there are at least two more people out there, conceived from my donations, Oscar and Sarah; how many more could there be?

I could just get back in touch with the clinic, explain my concerns, and see if they will fast-track everything confidentially; after all, it would be in their interest also if this stayed out of the public domain, but can I trust them? Can I trust their personnel not to sell the information to one of those two-bit rag newspapers or social media sites for a bundle of cash, easy money for a scandal scoop?

This is so fucked up.

Kate calls out from downstairs, 'Paul! Breakfast is ready.'

'OK, I'll be there in a sec.'

I'll have to make out I have a medical complaint or something, an issue in the lower regions, say that it's painful when I get aroused, that I need to see a doctor when I get back. Yeah, that could play out for a few weeks or more. She'll not pressure me for sex then, and it'll provide a suitable reason for my recent conduct, and I can be all apologetic. Then, if the results are favourable, and we are not related biologically, I can say the problem is going away, and I'm recovering.

But as I mull this over in my head, I realise this will be the second time I have lied to her.

# 25

## Kate – The Cottage, Crickleham

'Oh my god, Paul, why didn't you say something earlier?'

'I don't know, embarrassed, I suppose. I'm sorry.'

'Don't be sorry, oh, you poor thing. We just need to get you mended. We'll make an appointment with the doctor as soon as the surgery opens on Monday morning and try to rush you through. We can phone from here before we set off back for home.'

'Thank you, yes, we can do that. I felt awful, shunning you, trying to avoid sex, but the pain is getting unbearable now. It's fine right now, no issue, no pain or discomfort, but as soon as I get aroused, then, wow.'

'If you had said sooner, we could have postponed this weekend and focused on getting you better. I thought something was wrong, but I just thought it was the work pressure. Oh, planning this weekend is so insensitive of me now that I know what the problem is. It should be me apologising.'

'No, no, nonsense. Look, we can still enjoy our time here; there is no sense in cutting this break short; there's nothing we can do until Monday anyway. I'll lock my laptop in the car, forget work altogether, and we can go for a walk into the village or just stay here and chill; whatever you want to do.'

'You're OK walking?'

'Yes, absolutely fine, so long as Lady Godiva doesn't come down the high street.'

We both laugh, which helps change the atmosphere, lightening the mood. I never would have thought it was this kind of problem; it's the first time I've heard of it, but we'll get him fixed and back to how we used to be.

I throw my arms around him, and we hug, and he pulls away after about five seconds, smiling at me with pleading eyes. 'I'm only trying to comfort you,' as I say it, it dawns on me, 'Oh, yes, of course, I'm sorry.'

'You're such a sexy woman, even a comforting embrace can get me aroused.'

'Got it; I'll keep my distance, for the time being, I promise. I do love you.'

'And I love you too.'

I turn to the table and start to clear the breakfast plates and cutlery, and Paul assists by loading the dishwasher. How could I possibly think he was having an affair or struggling with the pressure of work. Paul has always been a workaholic and is the best person I know at handling stressful situations. As for him having an affair, well, being acutely aware I was once the other woman, it wouldn't be that much of a stretch for it to happen again.

This pain he is experiencing, though, we do need to get to the bottom of it; it could be quite serious, he may need some medication or worse, an operation and continued treatment. Why couldn't he just tell me? Is it a man thing? It's nothing he should be embarrassed about, and we promised each other to always be open and truthful with each other.

# 26

## Paul – The Cottage, Crickleham

We are lying on sunbeds on the patio at the rear of the property, relaxing. Kate, wearing a large brim floppy hat and sunglasses and very little else, is reading the latest escapist romance book from her favourite author. She wants an all-over even tan and is working hard at achieving it naturally.

I'm lying back, feet up, shades on, pondering, thinking of a way to get a DNA test done and being able to compare it to Kate's matching results to see if there is a match or not. The medical condition ruse worked, which is buying me some much-needed time, and it has Kate consciously not instigating anything sexual, no contact; perfect.

If Ally hadn't started this ball rolling a couple of months ago, taking their samples and sending them off for testing, we wouldn't be in this bloody problem now; we would be utterly oblivious to it and enjoying ourselves.

Of course! That's it! I nearly jump up off my sunbed. Ally!

I can purchase two kits; have one delivered to our home address and the other delivered to my apartment in London; the address will look like a regular home address. Then I'll get my best mate, Graeme, to provide one of the samples, and I'll do the other, but before submitting the samples, I'll swap the tubes, so his sample is under my reference identifier and my sample is under his. I'll tell him I'll return them as I'm going to the post office, so he doesn't see the use of my home address anywhere for his sample. Then, when the results are ready, I'll receive both letters and log on to see the results. My results will be uploaded to the test house web page in Graeme's name under his I.D., and I can push the match button to see if my results, in his name, match up with Kate, Oscar and Sarah. If they do match, no doubt Kate, Oscar and Sarah will try to contact Graeme, thinking he is their biological father, but only I will see their request, and I can just ignore them, so they'll never get Graeme's identity or mine. Then, if this is the outcome, that I am their biological father, I know what I must do; we'll have to divorce. I'll make it look like it was all my fault, which won't be hard as my actions have been the cause of a divorce already. However, what I need and am desperately hoping for is that there is no DNA match to my sample, that we are not tied by DNA, and we're safe to continue as husband and wife, and no one will ever know any different; I will simply tell Kate my medical problem is improving, and we'll be back to full working order quickly, normal service resumed, and this way, no one is hurt.

I feel elated, I have a plan, but this will only work if I can convince Graeme or one of my other mates to play along with it, as I need another male sample. When the results come in, I can tell Graeme his origins break down, and he won't even know I've used his name for the matching test; I'll just say I got my P.A. to send the samples off, and she messed up the postal addresses. Or better still, just tell him our samples were damaged in transit and that we have to do it all over again but use a different provider this time. Will this work? It feels like there are a couple of loose ends to trip me up, especially if Graeme doesn't agree to do it; I need to develop this a bit more, but it's the start of a plan.

Now, I need my laptop to check out the finer details on the testing company web page, proof of identity, postal addresses, payments and so on, so that I don't raise any red flags with the testing company. But this will have to wait; I have already locked my laptop in the car and promised Kate I wouldn't get it back out until we're home again. I'll have to do my research on my smartphone, I can't wait another two days to get this plan rolling, and should Kate ask what I'm doing, I can simply say I'm surfing the internet, looking for ideas for our next holiday together.

Moving my head slowly, looking across to Kate, I admire her elegant form; she is stunningly beautiful. I need this outcome to go the right way so we can stay together, stay married, and plan the family that she wants.

I pick up my smartphone, type NeuvaGen in the search engine, locate their web page address and click on it. Working through pages of information, I carefully read the small print, scrolling through whatever I can find to absorb. Once I've read through everything, a couple of tweaks are needed to my plan, but it could work with a fair wind. I just need to convince Graeme to provide a sample that he's happy for me to post.

There's nothing more I can do now other than enjoy the rest of this weekend, although it would be a far better weekend break if Ally had not convinced Kate to do that bloody test in the first place. That test created this secret anxiety over Kate's parentage, an invisible and private menace coming between us, a menace that only I am aware of. I want to talk to someone about this as it's slowly eating at me from within, the frustration of this unknown outcome, but I can't; no one but me must ever find out about this or the outcome. This must stay my secret.

Out of the corner of my eye, I register Kate turning her head towards me, 'You're not working over there, are you, Mr Hunter?'

I look at her, her peering over the top of her lowered sunglasses. 'No, I am not, I'm just making some plans for the future, our future.'

'Nice, I like the sound of that,' and she blows me a light air kiss across the gap between us before returning to her book, hopefully, a gap that will narrow and close fully in a few weeks' time.

Hopefully.

# 27

## Kate – Back at Home

Within half an hour of arriving home, Paul is in his study, sitting behind his laptop typing away. Although he was good at his word and didn't do any work during the rest of the time we were away, it looks like he's catching up on it now. He's called the surgery and arranged an appointment with the doctor for tomorrow afternoon; it's a minor miracle, as I can never get one that quickly. He must be concerned; I thought he would put this off and prioritise his workload, so I'm glad he's taking his health and this condition seriously.

I unpack our clothes and put the first load in the washing machine; unfortunately, the laundry doesn't do itself. The foodstuff we returned with I place in the fridge or cupboards, and within an hour or so of arriving home, I'm on top of things.

Pulling out my laptop and sitting at the breakfast bar with a glass of water, I boot up and go to NeuvaGen's web page, login and go straight to the message board. There's a new message from Sarah but nothing from Oscar. I click and open it:

> *"Hi Kate, I'm really looking forward to meeting you on Saturday, and I know Oscar is too. We video-called each other over the weekend and*

*thought it would be good to send you a photo of the two of us so you know who to look out for next weekend (attached). Hopefully, we're not too scary ☺ You don't have to send us a photo back, it's fine. Oscar mentioned you have offered to pay for lunch, that's very kind, but I'd prefer if we split the bill three ways if that's OK with you.*
*I was wondering, are you interested in finding out more about our biological father? We would like to. I thought I'd ask as it'll be something we'll bring up on Saturday and I didn't want to spook you, so you have some time now to think about it before we meet.*
*Be great finally meeting you at last. Luv Sarah xx*"

I click on the first of the two photos, and it's Oscar; he looks handsome and stylish and has a lovely smile. I click on Sarah's photo, and she is in total contrast to Oscar, with some ear piercings, a short and coloured haircut, and a tattoo on her neck, wearing a leather jacket and t-shirt. I enlarge the photos and put them side by side to look for similarities, and to be fair, I don't think you can tell they are half-siblings; there are no apparent similar characteristic features; the only thing that seems to be in common is that we all have blue eyes.

I'll send them both a photo of me to show I'm comfortable with sharing information; however, I'm not going to mention yet what I want to do about our biological father. I want some more time to think about this as I'm not sure how Dad will feel about my search for the donor. Besides, if our biological father wants to stay anonymous, then we'll never get to know his identity, and there's nothing we can do about that.

Searching through some recent photos, I select one of me and attach it to my reply message, indicating Sarah can share it with Oscar if she likes, and press send.

I return to the photos of the two of them on my screen: my brother and sister. It's hard to believe after all these years of never knowing I could possibly have a sibling, never mind two; I now have them, and we're going to meet for the first time. Looking at Sarah, and her outward image and her comment about paying for lunch, I sense she is an independent and strong character, knows what she wants and is not afraid to say the wrong thing, whereas Oscar, I imagine as gentler, polished, conservative in nature; could they be so different? I suppose who you are depends on your upbringing and the environment of your formative years. I think it was Aristotle who said, "*Give me a child until he is seven, and I will show you the man*", and looking at the two photographs, there may be something in this.

After several hours, Paul emerges from his study and briefly hugs me, 'Thank you darling, I just needed to get those emails done.'

As he releases me, he continues, 'I've got that appointment tomorrow at four o'clock with the doctor, and I was thinking, I might call Graeme and meet him down at the cricket club afterwards, if that's alright with you? We can have some practice time in the nets, letting me blow off a little steam.'

'Of course, that sounds like a great idea. You have been working too hard and need some escape time from work. Do you want me to come with you to see the doctor?'

'No, I'll be fine, thank you. The doctor will probably just ask a few questions, a quick examination, and then refer me for some tests, so I'm not expecting to receive any diagnosis tomorrow.'

'Of course, but if you change your mind, let me know.'

'I will, thank you.'

I'm pleased he's thinking like this now, our weekend away, and his problem seems to be making him think about his own health, both physical and mental. I watch him turn to the sink to fill the kettle and think of how much I love him.

# 28

## Paul – Cricket Club House

It's now or never; I have to convince Graeme to provide me with a DNA sample. I managed to pick up two test kits from the local pharmacy this afternoon; ironically, at about the same time that Kate thought I was attending my appointment with the doctor. I have everything ready now, so here goes.

'Hi Graeme, do you fancy a beer?'

'Yes, that sounds good, the usual, please.' As Graeme says this, the bartender is already preparing our drinks, knowing what our usuals are.

'I have something to discuss with you; do you want to grab a table over by the window? I'll bring the drinks over.'

'No probs.'

I watch Graeme walk across the room, dropping his kit bag beneath the table and pulling out a chair. Every which way I played this and tried to come up with a story to do a DNA test, it sounded strange and would have Graeme questioning why he should do it. Ally's approach with Kate was a bit of fun, linked to the Hen Party originally, but inviting Graeme, out of the blue, to do a DNA test sounds ludicrous; it's just not what we would do, and he'll start asking questions, especially if I'm controlling the sample posting.

I pay for the two beers and join him at the table. As I offer him his beer, he looks up at me, and I say, ‘Cheers, here’s to the first eleven against Burrowford; I’m convinced we have this in the bag this year.’

‘I’ll second that,’ he replies, and as he raises his glass towards his mouth, I stop him.

‘Ah, just a sec, we need to discuss something before you take a drink.’

‘Now, this is getting all mysterious,’ placing his glass down on the table. ‘So, what is this thing that is keeping me from my beer?’

‘Well, it’s a little sensitive, and the Membership Committee have asked me to do this quietly and discretely.’

‘Umm, this sounds interesting. At long last, they’ve come to their senses and want to make me club captain.’

‘Er, well, no, not exactly,’ I pause slightly, keeping eye contact with him. ‘There has been an anonymous complaint made against you, and because it’s anonymous, the Committee thinks it prudent to keep it low profile. So, they have asked me, as your friend, to help handle this discretely.’

‘Oh, and this complaint is what, exactly?’

‘Well, it’s nonsense, really, and I said as much to the Committee, but they don’t want the club’s reputation tarnishing, hence asking me to assist with this matter. The club has some young talent coming through that are destined for County and potentially the national squad, so you can see why they want this handled quietly.’

‘And what is this matter, this complaint that needs to be handled quietly?’

‘Well, the complaint is about inappropriate drug use.’

‘What! Me?’ he replies loudly.

I notice the bartender looking over to us, 'Shh, yes. Performance drugs or recreational drugs, the complaint isn't specific. Still, you can imagine the old guard in the corridors back there mumbling about a potential scandal, something that could taint the club's impeccable name and reputation.'

'Well, for sure, I have never used drugs for either; what utter nonsense.'

'Exactly, that's what I said; we've known each other since primary school.'

'Who the hell has made this complaint?'

'As I said, it's anonymous, so they want to keep this low key, but, as it was put to me, often there is no smoke without fire. I said it could just be someone disgruntled with you or want to create a nuisance for the club.'

'I don't believe this.'

'Look, Graeme, this is easily resolved. All they are asking is that you do a simple drugs test.'

'Sod off! You're kidding, right? A drugs test. For God's sake, we're not the All England Cricket Squad?'

Graeme's raised voice is attracting some further attention around the room. I knew he wouldn't take this well, but it was the only way I could think of to get him to provide me with a sample. The bartender has left the confines of the bar and is approaching us, 'Gentlemen, is everything satisfactory?'

I reply before Graeme says the wrong thing. 'Yes, everything is fine. My friend has just received some upsetting news. I'm sorry; we'll keep our voices down. Our apologies.'

'Very good, sir, thank you,' and he turns and heads back towards the bar area.

I look back to Graeme and, in a low voice, continue, 'Look, Graeme, it's nothing heavy, OK. I know you wouldn't take drugs for anything other than a medical condition. All the Committee wants is some reassurance. We can do that, can't we?'

Graeme takes hold of his beer glass and lifts it from the table, and I react, 'Just a second,' placing my right hand over the top of his glass. He gets the message and puts his glass back down.

'So, just because someone has a grudge against me, the Committee think I need to prove my innocence; is that it?'

'In a nutshell, yes.'

'The Committee here loses its way sometimes, nothing but a bunch of stuck-up old…'

I cut him off before he finishes his sentence with an expletive. 'Graeme. Please.'

'Well, you know what I mean.'

'I do, but we just do this quietly, and it'll all blow over, OK?'

His sigh sounds as though it's loud enough to be heard outside on the far crease. 'OK, OK. When?'

'They have given me a test kit; you just need to provide a saliva sample in a tube. It's as simple as that.'

'Really, a spit sample? They don't need me to provide a urine sample? No, of course not, why would they; they're already taking the piss.'

'Hah, that's the spirit.' I reach into my kit bag and extract the plastic bag containing the sample tube. 'Here, it's this simple. Do you want to go into the toilets and do it there?'

'No, give it here, I'll do it now.'

I open the plastic bag and hand him the sample tube. 'You'll need to fill it above the line.'

He nods and removes the screw top; turning his head away to the corner of the room, away from general sight, he provides his sample and refastens the lid.

'There,' handing it back to me. 'What now?'

'That's it. I'll drop it off with them, and the results will be through in a few days. Nothing to worry about.'

'Well, I know that. Can I have my beer now?'

'Yes, of course; I just didn't want the sample contaminated with alcohol.' I raise my glass to him, 'Cheers, Graeme, I'm sorry I had to ask you to do that.'

'Not a problem; I know it wasn't coming from you. Just another waste of club fees again, no doubt. Cheers,' picking up his beer glass again.

'Yeh, you know how it is,' I reply as I watch him take a sip of his beer.

# 29

## Paul – Study at Home

Getting Graeme's sample was much easier than I thought it would be. I could get used to this deception lark; it seems I am pretty good at it.

Completing the respective paperwork and address details, I package up Graeme's sample masquerading as mine and my sample in Graeme's name, complete with my apartment address. I have created an email address and log-in account for Graeme and created an account for me. Now, let's see if this works.

I made sure to use the same testing company, NeuvaGen, used by Ally and Kate, as I need the ability to match with the DNA records they hold if, indeed, there is any match, which I very much doubt. Now, it's a matter of waiting; all I can do now is concentrate on work and keep the fictitious testing of my mystery ailment ticking along with Kate until I get the all-clear on the DNA front. Kate is being patient with me, and when she asked last night on my return home about what the doctor had said, my reply was innocuous; nothing obvious was identified by the doctor, and some tests are needed. Kate thinks the tests I need are all going through my private medical insurance, who will be communicating with me by email and my mobile phone, so I've nothing to worry about on the postal front with Kate; we won't be receiving any mail at home; Kate is accepting and following what I tell her. I mentioned to her I had done one of those DNA tests for fun and sent it off, so the only thing arriving by post at home will be a DNA test results notification letter, which, if Kate picks it up first, I can ask her to open if I'm not there, confident that it will be referring to Graeme's sample results and not mine.

As I'm in London quite a lot these days, it was easy for me to say that my medical tests are being conducted by London specialists, thereby helping deflect Kate from wanting to accompany me. She is clearly worried about me, but I can't tell her what is really going on; it would create such a strain on us that I genuinely believe isn't needed; it's pointless worrying about something until it's definite, save the worrying for when there is something to worry about. I feel bad deceiving her like this, but I am doing this with the right intentions; I am protecting her.

Anyway, I'll be back in London for the rest of the week, and Kate is preparing for her meeting with Oscar and Sarah on Saturday; I hope all goes well for her when they meet. I want her to be happy, and yes, while I accept that having a sibling can be frustrating at times, it can also be enjoyable.

# 30

## Ruth – at Lauren's Home

'Mum, can you sit for a second? I have something to tell you.'

'What is it? You're not in trouble again at work, are you?'

'Mum, no, I'm not. Come and sit down; I bumped into Ally the other night, and she told me something about Kate.'

Sitting down in her armchair, Mum replies, 'I told you to not mention her name in this house. Your father has decided to spend the rest of his life with her, so, as far as I'm concerned, they are both gone from my life, and I have no further interest in them.'

'I think you'll want to hear this though,' pausing to let her calm a little, 'It turns out Kate and her parents have a family secret.'

'And how is that of any interest to me?'

'Because Dad didn't know about it either.'

'How is Ally? I've not seen her since all this trouble with your father started. Nice girl: I once thought your brother had an interest in her. What is she doing these days?'

Mum is trying to deflect again, trying to change the subject; anything to do with Kate and Dad is off-limits as far as she is concerned.

'Mum, he did, but it was short-lived; Ally is fine. Anyway,' shaking my head slightly, 'it's what Ally told me about Kate that surprised me. I bumped into her in a bar at the weekend, a little worse for the cocktails she had been drinking, I think, and she told me that Kate's dad, Duncan, isn't Kate's real father, and Kate has only just found out.' As I say this with raised eyebrows, I know I'm starting to sound like a gossip, but anything that puts Kate in a bad light is good, in my opinion.

'Oh, right, so, who is her father then?'

'Well, apparently Kate's mum and dad couldn't have a child, so they used a specialist clinic and artificial insemination. Kate's mum is her real mother, but her real father is unknown, and since, Kate has found out she has a half-brother and a half-sister.' After saying this out loud, I realise how thoroughly bitchy it sounds. Why did I think Mum would be interested in this gossip?

'Oh, well then, good for them.'

'Mum? What do you mean?'

'You'll find out one day, assuming you want to bless me with grandchildren. Being a mother is a beautiful, wonderful thing, and if that's what her mother needed to do to achieve it, then I have no problem with that.'

'Oh.' I didn't expect Mum to be so magnanimous about this; I thought she would… actually, I don't know what I thought she would do with this information. 'So, you're OK with this?'

'Why wouldn't I be?'

'I don't know. I thought anything that would upset Kate would make you happy.'

'Now, Ruth, I'm not vindictive. I'm not at all happy with Kate, but I don't wish her any harm. If I wanted harm to come to someone, it would be to Paul, your father; he's the one who betrayed me, betrayed us. He's the one that left us when he should have kept it in his trousers.'

Pausing, thinking I need to change the subject now as I can see Mum is channelling on Dad again. I pick up on the grandchild comment as deflection, 'It'll be some time before I'm ready to have children and give you a grandchild, it'll be up to Ben in the near future rather than me.'

'Why? Is Ben going to be a dad? Are they having a baby? He never said.'

'No, Mum. No, he's not. Oh, forget it.'

# 31

## Lauren – at Home

'Bye, sweetheart, see you next week.' It's good to see Ruth; I just wish Ben would call around more; I'll give him a call later.

When Ruth told me about Kate's parentage, I made out it was nothing but a good thing; I don't want Ruth being burdened with more anger and frustration, the way it has been with me, wearing me down, clawing at me, but the reality is, if that artificial insemination had of failed, Kate would not have run off with my husband; she wouldn't even be here.

Who am I kidding? I've never really put our divorce on Kate; the divorce was all Paul's fault in my eyes. Although I will never forgive her, I am a realist; if it wasn't Kate, I'm sure it would have been another woman, as he was willing to entertain another relationship, but what made this worse was that he did it with one of Ruth's friends. Paul was old enough to know what it would mean to me, and to Ben and especially to Ruth, but he still went ahead with his dirty, disgusting affair. He cheated on me and our children, and that was enough for me; I wouldn't have had him back after that. He hurt us so badly.

Clearing away our cups to the kitchen, I mull over what Ruth said about Kate's biological father being a sperm donor. Placing the cups in the sink, I'm pretty sure donors stay anonymous; Paul said that to me once when he told me what he had done before we met. I didn't want to say anything to Ruth, but Paul used to make donations when he was younger and working in London. He told me not long after we were married, when money was tight with our first mortgage and living costs were rising, suggesting he could do it again to help with our money needs. Paul being a donor freaked me out a little at the time, but afterwards, I realised it was, on balance, a good thing, the general act of making donations to help others. However, as we were then married, I made him promise he wouldn't do it again, and I trusted him to honour that.

Ha, I trusted him. The bastard. I'll certainly never trust him again.

Looking out of the kitchen window, it starts to dawn on me that I could use this information to freak Paul out, to make out he could be Kate's father; it'll unsettle them both, make them worry about something that he had done years before and it now coming back to haunt him. He told me he donated to a few clinics in London, making out he was a medical student or something. I can't recall any names, but he did it before we were engaged to be married. How can I use this small piece of information to make them uneasy with each other, to generate doubt about their so-called perfect marriage, and drive a wedge between them? Oh, the more I think of what I could do with this information, the more satisfaction it is giving me.

Further information will be helpful, as it will make it sound highly probable rather than just an outside chance. Kate's age would fit around the time Paul was in London making his donations, I think, give or take a few months. Did Kate's mum and dad use a London clinic? I don't know; I wonder if Ally does? Maybe a chance meeting with Ally could be useful so I can gather more information.

What if I just wrote an anonymous note to Kate's parents? I wonder what effect that would have on them and on Kate and Paul's marriage? I bet it would freak them out. Could I do that to her parents? I know they didn't do anything wrong here, but they didn't talk their daughter out of the wedding, did they? It wouldn't be right to penalise them for their daughter's theft of my husband, would it?

The pain and anguish I could cause Paul and Kate would last until they managed to get some tests done and show they are not linked, but that pain and doubt could then linger, fester inside long enough to create a deep-seated mistrust between them. Oh, that would be good.

I need something, though; a fact or two to make this a viable outcome, something tangible to sow the seed of doubt.

It's my turn to dish out some pain now, I shouldn't be the only one suffering, and to think, I can do this with just a few choice words.

Perfect.

Now, how do I orchestrate a chance meeting with Ally?

# 32

## Kate – Cheltenham

I decided to drive to Cheltenham, as this gives me the freedom to leave at whatever time suits me. The trains have been erratic over the recent months, especially with weekend maintenance work, train driver overtime bans, and the use of replacement bus services.

Entering the spa town, the extent of Regency architecture is a testament to the days of wealth and health retreats of the eighteenth and nineteenth centuries. Relying on my car's satnav, I navigate the one-way system and park near Pitville Park. Leaving my car, I walk across to the Heritage Café within the Grade I listed Regency Pitville Pump Room, our designated meeting place. I thought we could meet here first, chat over tea or coffee, then walk across the park to the restaurant I have reserved for lunch. This will help break the ice, and the walk allow us some space and time to talk a little before we sit close in the confines of a restaurant.

Walking up to the café, both Oscar and Sarah are already there, standing near the entrance chatting and smiling. I feel slightly nervous and stop for a second, watching them both; they seem comfortable together and confident. Oscar is wearing light-coloured chino trousers, a dark blue jacket, and an open-neck white shirt. In contrast, Sarah is wearing tight-fitting jeans, slightly frayed in a distressed fashion, a short black leather jacket and what looks to be a red t-shirt beneath. Looking at them, it would be almost impossible to say they were brother and sister. And now there's me, dressed in a light pastel summer dress, with a plain, light green cotton shawl draped over my shoulders, topped with a straw hat and green sunshades.

As I remove my sunglasses, Oscar spots me and waves; Sarah turns slightly towards me and, raising her hand to just above her waistline, waves slightly. I take a deep breath and take the final steps towards my half-siblings.

Approaching them, Sarah steps forward and throws her arms around me, kissing my cheek, 'Hello, sister.' Her embrace is genuine, loving and warm.

'Come on, Sarah, let her breathe, will you? Poor Kate, let go, or she will have some broken ribs to remember our first meeting by.'

Sarah releases me, 'Sorry, I'm just excited to meet at long last.' She steps back, and Oscar approaches me with his right hand outstretched, looking for a handshake greeting. I take hold of his hand, and as we close, I embrace him, putting my left arm around his shoulders and pulling him in. He wasn't expecting me to, and I sense him feeling a little on edge, the opposite of Sarah. 'Hello, brother,' I say quietly in his ear.

He pulls his upper body away from me, slowly, not forcibly in a bad way, while simultaneously replying, 'Hello, Kate, I'm pleased to meet you,' and shaking my hand firmly. I assume he is a little less comfortable with meeting a stranger than Sarah is, and he is not big on hugging and embracing.

I look at them both, both smiling and looking back at me, none of us speaking. The silence is broken when

Sarah laughs, and Oscar and I join her. The release of nervous tension is clear in all three of us.

'Shall we step inside and get a drink? I reserved a table for us just in case it was busy.'

Oscar responds, 'Yes, that sounds good. Excellent. Good forward planning there, Kate.'

He comes across as quite formal, almost regimented; I'm not sure if it's being around women, a newfound sister, or that is just how he is. Time will tell, I suppose; we just need to get to know each other better.

As we enter the Orangery to the side of the café, I mention my name and our reservation, and we are guided to a table in the middle of the room. After ordering drinks, we sit looking at each other, again in a kind of mutually accepted silence. I decide to open the conversation.

'Well, until a couple of weeks ago, I never knew I had any siblings; I thought I was an only child. The surreal thing is, I had no reason to go looking; this was all by luck, I suppose. It's wonderful to meet you both.' I put my hands on the table with palms up, inviting Oscar and Sarah to place their hands in mine. Sarah does it instantly; Oscar hesitates slightly, then follows Sarah.

'So, what are your first impressions of us?' Sarah asks.

'Wow, a loaded question there,' as I titter slightly.

'Oh, sorry, I didn't mean to…'

'No, it's fine, honestly. My first impressions; well, I think you both look gorgeous, are both very brave, and are both very fortunate to have such a fabulous sister.'

We all laugh at my last comment; a little nervous laugh but enough to ease the atmosphere around us. We talk about various things for the next hour or so, taking extra tea and coffee. When the invisible barrier is removed, Oscar is clearly a wonderful orator, well versed in various topics, and exceptionally educated; breaking through that somewhat rigid façade is a beautiful person. Sarah seems to have had a good working-class upbringing, polite, well-mannered and softly spoken with a broad accent, speaking with a passion about her current life; she doesn't mention much about her childhood growing up, only snippets, whereas Oscar is quite open about his time in private schools and holidaying overseas but to places of history and culture rather than beaches and swimming pools. Our three lifestyles are so contrasting that sitting at a table across from us, it would be impossible to believe the three of us are related. It's then I recall what Paul mentioned: we only have some blood and biology in common, nothing else; to all extents and purposes, we are strangers, or at least I am at this time. Our meeting weirdly reminded me a little of the films Pygmalion and My Fair Lady, which I watched with Mum when I was younger, observing class differences between people with different backgrounds but, beneath it all, are people who have a heart, a passion, and a spirit for life; as Sarah speaks, the phrase "*the rain in Spain stays mainly in the plain*" keeps coming to mind for some ludicrous reason.

As requested by Sarah, we split the bill equally three ways before leaving the café.

The weather is nice and warm, with a light breeze. Walking across the park, Sarah links my arm while Oscar strolls alongside us almost formally.

By the time we reach The Bishop's Mitre restaurant for lunch, we know each other's general background and have managed to avoid asking the question of our biological father. After placing our food order, Sarah crosses that divide.

Looking at me just after a witty comment about a television series documenting similar events as ours, she asks the question outright, 'Have you ever thought about who our father might be? I know we have.'

Even though I was expecting a discussion on this, her direct question catches me out a little. 'I have thought about it, but I haven't decided yet if I want to know his name or if I want to contact him at all. He does have a right to retain his anonymity, and I think that should be respected.'

'We know, and we do, but if we did eventually identify him and, say, contact him, would you want us to tell you his identity, or would you want to remain oblivious?'

'Wow, Sarah, that's a tough question. I don't know, although it would seem crazy that you would both know his name, and I wouldn't; it would create a weird known secret between us.'

Oscar interjects, 'So, I take it then you would want to know if that was the case?'

'Well… then, if that was the case, I suppose I would want to know, yes.'

I lift my glass of water and take a long, slow sip, looking at them both over the top of my glass, noticing them looking at each other, eye to eye, almost as though they were communicating telepathically.

*Do they already know who he is?*

# 33

## Duncan – at Home

It was Julia who told me this morning that Kate was meeting her siblings today in Cheltenham; I was upset that it wasn't Kate herself who told me. Is she already seeing me differently? Julia says I'm being a little paranoid, but I don't see it that way; Kate has never kept anything from me, well nothing as important as this, that is.

Julia is relieved this is all out in the open now, and I honestly thought I would be; after all, I wanted to tell Kate years ago, but I'm not so sure now. Meeting her half-siblings, I expect, will trigger her wanting to find out who her biological father is; this could be fraught with all kinds of worries and implications and could backfire on Julia and me. When Kate sets her mind on something, she goes for it full steam ahead; it's one of her redeeming features, she never quits. But if the donor doesn't want to give up his anonymity, then there is little chance of finding out who he is, and that could be hard for her to accept.

Julia and I are apprehensive about the thought of Kate meeting up with her half-siblings, but Kate is meeting up with them, come what may. Outwardly, Julia is embracing Kate's enthusiasm at finding out she has a half-brother and sister, but inwardly she is just as concerned as I am about what this could lead to. Oscar and Sarah are adults; they are people Kate doesn't know;

they are not really family like we are; they are strangers with some genes in common, that's all.

I wonder what Paul makes of all this. I presume he must be supporting Kate, like I did with Julia when on her own personal journeys. I had my doubts about Paul when they first announced their relationship, thinking he was just some older guy who had found a younger woman, him taking advantage of her in some way, having a secret affair, but no, he seems to be genuine, he loves her and wants the very best for her, and I respect that.

I do feel sorry for Lauren, though, his ex-wife, she must have been devastated when the affair came to light, and he chose Kate over her. That's probably why I still have a niggling doubt about Paul; that he could hurt a woman he had already made a commitment to and then reneged on it, never mind how it would affect his own children; I suppose that niggling doubt will never really go away. There was always going to be someone for Kate, someone that she would decide to share her life with, and we resigned ourselves to that outcome some years ago; the issue is that we don't want it to disrupt our small tight family unit; we want nothing to upset the balance we've worked hard to achieve.

All I can do now is to be here for Kate if she needs me like I always have been.

Walking into the kitchen, Julia is by the island, wearing her favourite apron, holding a bowl in the crook of her left arm while mixing briskly with a large spoon; she loves to bake and doesn't need a reason to do so.

'Oh, and the special occasion is?'

She looks up at me, peering over the top of her reading glasses, 'No special occasion, just the charity cake sale tomorrow down at the church, raising funds for some new preschool play equipment for the little ones to play on during the coffee mornings.'

'Ah, good show.' I walk towards her and mockingly attempt to put my finger in the mixing bowl and receive the obligatory wrap on the knuckles with the mixing spoon, one way to taste the mix, as I lick the back of my hand.

'Ouch.'

'You're so predictable; you do it every time.'

'I know, but you'll miss me when I'm not here to do it.'

'Come here, Mr Leyden, and give me a kiss.'

As I approach Julia and lean across to kiss her, she dabs my nose with the back of the spoon, leaving a splodge of cake mixture behind; 'See what I mean, so predictable,' and she leans over and kisses me.

Taking a step back, I pick up a kitchen towel to wipe my nose and the back of my hand. 'I hope all goes well today for Kate and that her half-siblings are pleasant.'

'It'll be fine, you know she'll be OK. I'm sure they are wonderful people in their own ways,' Julia replies, returning to her cake mixture.

'You always see the best in people, don't you?'

'Yes, why wouldn't I? Is there something wrong with that approach to life?'

'No, I suppose not, but not everyone is as honest and kind as you would like them to be. I'm a firm believer that trust has to be earned.'

'I know, but I've not been wrong to date, have I?'

'No darling, you haven't, but it only takes the once.'

'Oh, sometimes, you do frustrate me. A glass half empty person to my glass half full.'

'No, I'm just practical; the glass is half as big as it needs to be,' I reply, smiling.

'Go on, back to your garden, shoo. I'll let you know when one of my cakes is ready for testing.'

I blow a small kiss across to her as her head lowers to the bowl again, and she raises the spoon out of the mixture to check the consistency.

I do love this woman… and her baking.

# 34

## Sarah – The Bishop's Mitre Restaurant, Cheltenham

Kate seemed a little guarded when we met earlier, only natural, I suppose; after all, she doesn't know us yet. It was a good idea to meet first for tea and then take a short walk, as the change of environment allowed us to mix up topics of discussion, and I feel we know more about each other now; there is more confidence to introduce some of the more sensitive subjects into the discussion.

Oscar and I are glad she has indicated she would want to know who our biological father is, and the more of us involved in the search, the better opportunity we will have of finding him.

Kate excuses herself between the starter and main course and heads to the washroom. I look at Oscar and, in a low voice, ask him, 'She is nice; I think we'll all get on well together. What do you think?'

'Yes, I think so; she is pleasant enough.'

We are all so different in our peculiar ways. Oscar can be so particular, at times, a result of his upbringing, I presume, with his father being a senior officer in the military and him being in boarding schools for most of his youth.

'Lighten up a little, Oscar, you're always so... *formal.*'

'Sorry, I know. Yes, Kate is very nice.'

Well, for Oscar, “very nice” is an improvement on “pleasant enough”. I continue, ‘I’m going to tell her where we are up to on the search for our biological father.’

‘Is that advisable? It may upset her; she only said she was interested in his identity after we asked, and then, only if we found out would she want to know.’

‘I know, I know, but…’

‘I think we should hold off for the time being, this is our first meeting, and there will be plenty of opportunity to discuss this later. Let’s not pressure Kate just yet with some tough decisions.’

‘OK, but I really do want to push this along.’

‘That I know, Sarah; however, please show a little restraint for now, please?’

Nodding slightly, I turn my head from him and look out over the flower gardens and terracing.

Twiddling with the piercing in my left ear, I say quietly, ‘That was interesting, don’t you think? Her husband is twenty-three years older than her; he’s old enough to be her father. To look at her, you wouldn’t think she could have been the other woman, the younger mistress in an affair.’

‘Sarah, please don’t think such things; you are far better than that, and you know it. We don’t know the full story, do we? So, let’s not speculate.’

‘Sorry, no, I suppose we don’t.’

Oscar places his left hand on top of mine on the table, and I turn back to him, ‘Have you heard back from the clinic?’ looking directly at me with his piercing blue eyes.

‘No, not yet, you?’

‘No, nothing.’

I see Kate walking back through the restaurant, returning to us. Oscar follows my eyes and sees her, quickly releasing my hand. As Kate puts a hand on the back of her chair, Oscar partially stands, his polite upbringing still shining through. I note Kate registers this and smiles at him.

'So, do you think there are any more half-siblings out there?' Kate asks as she sits, which surprises me a little.

'Er, well, I suppose so, it's possible,' I reply.

Kate continues, 'I was reading of the experiences of others on various web pages and chat rooms. Some half-sibling groups are ten or more. I can only imagine what this must feel like for the biological father if he found out.'

As Kate says this, I turn to Oscar, who has not flinched and remains composed, looking at Kate. She adds, 'Especially if, say, all ten wanted to get to know him, and he already has a wife and family of his own; it would be quite a daunting experience for him and his family.'

'No doubt it could be,' replies Oscar.

Oscar was right; Kate is unsure if she wants to know his identity, but I think it's more for the donor's sake than ours. Kate comes from a supportive family background, which would have been wonderful, whereas Oscar, although he has a mother and father, they are estranged from each other, with almost no apparent affection between any of them. My parents split and divorced not long after I was born. Apparently, it was all Mum's wish to have a baby; however, I haven't really felt any maternal love and affection, and no paternal love whatsoever, just a lot of constant change as Mum and I moved between rented properties and her working irregular hours in low paid jobs trying to make ends meet. I was often left with neighbours or friends and sometimes left alone to fend for myself. My grandparents on Mum's side passed away before I was born, and my dad's parents didn't want to know us after their son abandoned us.

So, yeah, I want to find out who my biological father is and if he wants a relationship with me. Oscar knows this but insists I'll only be let down again and should let it go. But I need to know. I spend a lot of time looking at men in the street, in bars, and in my workplace, looking at their features and wondering if they could be my father. I know my need to know can become distracting at times and that I need to regulate and control my urge to find him before it consumes me entirely, but I want to belong to something, something more than a distant mother; I just need to find it. Oscar sees things differently from me as he has parents, and they haven't provided the love that he knows I want, his experience being the evidence that I'll not find what I long for.

But I'm not for letting this go just yet.

Addressing Kate's comment, 'Should that be the reason why we can't at least try? He has the right to decline our request and retain his anonymity, so he will always hold the trump card, although it may be that he actually wants to know us; it's just that he's not thought about it yet because he doesn't know we exist; but we do, and if we don't ask, none of us will ever know.'

Oscar looks at me and frowns; although Kate doesn't see his expression, I can tell he's frustrated with me for pushing this. So, I go for it, 'We've already contacted the clinic to ask them to contact the donor.'

Oscar looks at me sternly and widens his eyes in a sort of *how dare you* look. Kate looks at me, then switches quickly to Oscar, and she sees his glaring look at me.

'Oh, right, so you have started the ball rolling then?' Kate asks.

I reply before Oscar speaks, 'Yes, we have both written to the clinic with our requests; we are just waiting to hear back now.'

'Ah, so that's why you asked if I would want to know if you found out.'

'Yes,' Oscar replies.

Kate looks at us both in turn, pondering her next comment.

The waiter returns with the main course serving and places the plates before us, remembering who ordered which dish. 'Please, enjoy your lunch.'

'Thank you,' Oscar responds, smiling gently, always polite.

In turn, Kate looks at us both, 'And if he doesn't want to waive his anonymity, then what? You'll be happy with his decision?'

Instantly, Oscar replies, 'Yes.'

Kate looks at me, and I try to avoid answering, choosing to look down at my food, fork in hand, and turn over a small potato.

'Sarah?' she asks.

I hesitate a little longer, knowing I wouldn't be happy with that as a final outcome. 'I would have to be, I suppose,' then looking up at her, continue, 'but there are other ways to find out.'

'Sarah! No.' Oscar is sharp with me, 'We have been through this; the man is entitled to his privacy and anonymity.'

'Yes, but I…'

Kate interrupts me, placing her left hand over my right hand, gently wrapping her fingers around mine, 'Oscar is right, Sarah; we have to respect he may never want to know about us or want to get to know us.'

'I know that, but it's not fair. Since 2005, donor-conceived adults have the legal right to know who their biological father is.'

In a calming voice, Kate replies, 'Yes, but the donors after this date know that before they make a donation, that wasn't the case back then; he was told he would remain anonymous forever; fairness has to cut both ways for it to be fair.'

'But we don't have a say in it, so how can that be fair?'

Oscar chips in, 'Our thoughts weren't considered back then; it was fairness between the donor and donation recipient; it was subsequent consultation with donor-conceived adults that talked of their feelings and concerns, and consultation with some donors, that brought about a change in the law. It's just that a change in the law can't be applied retrospectively.'

I look up, Kate is looking at Oscar as he looks at me. I know the outcome of this conversation; Oscar and I have had it so many times. 'I know, but it still frustrates the hell out of me.'

'Look, you've written to the clinic; that's the first step; let's see what comes from that,' Kate adds, tightening her hold of my hand, gently moving our hands up and down slightly in a supportive gesture.

I look back to Kate, 'Will you write to them as well, please?' From her reaction, Kate wasn't expecting that.

'Er, well, I could, but it may not make any difference.'

'It would to me,' I reply.

# 35

## Lauren – Lunch at The Old Yew Tree

Ruth mentioned on the call last night she was meeting Ally today for lunch at the Old Yew Tree. I made out that I would be in the area about lunchtime doing some errands, and Ruth suggested I pop in if I was free to say hello. I think this was Ruth just being kind, and I said I'd see how things were going and maybe I would pop in. However, I decided instantly I would drop in on them as soon as she said it; it would allow me a perfect opportunity to speak with Ally and try to find out some further information about Kate and her donor father.

Watching from across the street, I see them both enter the café before leaving them to run one of my short errands. Returning about fifteen minutes later seems the perfect time to walk and say hello; they'll have ordered their lunch, and I can simply stay a few minutes for a cup of tea.

As I enter through the front door, Ruth spots me almost instantly and waves, quickly saying something to Ally, who looks over her right shoulder in my direction. As I approach the table, Ruth stands up and moves over to an empty chair, allowing me to sit in hers opposite Ally.

It takes some self-control not to ask Ally outright questions, and I adopt a slower circular approach, 'Hello Ally, it's been a long time; how are you doing?'

'I'm fine, Mrs… er... Hunter.'

Her hesitance was probably from realising she only knows me by my married name, and things had changed.

'No, it's Lauren, please; I'm putting all that Hunter business behind me now. How is your mother? I've not seen her for some time. I must say, you are looking well.'

'Oh, er, yes. Thank you. Yes, my mum is OK, she is as busy as usual.'

'Good.'

Ruth interjects, 'We've just ordered, Mum; would you like me to ask for a menu for you?' partly raising her hand to attract one of the young student types waiting on tables.

'No, it's fine, thank you, I don't want to interrupt your lunch. I would love a quick cup of tea, though, if that's possible.'

'Of course, Mum.' Ruth attracts the attendant, and as she orders a tea, I look across at Ally.

'Are you working now, Ally, or are you still studying?'

'I'm working now Mrs, er, Lauren. I work with a small law firm just around the corner. Nice place and people, the money is OK; it suits my needs for now.'

'Good, so long as you're happy.'

'Yes, I am, thank you.'

Ruth asks about my chores, and I rhyme them off in an almost boring fashion, making out that I'm keeping busy with mundane things. Ally listens, sipping her drink, and politely adds to the conversation.

The table attendant returns with my tea, along with two plated, open sandwiches for Ruth and Ally, and places them down.

Ally picks up her cutlery, allowing me to scoot in with my first real question, 'Do you see much of Kate these days, Ally? You were all such good friends before that thing happened.'

Ruth jumps in before Ally replies, 'Mum, really?'

'Oh, I'm sorry, I didn't mean to… oh yes, sorry, I see what you mean,' my reply, feigning an older, forgetful mother.

'No, it's fine, Lauren,' Ally replies, 'We still speak whenever we bump into each other; we're still friends; in fact, I bumped into her not long ago, and we had a good catch-up.'

'Ah, good; I'm glad you're at least staying in touch with each other. Ruth mentioned the issue with Kate's biological father; that must have been a massive shock to Kate?'

Ally cuts a glance to Ruth, who raises her eyebrows, and I catch Ruth mee-mawing a sorry to Ally.

'Er, yes, it was,' Ally replies.

'Ruth told me it all worked out alright though, with her mum and dad, and they're all still talking and being a family; that's great, don't you think? Ruth?' This put Ruth on the spot a little, but I want to portray that I have no issues with Kate as a person; outwardly, that is.

'Er, yes, I suppose so, Mum.'

Looking at them both, I add, 'A child doesn't pick their parents, so I'm glad it is all amicable. It's the mother in me, I suppose.'

Ally places her fork down and looks across to me, 'I must say, you are taking this all quite well, better than I think I could have done if it happened to me.'

'Don't get me wrong, I have very little time for both Paul and Kate, but I don't wish them any harm; what happened has happened; there's no changing that. Ruth, Ben and I are still a family, and we're working through this, aren't we, Ruth?'

'Yes, we are.'

I try my move as Ally lifts her fork and continues picking at her side salad.

'Paul, Ruth's father, once donated to the same kind of clinics when he was younger.' Ruth's fork slips from her grip and clatters on the side of her plate. 'He did it before we married; he wanted to help other couples have children, and of course, there was a money element in it for Paul, a payment received for each donation.'

'Mum! Really? What are you talking about?'

'Oh my god, I'm sorry, Ruth, it completely slipped my mind; I thought you already knew; oh my, I'm so sorry.'

There, the first seed of doubt is sown.

Ally had stopped playing with her salad; this was obviously news to her too, and I have a feeling this is the kind of gossip that Ally will thrive on; after all, she told Ruth of Kate finding out about her donor father without too much trouble or any thought for Kate's feelings and privacy.

I continue, 'I can't really remember where he did it, around the London area, I think, when he was working down there; two or three clinics he mentioned, but knowing Paul as I do now, he would probably have done a lot more than what he told me; although I suppose there wouldn't have been too many clinics operating back then as it was only just becoming a thing here in the UK. What they can do now in medical science is fantastic, don't you think?'

The second seed of doubt is planted. These will take root in Ally's subconscious for now.

'Mum, can we talk about this later, please?'

'Oh, of course, darling, I'm sorry. Look at me, jabbering on and interrupting your lunch.' I pick up my teacup and take a sip, keeping a close eye on Ally and her raised eyebrows, averting her glance from Ruth. No doubt Ally will feed this back to Kate at some point, and when this information coincides with the other things I'm planning, it'll create quite a conundrum for Kate and Paul to address. Even though there will be nothing in it, it will still upset their perfect little marriage enough until they sort it all out.

How I delivered this snippet of information may be a little upsetting for Ruth, but we've been through worse. I'll apologise to her later, but it is time she found out a little more about her father's past.

It's not like I have to keep *his* secrets anymore.

# 36

## Ally – Back in the Office

So, Ruth's dad was a sperm donor; now that was a well-kept secret, and from her reaction, I don't think Ruth knew about this either. Is Lauren playing me, or is she just not bothered about anything anymore, being lonely, wanting to talk about anything to anyone?

But the information is not lost on me; she said Paul was a donor; is there a slight chance of him being Kate's father? Although I suspect the odds are heavily stacked against that being the case, they will be greater than playing the lottery, won't they?

Is she saying this just for devilment?

Lauren continued chatting with Ruth about something this weekend, including them both and Ben, some family get-together, but I wasn't really listening to it; my thoughts were wandering elsewhere.

*Could Paul be Kate's father? Is it possible?*

No, surely not. But he is old enough to be; in fact, he's probably about the right age; Lauren said it was a London clinic; well, I think she did. Yes, specialist clinics in London. I can't remember if Kate said anything about a London clinic being involved; I can't recall.

No, it's nonsense, not a chance. Anyway, Paul knows that Kate's biological father is a donor, and it hasn't phased him, so why am I thinking about it? Probably just Lauren babbling on about nothing.

Nothing.

Is it, though? Oh, it's making me think about it. Should I ask Kate if her biological father was involved with a London clinic? But that'll sound odd; she'll want to know why I am asking. Or do I just tell Kate what Lauren said? But then, she'll be peeved with me having lunch with Ruth and Lauren. I've known Kate for far too long to let this sit without mentioning it to her; she has a right to know, especially if there is an outside possibility that Paul could be her father.

The two partner solicitors are in court this afternoon, leaving me to look after the office. Using the chance to call Kate, I wander into one of the meeting rooms and close the door; I don't want the other paralegals and office juniors overhearing me. I dial Kate's mobile, and she picks up almost instantly.

'Hi Ally, are you OK? I thought you didn't want to chat during working hours.'

'Hi, yes, I'm fine. It's just that, well, I overheard something today, and I thought you should know about it.'

'Ooo, something exciting?'

'I'm not too sure how to say this now, so I'll just go for it. Remember, it's just something I heard in a conversation, so there could be no merit in this whatsoever.'

'Now you have me interested. What is it?'

'Firstly, don't freak when I mention names; promise me?'

'Ally, what do you take me for. What have you heard?'

‘Well, I was having lunch with Ruth Hunter today and…’ and as soon as I mention her name, Kate is already talking over me.

‘Ruth Hunter? Why are you having lunch with her?’

‘It was just a catch-up; we are friends as well. We all were.’

‘I know, but…’

‘Anyway, her mum happened to walk in and sat with us to have a cup of tea.’

‘Lauren?’

‘Yes.’

‘And you sat there? With her?’

‘Well, yes. I was sitting with Ruth; we’d ordered lunch and were chatting, just catching up, and then Lauren came in. Ruth spotted her, and the next thing, she sat with us just as our food arrived and…’

‘Sounds kind of cosy.’

‘No. In fact, it was far from cosy; it was quite awkward, actually.’ I thought she might be bothered by this. ‘Look, I wasn’t expecting Lauren to appear, but she did. I have no axe to grind with anyone when it comes to you and Paul; you and Ruth are both my friends, and I don’t want to pick one over the other.’

‘I never asked you to, but you are my best friend, my Chief Bridesmaid.’

‘I know. Kate, let me tell you what I heard. OK?’

‘Yes, well, if you must.’

‘Oh, right. Look, please don’t be like that. I never mentioned you or Paul or the wedding or anything; it was Lauren who dropped the bombshell.’ As I say it, I know I didn’t mean to say it that way. Why did I use the word bombshell?

‘What is she doing now? What bombshell?’

'Sorry, that was probably the wrong word.'

'She did all kinds when Paul and I became an item; you know that more than anyone. Is this another one of her games?'

'That thought crossed my mind, but I don't think she would have said what she did in front of Ruth if it was all just another of her distractions.'

'Distractions? That's a new word for it. Anyway, what is it this time, this *distraction*?'

I'm beginning to think I should have just dropped this and put it down to gossip from Lauren. Kate is getting annoyed; I half expected that, but I don't want her to hear this from someone else, and she gets upset.

'A question first; do you know if Paul ever… erm, has he mentioned if he…'

'What, Ally?'

'Has he ever donated his sperm to a clinic in London?'

'What? What are you talking about?'

'Lauren said, when Paul was younger, he donated his sperm anonymously for cash.'

'And?'

'Well, did he?'

'I don't know, he's never mentioned it. Not sure he had to. Where is this going? That bloody Lauren, she's always meddling, trying to upset us.'

'Oh right, so he hasn't then. That's good.'

'Why is that good?'

The door to the meeting room opens, and one of the paralegals is standing there with a client. I cover the phone's mouthpiece, 'I'm sorry, I'll be done in a minute,' but still have the earpiece to my ear, and I can hear Kate asking me again. As they close the door, I reply to Kate.

'I'm sorry Kate, I have to go. Can we talk later?'

‘Just a second, why is that good?’

‘Well, I was thinking about what you told me about your dad, and I got to thinking…’

‘No, she did. She’s found out a little bit of news and decided to play games with it to get Paul and me all wound up yet again. But I won’t entertain this now; you know what she’s like.’

‘I do. I’m sorry, Kate, it’s been playing on my mind, and I thought I’d better say something to you. I do know what she’s like, I’m sorry. Forget what I said. I’ll call you later, OK; got to dash.’

# 37

## Kate – At Home

That bloody woman, how dare she! She just can't accept the fact that her husband loves me instead of her, that they're divorced, and that we're now married. She makes my blood boil at times; she really does. If I didn't know any better, I'd say she's becoming a bitter, twisted, old woman rather than accepting her lot and moving on with the rest of her life.

Ruth was hurt when Paul and I got together, but she seems to be coming to terms with it; attending the wedding was a good step forward for her. Ben accepted it quite quickly after his first reaction, which was understandably upset and angry, but he seems to be a real pragmatist, and I'm glad he's staying in touch with Paul.

What do I do about Lauren? I'm certainly not going to ask Paul about what he did or did not do when he was younger; that's exactly what she wants me to do, and I refuse to react to her stupid games anymore.

If he did make donations, so what? There's no way he'll be my biological father. No chance. No, it's just her again, trying to get between me and Paul after picking up some information about my dad, but I'm wise to it now, and this time it's easy to ignore it. I'm going to let this wither on the vine. If she tries to move this around to get traction with others, it will show her up for what she is.

I'll keep quiet and see if Paul mentions it to me; if he does, then it'll only have come from her and will show how she is spinning her twisted words with others.

Besides, what with the new deal and his medical issue, Paul has enough on his plate right now. I must ask him what the latest is as it's been some time now, and I don't think he's even told me what his affliction is called, and he's certainly not mentioned what treatment he's going through.

*Is he worried it's more serious than he's letting on?*

# 38

## Paul – Apartment, Southwark, London

It's been over five weeks since I sent off our two samples to NeuvaGen. The first set of results, in my name, which was actually Graeme's sample, arrived on Monday at home, and I managed to pick up the letter quickly before Kate saw it. I told Kate that I needed to be in London urgently and caught the afternoon train down yesterday, anticipating my results would be awaiting me at my apartment; I was disappointed when they weren't.

On opening the first results on the train travelling down, I knew there wouldn't be anything to worry about as these were actually Graeme's results, but when I logged in using the code provided, there were three matches waiting for me within the DNA register matching Graeme's DNA. Shit, I never thought of this outcome, and I suddenly realise this could be a bit awkward now if Kate asks me about the results; I just assumed Graeme wouldn't have any matches. I'll have to tell her my results were boringly negative, there was nothing to report, and so I just kept it to myself, adding it was a waste of my time and money. Hopefully, she'll accept that.

Since I picked up that first letter at home for Graeme's results, I've been anxiously expecting the second letter, the results of my sample, eagerly awaiting receipt of my notice addressed to my apartment.

This morning, it arrived.

My first action was to email my P.A. asking her to postpone my scheduled meetings this morning, vaguely alluding to a family matter I needed to address; this will afford me some time to take on board what the results may contain.

Looking at the envelope on the kitchen worktop, now it's arrived, I can't seem to muster the courage to open it; I sway from not wanting to know the results back to I have to know. For Kate and I to carry on, I have to know, as I cannot continue with this uncertainty between us, and I need to close out this fictitious medical matter I'm supposedly suffering with before Kate starts to suspect something else is afoot. All this is compounded further as Kate wants to start a family with me soon.

So, I must know the truth.

Picking up the envelope, I slowly peal open the flap and extract the single page letter. The content is brief; just like the other letter I received, my results are ready, and there is a reference code to insert on the web page to access my results.

My laptop is open on the worktop, logged in to NeuvaGen, ready, with the cursor slowly blinking at me.

I turn away from them and walk to the window, procrastinating, delaying the inevitable. Looking out and down onto the bustling street below, I start to admire unknown people going about their everyday business, all of them unaware of the dilemma I'm in here, above them, all alone.

My head is playing over possible outcomes again, stupidly, as the results on that computer screen will define the outcome as I'll have the definitive answer.

Come on, Paul, just get on with it.

Taking my computer and the letter to the breakfast bar, I sit down and type in the reference code; the screen changes and I see it.

I have matches.

'Shit!' is the first thing I say out loud to no one but me. 'Fuck!'

But then, slowly I realise, that was always going to be a possible outcome, like Graeme's results; I have a wider family, and the matches could belong to them. I try to slow my breathing a little and take a large swallow of coffee, staring at the screen in front of me.

# 39

## Sarah – Lunch Break at Work

It's almost routine for me now to collect my sandwich box and protein drink from the fridge and sit in the far corner of the canteen where I won't be easily interrupted or distracted. I pull my tablet screen from my messenger bag, and as I bite into the first half of my sandwich, I click on the tab for the NeuvaGen web page and enter my login details.

Instantly, I notice new messages are waiting for me, and I tap my finger on the icon… more DNA matches!

I, we, have more matches. Opening the link, the next words on my screen seem almost surreal. The first match, and most surprising, is a paternal match! My biological father has been matched to my DNA! Our shared DNA; Oscar, Kate and I have found our biological father. We are now just one step away from finding out who he is. I need to share this with Oscar and Kate straight away in case they've not yet seen it; this is great news.

Opening the messaging app on my mobile phone, I type out a short message to our small chat group to alert them and tap send. The little green tick on the screen indicates Oscar has opened it almost immediately, and within ten seconds, he is calling me.

His first word before I can speak is, 'Really?'

'Yes, I'm looking at it now on my tablet, a paternal match. We've found him! It's great! Isn't it great, Oscar?'

'Yes, it is good news; I can tell you are excited.'

'Yes, I am, it's fantastic.'

'What else does it say?'

'A simple message that I have a paternal match, with 99.99% confidence. It doesn't really get any more accurate than that, does it? It's brilliant!'

'I'm just logging on now; give me a moment.'

While I wait for Oscar, I look at the screen again; my father, our biological father, has been found. All those years of waiting, wondering, and hoping that one day he would take a test and…

Oscar interrupts my staring at the screen, 'I have the same; yes, he's been found, well, matched should I say; we still don't know who he is. And what about this other DNA match, Sarah?'

In all the excitement, I had forgotten the message indicating more than one match is available. I click back and see the other match and at the same time, we both say aloud, 'Another sister.'

Then I follow on with, 'Wow!' Oscar knows how much I crave this kind of news, so my excitement won't phase him, but sometimes I wonder what it would take to get him excited. 'We need to let Kate know.'

'Yes, I agree. Has she not seen your message?'

'Message delivered but unopened,' I reply.

'OK. You telephone Kate and let her know, and I'll write to both our matches to introduce the three of us. We need to handle the paternal match very carefully, with a certain… tact; we don't want to scare him off at the first opportunity; we may have to work at this for some days and weeks to come, treading carefully to earn his trust.'

'I know, and you are far better at this than I am, thank you. Yes, I'll call Kate now. Oo, this is fabulous; I'm really excited, it's wonderful.' As I say it, I must have done so in a raised voice as a few others dotted around the work canteen turn to look at me. I smile back at them, then turn away from their gaze and quietly end my sentence, 'Thanks, Oscar; let's chat later this evening when I get home.'

'OK, bye for now,' and with that, he cancels the call with the detachment of a business call.

Another sister and our biological father. I wonder what they are like? Will they want to meet with us? Of the two of them, and this is me selfishly thinking of my needs, if I could only link with one of them, I want it to be our father. There is so much I want to hear about him, his name, his background, his hobbies, his likes and dislikes, do we look alike, what's his job, why did he make the donations? I know if I try to make the first contact, I will more than likely scare him off, my over-excitement being interpreted as something else. Oscar is well versed in sensitivity, caution and diplomacy; I've been likened to a bull in a china shop on more than one occasion; I know I need to slow down and think first before engaging in communications, especially with strangers in first contact, but most of the time I can't help myself.

I tap on Kate's contact number and wait for the ringtone. It rings once and cuts off almost instantly, so I try again and get the same result, with no opportunity to leave a voice message, which is unusual. I revert to typing a text message advising Kate to look at the web page for further match results and to call me when she can, then press send.

I finish my lunch, keeping a close eye on my mobile phone, eagerly anticipating Kate returning my call. She was hesitant when we asked her about wanting to know who our father is, but she came around in the end, I think; well, that's what I'm going with anyway. She will want to know, I'm sure of it.

# 40

## Kate – at Home

It didn't take long for Sarah to see the message and call me; she must be looking at the web page messages at every given opportunity; the match information was only uploaded a couple of hours ago. I know she will want to contact them both straight away, but hopefully, she'll take some time for the information to settle so she can digest it properly and think of the bigger picture and possible consequences on herself and others and what we want to do as a group of half-siblings.

*Are we better off knowing or not knowing?*

But my curiosity has been stirred again now, and it wasn't until I saw the match messages this morning that I knew what I wanted to do. I now want to know who he is, what he's called, maybe even meet him. And, of course, I have another half-sister to welcome; we are four now.

I feel bad now for cutting off Sarah's calls as quickly as I did, but I want her to slow down and take a breath. No doubt she will have called Oscar, and they will be planning to contact our new sister and our father. I have every confidence in Oscar to do so with finesse if Sarah leaves it to him.

My first big questions are, what do I say to Mum and Dad, and what will Paul think?

Paul didn't seem that interested in my going on this journey, but I know he's only looking out for me and my best interests; he doesn't want me hurt again. I wasn't in a good place when I first found out Dad wasn't my biological father, and my thoughts raced away with me, but luckily, it all turned out for the better, and it could be even more so. My biological father could be a leading doctor or surgeon or be doing extraordinary things in deprived countries in other parts of the world, bringing relief and care to those unable to help themselves; or, he could have gone into medical research, looking to find the next breakthrough in treatments for debilitating afflictions and diseases. I hope he stayed in the medical environment; it'll be great to learn more about him.

*But will he want to know me and my half-siblings?*

He's possibly married now with his own children, and there could be many reasons he wants to stay private and remain anonymous. Although, if he did, why would he do the test and then share his results?

He must have realised he could have donor-conceived children out there, the product of his donated sperm, and doing the test and sharing his matched information could open the door to those children wanting to contact him. So, my take on it is that he wants to be contacted.

I'll call Sarah and Oscar on video this evening, and we can discuss it further and make a plan together.

Now… Mum and Dad: I should tell them about this information, and if yes, do I do it now or wait to see if he wants to be contacted? If he doesn't, then I'll be no nearer to knowing who he is, so there'll be no benefit or otherwise in bringing this news to Mum and Dad just yet; if anything, it could hurt them, and me; I don't want to be the cause of anything like that. Mum and Dad kept their secret for what they believed were the right intentions, and I suppose we'll never know if they made the right choice. Being older and then finding out Dad isn't my biological father was a shock, yes, but I can now appreciate the pros and cons, and of the decision they made not to tell me. I know they both love me dearly, only wanting to protect the bond and relationship between Dad and me.

That's it, decision made, I won't say anything to Mum, Dad or Paul just yet; it's probably best this way, they only need to know when I have something more substantive to share with them; I can park this for now and concern myself with it when there is a need to worry about it. If my biological father remains anonymous and I cannot find out anything about him, I may never need to share the knowledge of my quest with Mum and Dad and Paul, adopting the "*what you don't know won't hurt you*" approach is best all round, I think.

Right, decided. Now that's sorted, I'll message Sarah and Oscar back.

# 41

## Jody McTee – Local Café

When I received the notice earlier that my results were in and available to view, the matches section indicated other DNA matches related to mine. This is what I need; having three half-sibling matches along with our collective paternal match is how I will find him.

It took me a long time to track down my mother if I can call her that; the woman who gave birth to me, but I did find her in that run-down hovel claiming to be a home for those fallen into bad times and infirm, but I did find her, and I got the retribution owed to me for her ruining my life. Killing her was such a release; that part of my story is closed.

Now it's his turn, whoever he is.

It was sold to me that I was the product of a one-night stand, but that wasn't the whole story. My father, oh, I so hate using that word for him; he was a man working in the same town as her, my mother. From what I've pieced together, she had just turned seventeen when they first met; he was about twenty-two or twenty-three. She thought it was love, but clearly, it was just sex to him. They had a brief kind of on-and-off relationship, and it wasn't long after they met that she fell pregnant with me. A classic tale; he didn't want to know and told her to 'get it sorted', which was against her and her family's beliefs.

She kept trying to contact him, but he ignored her, so she went to his workplace to confront him, and that's when she found out he had been using a false name and had been playing her along all the time; he didn't even work where he had told her, and so, she had nothing to go on. No doubt, wanting to escape the situation, he probably left town and disappeared, never to be seen or heard from again, and for that, I will never forgive him.

She tried to hide the fact of her pregnancy, but it was getting harder and harder until one day, her mum, my supposed grandmother, suspected and confronted her. Her mum and dad were furious, bringing shame on the family, and fights and rows broke out as she insisted on keeping the baby, me. That's when she was thrown out of the family home and left to fend for herself.

With very little money and nowhere to go, coupled with that low life of a father of mine having run away, she ended up sleeping rough in empty premises and old derelict buildings, mixing it up with the wrong types. That's when the drugs started, and she started doing tricks for cash to fund her habit.

She was good-looking back then, apparently, and a pimp realised the potential and took her in, but the reality was what he dragged her into was worse than what she was leaving. The pimp found a niche market of offering sex with a woman, a girl really, who was pregnant, and some of the dregs of life who get their kicks from having unprotected sex with pregnant girls came paying good money, but she never saw any of it; her payment was a bed and her next fix.

She was still being sold out for sex up to the day before I was born, and by that time, she was in a bad way. I was born about four weeks before full term, and social services swiftly moved in after my emergency birth in the hospital. She was in no way capable of looking after me, and quickly, I was taken into care, but who wants the child of a drug-addicted sex worker, especially a baby with some congenital health issues? That nailed my future within the "care" system for the duration until I came of age and could escape its confines.

Care homes, orphanages, hospitals, foster care, juvenile detention centres, I went through it all. It made me the tough and angry person I am today, and it made me a survivor, one hell-bent on finding the two people who created me only to abandon me to the various institutions without a second thought, turning me into what I am today.

I didn't think she would still be alive, but when I got out of the system and found some work, I started planning my payback. It took me nearly two years to find out her name, to track her down, and then kill her. But before I did, I told her of everything that had happened to me, in detail, that she caused. She went to her grave, knowing exactly what she had exposed me to. Back then, I blamed her the most; she was supposed to be my mother, my protector, but killing her didn't salve my dark side as much as I thought it would; if anything, it motivated me to want the same for him. Then it slowly dawned on me that it was him; he was the one who should have provided us both with a safe home and some security, that he knew what he was doing, and so then, he became the focus of my attention.

But I had nothing to go on; there is no name on my birth certificate or in my care records about his identity, just "*father unknown*"; no photos, no work leads, nothing.

Then I saw this advertisement on a bus for DNA testing and looked further into it. It was a long shot, but it's now given me the best lead I've ever had. NeuvaGen know who he is, and I have half-siblings who hopefully will want to know who he is too; they might do my work for me, find out who he is, and provide me with a name, and then I'll get to meet him too.

I have waited a long time for this; I always knew I would find him.

And what of my half-siblings? What are they to me? Nothing; they're just fellow passengers on life's journey through hell, but they could be of some use to me.

Patience: the one thing I've learned over the years is that patience is essential to achieving what I want. I'll wait a little to see if they reach out first, as I don't want them to think I'm eager to meet up. To be honest, I don't want to acknowledge them in any way, I have no real interest in who they are or what they are about; they are simply a means to an end, to his end; that's all they mean to me, nothing more, nothing less.

I finish my sandwich and drink and settle my bill before leaving the café and heading across the street to the Town Library.

# 42

## Paul – His Apartment, Southwark, London

I've not moved for nearly five minutes now, my eyes fixed on the words on my screen, staring through the screen words "My Matches".

I click it. It shows my DNA has four matches: all my children and my offspring. My DNA is shared with four people, one male and three female: a son and three daughters.

This can't be correct, can it? How can this be? Who are the four?

Then it dawns on me, phew, well, that's a relief. Kate only mentioned Oscar and Sarah, and with her, that makes it three, not four. Could Ben and Ruth have done DNA tests that I'm not aware of? That would account for two of the four, and maybe the other two are the result of my donations being used with random couples all those years ago. Yes, of course, that makes sense.

Watching the cursor blink at me, willing me to make a move, I can't decide what to do next. If my theory is correct, I am not related to Kate, and we can move on together. But is this enough? Can I rely on my theory? The trouble is, it's not concrete, is it? There is no certainty in what I'm reading on screen and my hopes, and I'm tying it to a theory that provides me with my desired outcome.

Is it just wishful thinking? I must be sure; otherwise, I'll be no better off.

I recall some of the replies I read weeks ago to the frequently asked questions on NeuvaGen's website, that to find out more about my matches, I need to share my results with my other matches, but then, and it's the scary thing that worries me, that when this is done, there is no turning back.

So, if Ben and Ruth account for two of my matches, I could be opening linkage to two other donor-conceived persons biologically related to me. Do I want to do that? Do I need that distraction in my life just now?

But, if Ben and Ruth have not done DNA tests and they are not two of my matches, I'll have four others out there that I helped to create, making six in total as a biological father. The thing is, they could be anyone, and I suppose that could include Oscar and Sarah and… Kate.

Can I stick with the deduction that Kate is one of three, only three offspring from my donations, so she can't be one of my four matches? Can I hold on to this to show we are not biologically linked? I want to. But can I?

My head is spinning again.

I close the laptop and drop my head in my hands. I'm no better off now than when I started this; I still do not have a definitive answer, and the only way to close this down is to share my information.

Walking to the window again, looking out and downward, the scene hasn't changed much at all, much like my position. Any one or all of my matches may try to contact me shortly to share information, and if they did, then what do I do?

The implications if she turns out to be my daughter are enormous and blow my mind. But it just can't be so;

the odds are surely against it; this is the only thing keeping me sane at the moment.

Kate has been magnificently patient with me, holding on to the belief I'm working through some treatment for my fictitious genital problem. I feel awful for lying to her, telling her I'm going to specialist medical consultations that don't exist, and taking medication in front of her that is nothing but vitamin pills. Still, I need to keep the story alive so that we can become one again once I've proven to myself she is not my daughter.

Dropping back down on the settee, closing my eyes and covering my face with both palms, I scream quietly into my hands. What the hell am I going to do?

# 43

## Jody – Town Library

Having collected lots of information about my mother, her parents, her early life, and her friends, it allowed me to piece together her movements and how she met him, my father. Her best friend at the time, Julie, was a mine of information about the pair of them, but obviously, he was using a false name, making it impossible to track him down.

He was tall, just over six feet, with fair hair and blue eyes, and he had a passion for cricket. Julie remembered he would always want to know the latest cricket score or catch up on the latest match on a small radio he carried. She distinctly remembered one time when the three of them were out in the town centre, him stopping to watch a cricket match in the West Indies on TV screens in a shop window and my mother tugging at him to leave the scores alone and stop ignoring her. Julie recalled his accent wasn't local but more north home counties, and he often spoke of a good friend, but she couldn't recall his name; it was all a long time ago. She said he never touched coffee, preferring tea or real ale on a night out. No one had a photograph of him; in those days, the snappy world of mobile phones was in its infancy.

My so-called mother spoke to Julie a lot about him, and Julie said she was always trying to slow my mother down; she seemed too eager to want to be with him.

Flicking through my notebook, I read the information I've collected on him; it's sad how little I know. Apparently, I do have some of his physical looks, traits, likes, and dislikes, but none of these are substantial enough to prove a man could be my biological father. However, they are background, providing some basic supporting evidence. I have inherited his blue eyes and fair hair, but I've come to hate cricket with a passion, probably because he loved it so much.

The trouble is, my mother never had much information about him, and with him hiding his identity from her, it's been impossible to find out who he is until now.

Sitting here, in the library on the free-to-use public computers, I think of all the information available to me now, here at my fingertips, with the World Wide Web and national and local archives, but I don't know where to start looking. I know his birth certificate will be on the national register somewhere, but it's one of millions of records, and there may be other snippets from newspaper cuttings or local events, but which newspapers and which local events; I have no name and no idea of his hometown to focus on.

The DNA results I received yesterday are the best break I've had at identifying him. I am only one step away from naming him… and then we'll meet.

Logging into the NeuvaGen portal, I see the message waiting for me from one of my matches, Oscar; my three half-siblings, Oscar, Sarah and Kate, would like to meet me. So, they are in touch with each other; that could be interesting but also dangerous for me. I don't want to get too close to any of them, not with what I have planned.

I'll play elusive for the time being, see what information I can get from them, anything that will help identify him, and hopefully keep me at arm's length from them.

I start to type my reply to Oscar.

> "*Oscar, thank you for reaching out to me following our matched DNA results. I'm uncertain of my next steps, as a part of me thought this would not be successful, and I hadn't thought it through fully. I'm sure you can appreciate this is a surprise for me, especially on hearing I have half-siblings. I will be in touch again soon. J.*"

I keep it brief, indicating it's my half-siblings who are the shock, not my paternal match. Now that he is on the database, I can access his name when I break through their firewall. The best thing about a wayward upbringing, mixing it up with all kinds from all backgrounds, is learning all the dark skills they never teach you in an ordinary state school.

I pull out the portable hard drive from my backpack and check that no one is around before connecting it to one of the computer's USB ports. It's just a matter of time now.

This is the most alive I've felt since killing her, that woman, my mother.

# 44

## Paul – His Apartment, London

Lying back and looking up at the ceiling, it feels like I've been here for hours, thoughts dancing around my head of how to find out who my matches are without giving away my identity. Every which way I think of approaching this exposes me, and I can't risk that; I have to keep my identity secret just in case. I hear a gentle "ting ting" from my computer, and, not recognising the notice alert, I slowly sit up and rub my eyes before padding across to the laptop once more.

Tapping the mouse pad, the screen comes to life, and the small light beside the built-in camera flickers as the face recognition software activates.

The screen fully opens, and I'm still on the NeuvaGen home page, but the countdown clock indicates it will self-time out in two minutes due to inactivity. As I move the cursor around the page, the timer disappears and is replaced with a message alert in the middle of my screen, and I see the little envelope icon with a small red 1 in its top corner, indicating someone has sent me a message.

I click on the icon, the message opens, and I start to read:

"*Hi, my name is Oscar, and we have matched DNA.*"

What the fuck! Oscar! No, it can't be the same Oscar, not Kate's Oscar. I feel my pulse quicken and look away from the screen; no, it can't be. I take a couple of deep breaths to calm down before returning to the message.

> "*Hi, my name is Oscar, and we have matched DNA. I am writing on behalf of my half-siblings, Sarah and Kate, and I, and one other who has been matched with us just today; I'll be writing to her separately.*"

I drop my head into my hands and scream out, 'NO. NO. NO. NOOOO!' The rage in me is intense, and I just react, picking up the glass of water beside my laptop and throwing it across the room into the kitchen area, watching the glass strike against a wall cupboard, showering shards of glass and water everywhere. 'NOOOO!'

I can't read anymore.

# 45

## Kate – At Home

The call with Sarah and Oscar left us all disappointed to differing degrees. Our paternal match has yet to respond, and we've only received a brief reply from our newly found half-sister. I can appreciate our biological father will be thinking things through carefully; after all, there are at least four of us now that he never knew of, but he must have expected some news, someone matching his DNA, or why bother doing it. He knew he was a donor; he couldn't have forgotten that, although I suppose the testing kit could have been a gift from a family member or friend, and it never registered with him, this could be the outcome. Then again, it could be he is actively out there looking to see what his donations have created, although according to the NeuvaGen webpage, if he wanted to know this, he could contact them directly, and some information could be shared with him, so it's more likely that he just didn't think matches could be made this way; so I'm on the side of an innocent revelation, whereas Sarah is clearly thinking he's being selfish, and Oscar is just Oscar, neutral and willing to bide his time.

Our new half-sister, known to us only by her NeuvaGen reference code and the initial 'J' added to her message, at least replied, and I also appreciate her position of wanting some more time to think of what she wants next. Rereading her message, she is in the same boat I was in and needs time to process the information first; I can respect that. Oscar talked it through again with Sarah, reminding her that this is a significant milestone in someone's life, and they need to come to terms with it.

So, we are one step closer to identifying our biological father; it's all on him now; he's the only one who can lift the cloak of anonymity. Sarah wants to message him again, but both Oscar and I have convinced her to wait and let Oscar make contact in due course.

I'm sticking with my earlier logic of saying something to Mum, Dad and Paul only when there is something positive to tell them.

Contact with Paul is more sporadic than it should be anyway; if I didn't know any better, I'd think he is trying to avoid me. It's worse when he's away, and when he's home, he's either in his study or down at the cricket club, playing or socialising with his teammates.

Next time he's home, I need to pin him down and ask about his medical treatment; it's all a little too vague, and I'm starting to worry that there is something more seriously wrong with him. He carries his medication with him, never leaving it around for me to see and read the label. Could it be if I checked out the medication, it'll lead me to an ailment that he's trying to shield me from? I just want him to be honest with me; we said we would always be.

I did start to wonder if he had contracted some kind of sexually transmitted disease, as he's not even coming close to me anymore, but I know Paul, he wouldn't have cheated on me, he wouldn't have slept with another woman; he must be ill, he's concerned enough to get treatment and taking steps to prevent himself from becoming aroused. Poor thing. As soon as he's well again, we'll plan a lovely long holiday away in the sun, reconnect, and re-ignite that passion we've lost due to this bloody illness.

Everything is a waiting game these days, waiting and wanting.

# 46

## Jody – Dale Bridge Cricket Club

The address I have found for him is a rented apartment in London, but the current tenant on file has a different name; Paul Hunter. I now know my father's name is Graeme Oglesby; he probably used a friend's address to hide his tracks from his wife and his family, but that won't deflect me from my goal; I can see through such a simple deception; this Paul Hunter must be a good friend to him. Even though I know his name now, I still refer to him as him; my disdain and lack of respect for him prevents me from using his real name.

A search on the internet brought me only four hits globally for the name Graeme Oglesby, and I had to whittle these down to a final contender; lucky for me, he has such an unusual surname coupled with his spelling of Graeme. I looked at whatever I could find on each of them, age range, appearance, and family status, and I reduced it to two possible candidates that it could be. However, searching deeper on the internet, I found an old bio for one of them, which helped me eliminate him; he wasn't in the UK during the years in question; he was living in Singapore before the likely sample dates through to after my birth date; not a concrete elimination but I consider it highly probable it's not him. So, by deduction, I've ended up on the one Graeme Oglesby as the only likely candidate. His age now puts him in his early to mid-twenties when I was conceived, making him about five to eight years older than her, my mother, which fits with what I've been told about him. He is married with his own children, two, both younger than me. He was born and raised in Hampshire, eventually moving to the Dale Bridge area after they married, and from the posts, it looks like he works near home now after many years travelling with his job. He seems successful, and the photos online portray an air of self-confidence and almost arrogance; I feel I can almost read into the depth of his mind through those eyes as they glare back at me.

It amazes me that people don't lock down their social profiles; do they not know what a determined person can find out about them if they try?

The perfect family. The photos I can see of them online on various social media platforms make me sick. I could have had that life if he'd been honourable and done the right thing by her and for me.

Looking at his posts and photos, I see that his features tend to align with mine: fair hair, reasonable height, slightly larger off-centre nose, and blue eyes. Staring at his photo on my screen, it's satisfying to be looking at the image of my biological father, knowing that I'm meeting him in person soon. This is the man who took advantage of my mother and then abandoned her, resulting in me living the shitty life that I have. He is the root cause of everything that has happened to me, and I will let him know it.

His social pages don't indicate where he lives, but there are several photos of him posing wearing cricket whites, standing with teammates, and one photo in particular of him holding a trophy with the name of a cricket club on a sign behind him, Dale Bridge Cricket

Club. Julie said she remembered he had a passion for cricket. The caption beneath the photo also mentions a fellow team member, Paul Hunter, for scoring a half-century, the same name on the tenancy agreement for the apartment in London. So, I have him now on his home patch. Entering the cricket club name in the search engine, the club web page appeared as the first hit, and scouring the club images, I found him in at least three further photos. This is his club; now I know where to find him, and after searching the cricket fixtures list, I know when he'll be there. It wasn't that difficult after I had a name for him.

Sitting on a plastic chair in the main stand to the left of the steps up to the pavilion, I look at the cricket match, quietly sipping a cup of tea from my flask; men in white outfits pretending to be gentlemen. He's been in bat now for nearly thirty minutes and seems to be hitting many runs, with some local support applauding his successes. It sickens me that people are actually applauding him, massaging his ego, thinking he is a special person deserving of such reverence.

"How's that!" A cry from multiple players on the pitch, and the umpire has given him the signal for out. The home team stands, applauding their player, while the away team congratulates their bowler between the wickets. I look at him closely as he walks towards me, heading back to the pavilion, bat tucked under his left arm as he removes his gloves and hat with face guard, and even with his head bowed, I can tell it's not him; this isn't Graeme. He climbs the three steps near where I am sitting as a replacement batsman from the pavilion comes down the steps from behind me, and they stop briefly beside me. I overhear them exchanging a few words.

'Watch out for that mean backspin he's playing; he's damn good.'

'Are you alright, Paul? You're a million miles away today. That's the first time I've known you go for a delivery like that, an obvious wicket threat.'

'I know, I'm sorry, Graeme; I've too much on my mind.'

'OK, don't worry about it, pal, we all have a bad day now and again. Still a decent inning; I'll catch you later.'

'Cheers. Good luck, Graeme.'

hearing this exchange, my observations confirm I'm within a few feet of my biological father; this is the closest I've ever been to him, and it's hard to control my excitement, but I must, as I intend to get much closer to him later today.

Sitting, staring at him as he walks out onto the field, I keep thinking over what I intend to say to him. My thoughts flip from calling him out, here and now, in front of his friends, or remaining patient and waiting for a quiet moment when we're alone, but the decision is easy, given what I plan to do to him, I don't want to be noticed or remembered by anyone; I don't want any witnesses.

I haven't got a car, so following him home will be impossible. There will be little opportunity to catch him on his own here, and once he leaves in his car, I'll have to wait until the next match to try my luck again. I considered waiting in the shadows to note down his car registration plate, but hacking into the government driver licencing centre to find out his home address is too risky, so my mind is made up; I'll confront him here, but in the car park when he leaves; hopefully it'll be a little later and darker by the time he decides to go; at a time when we'll be on our own.

# 47

## Graeme – Dale Bridge Cricket Club

‘See you later, Graeme,’ Paul calls out to me as I open the rear door to the changing rooms.

‘Yeh, see you next week; I hope you get your worries sorted; call me if you want to talk about it. Cheers, mate,’ my reply as the door self closes slowly behind me.

Paul won’t let me in on what’s bothering him, but it’s clear to see it’s important to him; it’s affecting his game, so it must be pretty bad.

The sun set about half an hour ago, and I know I’ll be in for a grilling session from the missus when I get home. I should have been home nearly two hours ago for dinner, but she knows what I’m like, especially on serious match days like today; anyway, I’m never in trouble for long; she loves me too much. I’ll book us a couple of nights away soon as a little treat for us; I know she puts up with a lot from me during the playing season, especially her having to run the kids around to all kinds of events over the weekend, and that’s why I love her dearly.

I am surprised, though, how quickly it’s gone dark; thick clouds rolling in, and the absence of the moon isn’t helping. Raising my car key fob, I press the button, and the lights of my BMW flash, automatically turning on the headlights, illuminating the wall in front of my car, and back splashing a diffused light in my direction. As I approach the rear of my car, I sense another person nearby, and hearing soft footfall on the gravel behind me, I turn.

'Hello,' I call out.

'Graeme Oglesby,' is all she says to me as she closes towards me, slowly coming into the low light from my car.

'Er, yes, and you are?'

'I'm your daughter.'

'Sorry? My what? Did you say, my daughter? I don't think so.'

'Yes. I am.'

'No, I'm sorry, I think you have the wrong man,' and as I say it, a couple, laughing loudly, turn the corner of the pavilion building, heading towards some parked cars on the other side of the car park, their path interrupting the sensor to the security lights on the mast overlooking the pavilion, illuminating the car park. I notice her glance a look at them over her left shoulder, while simultaneously pulling down her baseball cap lower over her face, making it harder for me to see her now, especially with the brighter light behind her and the limited reflection of my car headlights.

She continues in a hushed voice, 'No, I haven't. You are my father, well, my biological father anyway. You got my mother pregnant and ran away, abandoned her… and me.'

'Uh, no way, now I know you have the wrong man, I have done no such thing.'

'In London, back in 1998; have you forgotten already?'

'What are you talking about? I certainly didn't get your mother pregnant.'

The rear door of the changing rooms opens again, and over her shoulder, I see Paul step out into the car park with his kit bag slung over his shoulder; he looks our way and stops to focus on us.

'Is everything alright over there, Graeme?'

'Yes, everything is fine, Paul; just some kind of misunderstanding we are trying to sort out.'

'Are you sure?'

'Yes, I'm sure.'

'OK. See you at practice next week, mate?'

'Yeah, sure, see you then,' I reply as I turn to look at her again. In a quieter voice, looking at the top of her baseball cap on her lowered head, I ask, 'What makes you think I'm the man you are looking for?'

She raises her head slowly, her eyes level with mine, and speaks with a slow, confident tone, 'You are Graeme Oglesby, aren't you?'

'Yes, I am.'

'Then you are the man I am looking for. You bastard.'

'Wow! There's no need for that tone, love.'

'How dare you call me love!' she shrieks at me, grabbing the sleeve of my pullover.

I pull away from her, breaking her hold, and move to my car, opening the door and throwing my kit bag across to the passenger seat. As I climb in, she tries to grab a hold of the door, but I slam it shut and engage the door lock. She stands there, pulling at the handle and thumping the window as I start the engine and put the car into reverse. I hit the gas pedal, and the wheels struggle for a second, searching for traction, but find some, and the car moves backwards quickly. She releases the door handle to avoid being dragged along with the car.

I spin the car around and accelerate off, leaving her standing there. She gets smaller in my rear-view mirror as I depart. My heart is pounding; I don't know why. I suppose the unexpected nature of her being there and her tone, coupled then with that sudden change in her attitude. She used my name, but that's either a mistake or a play. Was that some kind of scam? Was she trying to fleece me or something?

My mobile rings and Paul's name appears on the dashboard display; I push the button on my steering wheel to answer it.

# 48

## Paul – Car Park

'Is everything alright over there, Graeme?'

'Yes, everything is fine, Paul; just some kind of misunderstanding we are trying to sort out.'

'Are you sure?'

'Yes, I'm sure.'

'OK. See you at practice next week, mate?' I reply, sensing everything is not as fine as Graeme says it is.

'Yeah, sure, see you then,' Graeme replies, turning back to look at the woman; our brief exchange obviously now concluded. I turn and head for my car parked on the far side of the car park, open the back door and place my kit bag on the rear seat. As I close the door, I look over towards them, and they seem to be in a more heated discussion now. I see her grab at the sleeve of his jersey as she raises her voice, and he pulls away, turns and gets into his car. She reaches for the door handle and tugs at it, and without thinking, as if by instinct, I raise my mobile phone and start to video record them.

Graeme starts his car engine as she pulls again at the door handle and then bangs her fist on the glass window of the door. Graeme puts his car into gear and accelerates backwards, causing the loose gravel to flick up in a shower about her as the rear wheels spin, looking for grip on the loose stones. The noise of the sudden acceleration attracts the attention of another couple in the car park, who turn to see Graeme's BMW turn one hundred and eighty degrees and depart the car park at speed.

The woman watches him drive away, then looks at the couple, and then over to me, noticing me with my phone pointing in her direction. She instantly turns her back to me, lowering her head and pulling down her baseball cap to mask her face. She walks away quickly, turning the corner of the changing room building and disappearing from my sight.

What the hell was all that about? Graeme's not been having an affair, has he?

No, in all the years I've known him, I've never known him to be that kind of man. It must be something serious, though; she seemed well annoyed with him, and he was certainly in a hurry to get away from her. I stop the video recording and look at the phone in my hand. Shall I phone him to see what's been going on?

I go to my speed dials and press his name; the call connects in a few seconds, and on the second ring, Graeme answers it.

'Hi Paul, sorry about that.'

I can hear his heavy breathing, as though his adrenaline has kicked in and he is trying to calm down again.

'What the hell was that? She looked pretty mad with you.'

'Yeh, that was really weird and intense. I don't know who she is, a complete stranger. She walked up behind me in the car park, called out my name, and I turned, then started going on at me about knowing her mother in London and me having an affair with her. I told her she had the wrong bloke and that I didn't know her mother, and then she started to flip out. I think she's a bit, you know, unstable or something; probably let out for the weekend and off her meds.'

'But she called out your name?'

'Yeh, weird, right? Like she knew me.'

'Sounds like she's got the wrong Graeme Oglesby.'

'That's what I said.' I hear him exhale deeply and then continue, 'You don't think it's a stunt by one of the lads, do you? Or something to do with that bloody anonymous complaint?'

It could be the former, but it's definitely not the latter, that, I know for a fact, wasn't real. 'Possibly one of the lads, they're always pulling stunts, you know what they're like.'

'Yeah, but if it was, she's a bloody good actress; seemed real enough to me, her frustration and all.'

'It did to me too. I'll ask around, see if one of them is pulling your leg or trying to wind you up for some reason.'

'Cheers, mate. It did freak me though. Jeez, I'm shaking a bit here.'

'OK, I'll see what I can find out and let you know. Are you OK to drive home?'

'Yeah, I'll be fine, now I've got away from her.'

'Alright, look, take it easy, mate.'

'Yeah.'

'Catch you next week?'

'No, you won't, because I'm the best player around here, it's only sixes from me next week,' and he laughs to himself as he kills the call.

I can't see why anyone would want to wind him up like that, but then again, there are some crazy guys in this club. I don't think I've seen or heard him that rattled before, and we've been in some tight spots, the two of us.

Has he been seeing another woman, has my thing with Kate rubbed off on him?

No, not Graeme, I'm not having it. Graeme is as straight as they come.

I get into my car, and as I go to start the engine, I stop and lower my arms to rest in my lap. Kate will be in when I get home. I'm not ready yet for this, breaking the news that I am seeing another woman and want to be with her instead. It's the only way I can think of to break us up without anyone finding out our secret, no, my secret; she doesn't know anything about it.

She tried again earlier today to find out what the doctors are doing to sort out my "problem", and I did my best to deflect her questioning, but she will start again, no doubt, as soon as I'm home.

Kate, I love you. I punch the steering wheel; I must not think like that. We are done; through. I'll tell her next weekend when I come back up from London. I'll have to get my game face on, act it out, clear my things out of the house, freeze the bank accounts and block withdrawals, and make it look like the real thing; well, it shouldn't be difficult; I've had enough practice. But this will shatter me, as it will her, but she has no idea of the bigger issue, and I want it to stay like that.

# 49

## Oscar – Jody's Flat

It's a little colder tonight, standing inside the dark recesses of this shop door. My mind is turning over the events of the last few days, rehearsing what we are going to say to Kate, if anything, about our new sister.

The information Sarah gleaned from private messaging Jody was useful, allowing me to track Jody down. She is living in temporary accommodation, taking a flat above a tattoo parlour not too far from Kate's home, which is either freakishly uncanny or planned in some way.

I tried reaching out to Jody without success, but Sarah seems to have struck a chord with her, and they have been exchanging basic information about each other, with Sarah providing her with some background on Kate and me. After a few message exchanges, Sarah shared a few photos of her tattoos with Jody, and Jody reciprocated. One tattoo in particular caught Sarah's eye, and she offered up the artist's name, which Jody confirmed; Jody saying she was impressed with Sarah's eye for detail and knowledge of the particular artist. From this, we tracked down the tattooist's parlour, and a couple of days ago, I walked in, quietly asking for Ronan as I had a special request. I waited for half an hour for Ronan to become free and mentioned to him I particularly liked the

Medusa head tattoo my sister Jody has on her upper chest, reaching up into her lower neck and that I'd been considering a smaller one on my back. He said he could call out to her in the upstairs flat, and I hushed him quickly, saying no thanks, my intention being for it to be a surprise and to please keep it quiet. I made an appointment in a couple of weeks and slipped away quietly.

Sarah is convinced Jody's primary motivation is to identify our biological father rather than have any invested relationship with her wider half-siblings, and to some extent, I can respect that. It's always been Sarah who has wanted more bonding, and although I was also hesitant at the beginning, in my situation, I'm glad she did; I now have a sister I can talk things through with, and we support each other when things are a little rough and one of us needs cheering up.

Sarah is quite enthused with the relationship she is building with Jody, hoping that one day Jody will want to meet with us all and we can become close, or at least closer, but I'm not so sure. At times, I worry Sarah can be a little naïve when rushing into communicating and sharing with people, especially when it comes to engaging with other matches and her drive to want to identify and connect with our biological father. To me, Jody seems, I don't know, detached from it all in some way, and I don't want Sarah to get hurt in the process. In Kate's situation, she too was unsure at first but soon came around to the idea of meeting. When we met, it was clear we had some kind of bond, or at least something in common to bind us, but Jody's detachment from Kate and me leaves me a little, I don't know… sufficiently cautious to wonder at her motives.

I've spent quite a bit of time searching online for any information on Jody, but she doesn't seem to have any social media presence I can find, and I've searched many sites and forums. For me, it is unusual in this modern age that a person of her age and interests has no outward digital presence; or am I just being a little cynical?

So, now knowing where she lives, I decided to take some time away from work at short notice and follow her to see what she does and what she gets up to, and so far, it's been quite dull, with mundane work commutes and shifts at two local bars pulling pints and clearing tables. She doesn't seem to have any friends she socialises with, and as soon as her shifts are over, she returns to her flat above the parlour.

However, tonight, something is a little different. Jody left work at the usual time, and just as I was resigned to tailing her back to her flat, she took a left turn instead of a right, which surprised me. She continues walking towards the town centre, heading into the central business district, which is all closed up and quiet at this time of night, making it harder for me to follow her without being noticed. She climbs some concrete steps and walks into the middle of an open paved area. I watch her from the shadows as she stops to look at a tall office block, quickly referring to her mobile phone a couple of times before looking around the plaza area and then departing. Was she waiting for someone or is it the building that interests her? I waited a good ten minutes after she left before walking across the plaza over to the office building. Looking at the companies listed on the nameplates, I can't see anything special; it's just a list of regular companies, as far as I can tell. Taking out my mobile phone, I swipe for the camera to photograph the company names, and as I do so, the flash on my phone illuminates the doorway, attracting the attention of a night watchman I hadn't spotted sitting behind a desk in the reception area; he stands quickly looking at me, holding a walkie talkie in front of him, poised to speak. I wave and smile, raising my thumb to indicate all is OK, before turning to walk away.

Crossing the plaza again, I look around; there is nothing unusual to see, just a quiet space with empty bench seats dotted around planted areas; the only thing unusual is Jody's movements.

*What was that all about?*

# 50

## Graeme – Kelligg Lock

The sun is low in the western sky, warmer weather today, and it stays dry, perfect for a walk home from the office after a few drinks with the other partners. Crossing the plaza, I decide on taking the canal towpath route home, which is a little longer than sticking to the road, but the scenery is far better, and it will help burn off some of the small spare tyre that is starting to appear around my waist.

Within fifteen minutes, I'm out of the built-up area, enjoying the peace and quiet. A couple of ducks about twenty yards in front of me swim gently upstream, almost keeping pace with me before they turn into some reeds growing to one side of the canal. My mobile phone pings, indicating a message received, and as I fish it out from my jacket pocket, a female voice from behind calls out my name.

'Graeme Oglesby.'

Averting my look from my mobile, I slow down and turn to see who it is and register that it's that bloody woman again.

'Look, I don't know what it is you want from me, but I don't know you. I never had an affair with your mother, so I can honestly say you are not my daughter. You have obviously mistaken me for someone else. Now, if you don't mind...' I turn to continue walking the path home.

She replies, 'I know you, Graeme Oglesby. I know what you are. Just be a man and own it.'

This woman is starting to get on my nerves. I only want a quiet walk home after a few drinks; I don't need aggravation from some deranged, confused, strange woman. Stopping, I turn to look at her, 'Look, I'm sorry I can't help you; you are mistaken; I'm not the man you think I am. I don't know where you got my name from and how you have me confused with someone else, but I'm obviously a different Graeme Oglesby to the one you are looking for; have you thought of that?'

'I know I have the right Graeme Oglesby. There are not many Graeme Oglesby's around, and I know I have the right one because I've seen the DNA results, tracked you down, and we have things to talk about.'

She's just not listening to me. 'Oh, for God's sake, woman! What is your problem? I don't know you, and believe me, I don't want to,' but as I say it, I see a change in her body language; I've touched a raw nerve somewhere.

'You've not changed then, have you?'

'Sorry? What on earth do you mean by that?'

'It's always about you, isn't it? What you want, your terms; fuck everyone else, it's your way or no way.'

This rattles me a little; she is getting angrier by the second, and her tone is now menacing, so I need to calm this down. Raising both palms in a gesture of appeasement, phone in my left hand trapped by my thumb, trying to de-escalate the situation, I reply in a softer tone, 'Look, I'm sorry, it's been a long day, I've had a couple of drinks, and I just want to get home to my wife. Shall we start again?'

'Get home to your wife, Susan, to your nice comfortable home. Amazing how that never entered your head all those years ago when you got her pregnant.'

'How do you know my wife's name? Got, who pregnant, my wife, Susan?'

'No, my mother, you lying, cheating bastard. I checked online records; you were already married then, weren't you, when you had sex with my mother?'

The venom in her voice now is rising rapidly, her face is reddening, and I notice her clenching her hands into fists and releasing them, only to repeat.

'Look, I'm not him! I'm not the man you think I am. I've never been unfaithful to my wife, so there is no way I can be the Graeme Oglesby you're looking for, can I?'

'Like I said, I know you. I never really expected you would admit it, that you would come clean and own your actions; you didn't then, so why would you now? But I know it's you.'

This woman is deranged, and now I'm starting to get worried. I look past her, down the towpath and then chance a quick look over my shoulder; there is no one else in sight. This stretch of canal is not overlooked by any properties, so we're here on our own, and she is starting to frighten the shit out of me; she followed me down here to confront me again. She is not accepting that she has me confused with someone else, so either I convince her of her error, or I need to put some distance between the two of us and get home.

'Look, OK, we've obviously got some crossed wires here somewhere. Yes, I am Graeme Oglesby, but I'm not the Graeme Oglesby you think I am.'

'Nice try. You have the right name. You are the right age. Your DNA confirms I am your daughter; we are matched. You are my biological father; just accept it.'

'But I'm not; get it into your head! I am not him!' I can feel my blood pressure rising, adrenalin coursing through me is making my hands shake slightly, and I'm getting angrier; she is not listening to me, and she needs to.

'You have lived a life in denial for so long now you think it's the truth. I can prove you are my biological father, the man who got my mother pregnant and then abandoned her, the man who used a false name to entice a seventeen-year-old into sex, then turned his back on her and left her to her fate, a fate that I have endured for the last twenty-two years.'

This conversation is getting nowhere. I take in a big breath and exhale deeply. I've had enough now, I'm going home, and when I get there, I'll call the police; this woman is crazy; she needs help. I turn to walk away from her, and after a few paces, it dawns on me what she just said. I turn back to look at her, and as I'm turning, I calmly say to her, 'What are you talking about, DNA? How the hell have you got a hold of my DNA to compare it to yours?'

But she is right behind me with her left hand raised high and, caught off balance, I look up at it, not reacting quickly enough to miss her blow. She smashes downward at speed with an iron bar that crashes across my right forearm that instinctively I've raised over my head to offer me some protection. The pain is excruciating as I stumble and fall to my knees on the gravel towpath.

# 51

## Jody – Kelligg Lock

The sheer nerve of this man, denying everything, effectively, denying my existence. I came here to talk first, then kill him, but as he is not having any of it, I'll just get on with the killing. Turning his back on me is a mistake; no one does that to me anymore. I start walking towards him, picking up my pace to catch him up, while at the same time, I slightly release the grip on the hidden iron bar I have up my sleeve, letting it slip down into my left hand. Taking a firm grip at the end of the bar, I raise my hand, and just as I have it to full height, he stops walking and turns to me saying something, but I'm past listening to what he has to say. Bringing the bar down sharply, aiming for his head, he realises what I'm doing and goes to cower lower whilst raising his arm to protect himself, but that'll not save him.

I smash the bar down hard into his forearm, and I know I have inflicted some serious damage to him as he cries out. He falls to the gravel, collapsing on his knees, bringing his right arm down in front of him and cradling it in his left arm. He looks up at me with a look of sheer horror and only says one word: 'Why?'

I pull my left arm up high again and reply, 'You are the reason I suffered for as long as I did; be grateful your suffering is only going to be for a few seconds.'

'No!' He shouts, as I tip my right shoulder downward, using all the force and momentum I can muster and bring the bar down on his head. The crunch is audible, almost sickening, but deeply satisfying. His eyes, wide open, shoot upward, his pupils disappearing beneath his eyelids. His body jerks violently and crumples to the gravel, still in spasm, writhing in the dusty stones.

Within fifteen seconds, he's lying still, curled in a crumpled, almost foetal position. I look around quickly and see no one. This wasn't the place I intended to kill him; it was going to be at his home, possibly killing his wife also in front of him, but she's been lucky, although she'll suffer in a different way now. He just wound me up so much with his denials that I had to kill him now.

Bending down, I pick up his mobile phone and throw it as far up the canal as possible; it splashes and spooks some ducks hiding in the reeds, the phone disappearing beneath the surface with ripples dying out in seconds.

Bending to grab his body, I hadn't realised what a dead weight is like to move; the only thing I can do is roll him towards the edge of the canal. Looking around again to check there is still no one around, I bend, taking a grip of his jacket and trouser leg and lift, rolling him into the calm water about a foot below the stone coping to the canal lining. The splash is not big, and he remains face down. As I watch him floating, I register there is a flow in the canal, albeit slow, and I watch him gently floating away from me. Looking around to make sure nothing is left on the towpath, I pick up my iron bar, brush myself down quickly and turn my back on him, walking away slowly and confidently, upstream towards Kelligg Lock. It's hard to keep the smile from my face; the release is enormous. I even feel a spring and lightness in each step;

it's like I can now look to my future after divesting the baggage of two decades.

Although their suffering was far less than what they imposed on me, I got what I wanted.

My work is now done.

Just ahead, two ducks return to the water, skimming in and landing near another patch of reeds on the far bank.

I'm suddenly hungry, ravenous even; is there still somewhere open where I can buy something to eat? I quite fancy a bit of crispy duck.

# 52

## Oscar – Near Kelligg Lock

My position behind the bridge abutment provides a perfect place to observe her, and each time she looks up, I can easily duck back behind the stonework. She is clearly following this man in front of her, stepping out behind him after he left the office block, the one she was looking at last night.

I'm not sure why, but I've not been comfortable with Jody since she joined us in our sibling chat room; there is something about her that has me feeling uneasy and unsettled, and I don't want her affecting or upsetting Sarah or Kate; my sisters are precious to me; I love them dearly.

The two of them are standing and talking. Obviously, they know each other, but some of his body language is off. I can't hear what they're saying, but from the raised tones of the man, he's clearly not happy with her; maybe they are ex-partners, and she won't take no for an answer.

I see him turn his back on her and start walking away, stopping within a few strides and turning back to her just as she raises something above her head. In that split second, his natural instinct is to raise his arm as she strikes him, and he falls to his knees before she raises her arm again, but this time with a clear determined force to kill him. As she strikes him the second time, he collapses to the path.

I'm frozen to the spot, not sure what to do. I fumble in my pocket for my mobile phone, but as I pull it out, it slips through my trembling fingers, falling into the long grass at my feet.

The scene freezes me. She looks around again, and I duck back behind the bridge. Dare I look again? What if she turns back and comes this way towards me? What do I do?

I have to know. Chancing a peak around the stonework, I'm just in time to see her roll his limp body into the water. Fuck! This is serious. I duck back again. What has she got, a machete or a baton? I couldn't make it out but can't see it now. Come to think of it, I didn't notice her carrying something earlier; she must have hidden it somehow. I need to get away from her; she won't want any witnesses to her crime, that's for sure, and I have nothing to defend myself with.

Lowering myself slowly into a crouch, I search around in the long grass to find my phone and pocket it, deciding to scramble up the embankment beside the bridge and climb the stone wall to get onto the road above. This offers me the best chance to put some distance between us, and hopefully, we'll be heading in different directions.

The grass is slippery, mixed with brambles that snag and claw at my trousers. Losing my footing, I drop to my hands and scratch them badly on the thorns, but I've got to keep going, crawling up the embankment on all fours; she could be here any second, hitting me from behind. On reaching the top and the base of the bridge parapet wall, I crawl along it to a point low enough to climb over. Keeping a minimalist profile, I roll over the top of the wall, hoping she hasn't seen me, and drop down onto the narrow stone road behind.

Sitting behind the protection of the wall, I realise the only protection it affords is to hide me from view from the towpath; anyone can hop over like I did. Catching my breath, I stay low, move along the wall to the end, and then decide to go for it. I stand and run full pelt down the road towards the trees lining either side of the track, for that's all it is, some old path or farmer's driven track. I'm in the middle of nowhere.

Keeping going, putting distance between the two of us, my breathing is labouring, and I start to slow. Over the last half mile or so, I have been constantly looking over my shoulder, making sure she's not following me. My speed now drops to a brisk walking pace, my adrenalin levels lower, and my thoughts become clearer. The flight instinct for survival took over.

Who the hell was that man she just attacked and killed? The way his body rolled into the canal, he certainly looked dead. She murdered him in cold blood, in broad daylight, my God. The police: I need to tell the police what I saw; of course, I should, but… but this is my half-sister, and they will want to know what I was doing following her. Could I have prevented his murder? Will they try to include me in the crime as an accessory? Oh, I don't know.

Who was he? He may have been a villain or some other bad one, and she was exacting revenge, I don't know. Do I turn my sister in to the police? Christ, I wish I'd never followed her now. Will she harm Sarah and Kate? Go after me? Well, she will if she finds out I witnessed her killing him.

I must get in touch with Sarah and Kate to warn them. I fish my phone out but then realise I could be leaving a digital footprint, messaging or calling from the area, and swiftly put it away again. Think!

I need to get home, get out of these clothes, and prepare my story in case the police call on me. Then, speak with Sarah and Kate and tell them what I just witnessed; we can decide what to do together; this is our half-sister, but she can't be allowed to kill someone, regardless of whether he is a criminal or not; no, she can't do that.

Looking ahead, down the track, I'm not certain of exactly where I am, but I have a rough idea. I can see some rooftops in the distance, about half a mile or so away, and decide to aim for them, find out where I am, and then head back home.

That poor guy, he didn't stand a chance.

*What did he do wrong? Who was he?*

# 53

## Kate – At Home

Paul has not phoned again today; this is getting worse. I know he's busy, but he used to make some time free to call me or send a text message at least. Is he avoiding me? I hope it's not bad news about his ailment, and that the specialists are treating what is wrong with him. He's still not said what it is, not given me a name for it. I think this is more serious than he's been letting on, and he's keeping it to himself, trying to stop me worrying about him, but this is making it worse. He needs to understand we are one now, and we share things together; we're better as one, no secrets. I'll ask him the next time we speak.

The message from Oscar earlier was a little cryptic; he wants to speak with Sarah and me about something urgent, but he didn't say what and didn't reply to my follow-up message; he'll be calling in a few minutes. It could be about our biological father; I wonder if he's discovered something new?

I can't help thinking that if we want to find out his identity, we would have to do something a little… different, but such a thing would fly in the face of his right to anonymity. From his silence, he's obviously torn over this, holding back on identifying himself or meeting up. We need to convince him somehow that we're not after anything other than to know a little bit more about him and his family background to understand where we may fit into his family tree. I would like to know what drove him to make his donations to help out others who were struggling to conceive.

The conference call app on my laptop starts to ring; it's Oscar, bang on time, never late; I answer it. Our video images come on screen, and Sarah joins us within a few seconds.

'Hi Oscar, Sarah.'

Sarah replies, smiling, 'Hi'.

But Oscar remains silent, subdued, not really looking at us; he seems… lost.

'What is it, Oscar? What's wrong?' As I ask him, I notice the smile fall away from Sarah.

Sarah chips in, 'Oscar, is everything alright?' The concern on Sarah's face is real.

'Umm, no, far from it,' he replies.

'Oscar, what is it? Is it about our biological father? Have you found out something?' I ask him.

But before he can reply, Sarah chips in again, 'If it is, we should call Jody and include her in the news.'

'No!' The sharp reply from Oscar surprises Sarah and me alike. 'No. We're not calling Jody.'

'Why not include Jody? Is there something we don't know about?' I ask.

Oscar pauses again, he is struggling to tell us something. He doesn't look good and is obviously troubled. He looks down, averting his eyes from us.

'Oscar, why are we not including Jody?' Sarah asks him, both of us wanting an answer.

'She…' he pauses, visibly swallowing hard, 'She killed a man today.'

'What?' Sarah and I say that at the same time; I continue, 'What are you talking about, Oscar? What man? Where?'

'I saw her do it. I was following her.'

Sarah reacts, 'Why were you following her? What the hell are you talking about?' He's not making eye contact with us, his gaze remaining downward. 'Oscar, what man?' she asks.

'I don't know who he is, was. Something about her hasn't sat right with me since she connected with us, something that made me feel… uneasy. She has been vague about her past and not really engaging with us, don't you think?'

He has a point, 'Yes, er, I suppose so; she was shocked at first like we were. I know she avoids giving direct answers, but I just think that is her nature. Who is this man, for god's sake? Have you seen him before?' I plead with him.

'I don't know! I thought I'd try to find out a bit more about her, but I couldn't find anything on social media, no websites or accounts, nothing in her name,' he pauses, 'it's like… like she's a ghost,' he adds.

Sarah adds to his comments, 'I know, I tried to find out a little more about her but drew a blank as well. She has not answered any of the messages that I sent to her since, erm, last week. She's… like… distant, it was starting to feel like she was just using me, us, somehow.'

There is silence for a few seconds before I ask Oscar, 'What do you know about this man you think she has killed?'

'There is no *think* about it; I saw her do it, then push his body into the canal, up by a lock gate. It was brutal; she just hit him with a bat or a bar or something, twice, and he went down, and she just… just rolled his body into the canal as if it was like an old carpet or something.'

He is visibly shaking, 'So, what did you do? Did you call the police?'

'No.'

'Why the hell not?' I ask him, raising my voice.

In a low, purposeful voice, he replies, 'Because… she is our sister.'

We are all silent now, not knowing what to say next. Sarah stares directly into her camera lens as though her screen image is a photograph rather than a live video image; Oscar's eyes are still averted, and he is still reluctant to look up at his screen or into his camera. I break the silence, 'She may well be our half-sister, but she cannot go around killing people; you have to tell the police, Oscar.'

He looks up and snaps back at me, 'Oh, right, yes, and say what? A few hours ago, whilst I was secretly following my half-sister down a canal towpath, I hid behind a bridge and watched her brutally kill some stranger, then dump his body in the canal and walk away? *Oh, and what did you do, sir?*' mocking the tone of a police officer, 'Oh me, well, I just turned away and made a run for it, then I couldn't decide what to do. Meanwhile, she's making good her escape.'

He's in shock, he's angry, and he's confused, understandably so.

Knowing Oscar far better than me, Sarah says, 'Slow down, Oscar, you did the right thing. Slow your breathing down a little if you can. Have you got your inhaler with you? Do you need to take it?'

I didn't even know he used an inhaler. She is showing genuine concern for him and continues in a calm voice, 'Oscar, are you OK? Do you want me to come to yours? I can get the next train.' Her sincerity and concern for him is evident; of the three of us, she is the one who bonds us together.

'No, I'll be fine; it's just, well, wow,' he pauses, 'Kate is right, I have to tell the police. She must be stopped. He may have been a complete stranger to her, I don't know, but it did look as though she was following him now I think about it, and they were talking, like she knew him. If no one else saw her kill him, then I am the only witness.'

'So, you think she knew him?' I ask, but Sarah continues talking to him, ignoring my question to Oscar.

'Let me come over to yours, Oscar; we can go to the police station together.'

'No, I'm fine, I'll do it. I'll call them and tell them what I saw and who I saw do it. I'll not mention you two, there's no need to drag you into this.'

'Don't do this alone, Oscar,' Sarah says, 'We are here for each other, remember?'

'I know, but I've got this. Jody has to be stopped.'

No one speaks; we all just look at each other, staring at our screens. There must be more to it than this, he wouldn't have been a complete stranger. I break the silence.

'But it doesn't make sense to me all this, we need to understand what happened here. She wouldn't just kill a random person, would she? There must be more to it.'

'What?' Sarah asks.

'Well… she may have had a good reason to kill him.' As I say it, I can't believe these are my words, and I'm saying them out loud.

Oscar speaks, 'Really? Not thirty seconds ago, you said I had to report her to the police. Do you now think it's acceptable to go around killing people you may know because they deserve it? That it's OK to let Jody act as a public executioner?'

'No, that's not what I'm saying. But there must be a reason; surely there has to be, don't you think?'

'You didn't see her kill that man; it looked like… like she enjoyed it.'

'No, I'm not having that, Oscar; you yourself said you were hiding behind a bridge some distance away. How could you say she looked like she enjoyed it? You didn't stay around long enough to find out, did you?'

'Fuck you, Kate, I just saw her kill a man. Would you have hung around there for a chat with her afterwards? No, I guess not.'

Sarah speaks up, 'Stop it, please, the two of you.'

We all go quiet again. It's clear we are each torn with what course of action to take, and I understand it; my first reaction was to call the police, but then there has to be a reason why she killed this man, and we should try to find out why first. I speak quietly now, 'Yes, she has to be reported to the police, there is no question of that, but shouldn't we try to find out why she did what she did before we coldly turn her in?'

Silence again. From their expressions, they are thinking it over, wrestling with the dilemma before us. I try again, 'This is our newly found half-sister, and we know very little about her. Shouldn't we try to understand her and support her? It would be far better if she handed herself into the police rather than be hunted down following a tip-off.'

Sarah replies to me in an almost timid manner, contrary to her usual forthright manner, 'But… she killed someone, another person, and we should put that above everything else. Her reasons, if she has any, will come out when the police interview her.'

'I know, I am not saying we should let her get away with this, far from it, she will go to the police, either voluntarily or not. What I'm saying is we'll probably get the fullest response from her before the police are involved. What do you think, Oscar, you were the one following her?'

'I'm not sure; what if we find out her reasons and she, well, I don't know, kind of *wins us over*?'

'And how is that likely to happen?' Sarah asks.

'Well, what if he abused her or raped her, and she couldn't cope with it all coming out in public? I don't know, do we really want to try to understand why she did it?' he replies.

Silence again. This moral dilemma is only a dilemma because she is our half-sister, newly found at that; anyone else we would turn over to the police without a second thought.

Sarah wants to say something but stops herself at least twice, finding the courage to ask it on her third attempt. 'How and when do we ask her? It needs to be sooner rather than later. How do we get her to meet us somewhere private?'

Sarah is coming around to the idea, and I think I'm ready to do it; just Oscar to convince now.

'Oscar, how did you find Jody to follow her?' I ask him.

Before he can reply, Sarah answers, 'Well, that was me, Kate; I mentioned some specific artwork to Jody in some of her tattoos, complimenting the touch, and she indicated her favourite tattoo artist; the skills and style reflect in the artist's work, and an experienced eye can spot this. Anyway, finding that artist on the internet was easy enough, and…'

'And I went there and found out she lives above his tattoo parlour.'

'Oh, OK, very resourceful. So, where is she?'

'She is in Brown Heath, not far from you, actually. She took a six-month rental on a flat just off the high street, ironically over the tattoo parlour called Skin it Alive.'

'So, how do we get her to meet us?' I ask him.

'That's simple,' Oscar replies, 'I just need to mention something about her and canal, and I'm sure she'll meet me.'

Looking worried, Sarah asks, 'Isn't that dangerous? Won't she think about doing something to you… you know, to shut you up?'

'No,' he replies, 'remember, I am the one with tact and sensitivity.'

Seizing the moment, I jump in with an affirmative tone, 'OK, let's do it. Oscar, can you arrange to meet her somewhere near here in the next day or so? If we can all meet her together, I'm sure we'll get to the bottom of it. Can you both do this at such short notice?' I ask as they may have other commitments, and Sarah is an employee with a company who'll need some time off.

'Oscar, are you up for this?' Sarah asks.

'Yes. Sure. I can be there tomorrow.'

'OK, I can throw a sick day, and I'll join you both,' adding, 'but where do we meet her?'

It dawns on me that I have the perfect place. 'Paul is in London most of this week, and his office will be empty tomorrow evening. I have a set of keys and know the alarm code. It'll give us a nice private place to meet up.'

'OK, great,' from Oscar, 'send me the address and I'll arrange it. Shall we aim for seven o'clock tomorrow night?'

'Yes,' I reply.

# 54

## Paul – His Apartment in London

'Graeme is dead; we think he's been murdered.'

Oh, my god. Hearing Lauren say the words absolutely floors me, and I drop down onto my desk chair and lean backwards as the back support tips to its limit. She's pulled some stunts in the past, but this one takes the biscuit.

'No, he isn't, no, don't be so cruel, Lauren; why would you say such a thing like that?'

'Because it's true, honestly Paul, Graeme is dead. Did you not hear about the man found dead in the canal yesterday?'

'No, I'm down here, I don't get the local home news in London. No, sorry, you're just spinning me another one of your lines, aren't you?'

'No, Paul, I'm not, I promise. Graeme is dead.'

She actually sounds sincere. But the number of times she has spun me a line since we split up would make the little boy crying wolf look like a saint.

'Are you being straight with me, Lauren?'

'Yes, Paul, I am.'

'But… why? Who would…?'

'The police aren't saying much at the moment. When Graeme didn't arrive home from work on Wednesday evening, and it was getting late, Susan kept trying to call him on his mobile, but the line was dead; it was just tripping straight to voice message. In the end, she phoned the police, but they had no reports of anyone injured or unknown in the hospital, and they said he could just be out with friends and that his phone battery had run out. But she pleaded with them; she knew something was wrong. Graeme's not like that; he always calls her when he stays out late. Anyway, he never came home, and a body was found in the canal earlier today and… it's him. His death is being treated as suspicious by the police. Graeme's brother just phoned the house line here because you hadn't returned his calls, he was trying to get a hold of you to let you know. I'm so sorry, Paul, I know how close the two of you were.'

'I… I… I've been in meetings all day. Oh my god, Lauren… Graeme?'

'Yes. It's terrible.'

We both fall silent.

Then I break and ask, 'Do our kids know yet?'

'No, not yet. It's not something I want to tell them on the phone, but one of us will need to, it'll be public news soon. They were both close to Graeme; he was like an uncle to them; they've known him all their lives.'

'I know. Shit, I can't believe this.' My thoughts are all over the place. 'How's Susan? She's not on her own, is she?'

'No, her sister and brother are with her. She's in pieces, though, as you can imagine. He was such a wonderful person, a good husband, dad, friend.'

I can hear the upset in Lauren's voice, she is close to tears.

'Look, I'll get the next train home, I'll be there as quick as I can.'

'Don't forget, this is no longer your home, Paul.'

Her switch to such a cold statement stuns me, and I go into reaction mode.

'I know, don't start picking at my words, Lauren, for god's sake.' She is quiet, hopefully realising this is not the time to start a fight or slanging match. 'I'll call Ben and Ruth now, then pack a few things and head back. They'll be upset and will probably come over to yours,' emphasising the ownership. 'If you need me there, let me know. I must go see Susan as soon as I get there.'

'Right…' followed by a deep sigh, 'And don't forget to let your new wife know', with emphasis aimed back at me. The phone goes dead.

She'll never forgive me for what I've done, but at least she phoned me to tell me about my best friend. As two couples, we were all close, close up to the point I did what I did with Kate. Lauren initially thought Graeme must have known about Kate and me, and they fell out big style, and Susan sided with Graeme, naturally, but truly he didn't know; I hadn't told anyone until Kate, and I decided to have a future together. Lauren accepted the fact that the four of us couldn't remain close friends, her realising that Graeme and I had been best friends since our school days, well before he met Susan and I met Lauren. But Lauren will be hurting from this; I could feel it during the call; she always liked Graeme; shit, I never asked how she was coping with it; I should have asked her.

Oh, Graeme, mate, what happened? I let my mobile phone slip from my hand onto the desktop and bring my hands to my face, taking in a deep breath through my fingers. What the hell happened? It's got to be a random thing, Graeme wouldn't hurt a fly, and he certainly wouldn't get involved in anything dodgy or criminal, he is the most level-headed guy I know; I knew. I'm stunned by this; what do I tell the kids? Ben and Ruth were close to Graeme, he was my best man twice, their godfather at their baptisms, and was always around, chatting with them, appearing at birthdays and family celebrations; the three of them secretly planned an overseas trip for my fortieth birthday celebrations, and I didn't suspect a thing; they were as thick as thieves.

What the hell happened? She said he was found by the canal; what the hell were you doing by the canal, Graeme? I sit upright, pull my chair closer to the desk and start tapping the keys on my laptop, looking for any news or reports. Sure enough, there are local news headlines, but none identifying the man found or any leads or witnesses.

As I read the articles, a pop-up appears in the lower corner of my screen: an urgent message notifying me to install the latest upgrade package from NeuvaGen to enhance security protocols.

'NeuvaGen,' I say quietly to myself. The start of all my problems, those bloody DNA testing kits. If Kate hadn't done hers, and that whole conversation about donations from a London clinic at about the same time I was providing them with donations hadn't happened, we wouldn't be in this predicament now. I'd still be staying with Kate, happily married, and I wouldn't have needed to do those bloody DNA tests and hoodwink Graeme into providing that sample.

But Kate is my child, and I can't let this continue. I need to bring this marriage to a close; dodging Kate can only last so long. Why is this all happening at once? I've lost my best mate, my new wife; I'll be losing my mind next. I can't tell Kate now about a divorce, not with Graeme dying.

I close the laptop and start collecting charger cables together, a few paper files from my desk drawer and some other bits and pieces. I pull some clothes together along with my wash bag and throw everything into a holdall. Looking at my watch, the next train is in about forty-five minutes; I'd better call Ben and then Ruth.

I didn't want to end the call; Ben took the news badly, as I expected, but he said he would call Ruth, then call his mum, telling me I should focus on returning home. Since Lauren and I split, Ben has become quite independent and more confident and assertive; his development is probably the only good thing to come out of this whole mess I've created. I'm pretty sure, though, he'll not want to know me anymore when I tell him that Kate and I are splitting up; for sure, Ruth won't speak to me again.

Leaving my apartment, I close the door while I call my P.A., informing her I'm heading home urgently and that she can contact me through my mobile, but only if it's essential. I hear her asking me what the urgency is, but I'm already pulling the phone away from my ear and heading out the door before she finishes her sentence. She'll think I'm rude, and I'll apologise later; she will understand, I'm sure.

Lauren is right, even though technically Kate and I are no longer an item, which neither of them know of yet, I'll have to call her. But this will make things more awkward; Kate will want me to come home and spend time with her as we console each other, but I know what I know now, and I must remain detached from Kate; we can't be one ever again. I'll phone her from the station before the train departs.

Walking to the station, I play events over in my head; I deceived my first wife and now my second; I upset my children, deeply hurting them in the process, and probably about to alienate them when Kate and I split up;

and now my life long best friend is dead, I'll never speak with him again; all this since I met Kate. What kind of person I have become? I start to fear I'm stuck on a downward spiralling journey now, one in which the only outcome is me ending up being a bitter and lonely person in some dark, solitary place.

For god's sake, why is she not answering the phone, I don't recall her saying she was going out tonight. Come on, Kate, pick up or call me back. As the train exits the last tunnel on my journey home, I try one more time, but this time, the call cuts off shortly after connecting, so I decide to leave her a voice message,

> "*Kate, it's me. I have some terrible news. Graeme is dead; they found his body in the canal, and the police are treating it as suspicious; he may have been murdered, and his body pushed into the water. I wanted to let you know before you heard it cold on the news. Graeme's brother called Lauren, and Lauren called me. I'm on my way back on the train; I should get in around eight-thirty. Call me as soon as you get this.*"

# 55

## Kate – Outside Paul's Office

Parking my car around the corner from the office, I wait fifteen minutes after Magda, Paul's personal assistant, leaves and locks up before I go up to the front door and re-open it. I'm a little early, just before six-thirty, as I want to make sure the meeting room is clear of documents and materials before our meeting. I also want to set up a small video /audio recorder in case this situation backfires on us so we can demonstrate to the police that we were not in cahoots with Jody in this murder. However, I'm not sure how much such a recording will help us as we are already interfering with the police investigation, delaying the murderer's capture.

I managed to catch the brief report on the local news earlier, announcing that the body of a middle-aged man had been recovered from the canal earlier today and that his identity was being withheld until his family had been informed. The report did not confirm if his death was suspicious or not.

The clock is now ticking.

The meeting room is empty and clear, and I set up the recorder in one of the display cabinets at the end of the room. I have it linked to my phone, and I check the image and audio; everything seems fine.

From the kitchen, I collect four glasses and a large jug of chilled water from the water dispenser and place them in the middle of the meeting room table. The window blinds are already closed; the scene is set.

I've been anxious since Oscar called me early this morning to say the meeting was on. He spoke directly with Jody after exchanging a couple of messages in NeuvaGen's message room and providing her with his mobile number for a burner phone he had purchased from a late-night store last night. Oscar thinks of the minor things that could become important, which prompted me to think about recording our meeting with Jody.

As per our agreement, the first to arrive is Sarah, a few minutes before seven o'clock, and I let her into the building; she is nervous and a little jittery, so I take her to the meeting room and pour her a glass of water.

'Everything will be fine, Sarah; Oscar and I will do all the talking, but feel free to join the conversation whenever you want to.'

'Thank you,' she replies, 'I think I'll just sit and listen if that's OK with you?'

'Yes, absolutely; not a problem.'

I feel my mobile phone vibrate in my jeans pocket, and when I look at the screen, I see it's Paul calling. He'll have to wait; Jody will be here any time now; we need to stay focused, so I let it ring out.

Oscar remains outside, waiting quietly across the road, hidden from view, watching to make sure Jody arrives alone.

Sitting with Sarah, I watch the large wall clock tick past seven, slowly continuing to five minutes past. She's late. Has she changed her mind? Will she come? After all, she is a killer. What if she is planning something right now to silence us? As the minute hand creeps towards ten minutes past, I start to wonder if we're doing the right thing or not. Sarah keeps looking at her phone and then up at the clock face above the large LED television screen; Sarah's tension is now feeding off mine. I begin to worry about Oscar outside now, on his own; he's potentially more exposed than us.

Could she have got to Oscar? I start to panic; we didn't think this through thoroughly, and I need to contact him. I take out my mobile, and as I do, Paul rings again. This time, I cancel the call, and I see it is the fourth time he's tried calling me in the last quarter of an hour or so; sorry, Paul, you'll just have to wait, I'll call you later. I start to type a text message to Oscar's mobile phone, even though he told me not to as we're trying to minimise contact between us and avoid leaving digital footprints for others to follow, but I need to know he's alright, that's he's safe.

I press send and wait.

Nothing comes back.

The minute hand passes quarter past seven.

'Do you think she's coming?' asks Sarah, nervously nibbling her thumbnail.

'Oscar is convinced she will; he's in no doubt. She could just be delayed somehow or waiting to see what we do. I suppose from her perspective, she could be frightened of walking into a police trap.'

'Well, if she thought that, she wouldn't come, would she?'

'No, I suppose not. I'll message Oscar again.' I press send for the same message again.

A minute or so later, the only reply is an emoji of a thumbs up. As I look at the screen image, paranoia starts to creep in; did he send that, or has she got his phone?

'What did Oscar say?' Sarah asks.

'Nothing, it's just a thumbs-up emoji.'

'Shit, Kate. I think we should stop this; we don't know what we're getting into here.'

'You might be right; I'll go out and signal for Oscar to come in. If he doesn't walk to us from across the road but she does, we can shut and lock the door and call the police.'

'Kate, you're starting to scare me now.'

'Wait here. I'm going to call Oscar in.' I stand and start to head for the door.

'Don't leave me here on my own. Kate!'

'Sarah! Look, try to stay calm. If I don't come back in, call the police. 999, no messing about. OK?'

'Yes, but…'

'I'll be back in a few minutes. I promise.'

I leave the meeting room, closing the door behind me, and turn and walk down the corridor, heading for the large wooden front door. Before unlocking it again, I recheck my phone for any further message from Oscar; nothing, just a waiting voice message, no doubt from Paul.

I turn the key in the mortice lock, then turn the latch key handle on the day lock and pull at the heavy door. Stepping back to let in swing inwards, I can hear footsteps climbing the stone steps outside.

# 56

## Oscar – Paul's Offices

I've been here since before five o'clock, keeping a close watch on Paul's office building, watching other occupiers and tenants leave the building steadily since then. Kate mentioned that the last to leave usually is her husband's personal assistant; brunette, about five foot six, aged in her early forties, normally wearing a Mackintosh-type long coat and invariably with one or two small bags of shopping. On leaving, she sets the building alarm code and locks the big, blue-painted, wood front door for the night. As if it could have been scripted, Kate got this scene perfect, and her husband's PA locks up at six-fifteen, heading home for her evening dinner.

Keeping a vigilant watch on the surrounding area, I change position every fifteen minutes or so, seeking different vantage points to keep a lookout for Jody or any accomplice she may have enticed to help her. During one of these changes, I see her sitting at a window table in the small coffee shop a little further down the street. I don't let on; just keep an eye on her from behind this flight of stone steps to the last Georgian building in the row of elegant, white-fronted houses now converted to stylish office rentals.

Quietly watching her, my mobile phone pings, and I fish it out of my pocket. Looking at the display, I recognise the number as Kate's, slightly annoying me as I told her not to use this number unless it was in an absolute emergency. Yes, Jody is late in making an appearance at Paul's offices, only just, but she is here, watching the offices whilst being watched. My reply to Kate is a simple thumbs up, but when I look back up to Jody, she has left the window table, and I can no longer see her. That momentary distraction may have cost me my advantage.

I step back beneath the steps, out of view from most angles, change my baseball cap, pocketing the blue cap and donning a red replacement, flick up the collar to the small jacket I'm wearing and pull up my sleeves to show bare forearms. The little changes can make all the difference in snap observations and recall; well, that's what they say in those spy novels.

Now, I have to decide what to do next. Is she simply at the back of the coffee shop paying her bill, or did she slip out the front without me noticing her, or worse, charm the owner into letting her slip out the back door? I can stay here and hope she is paying her bill or move on the off chance she has made me and is cutting around behind me as I think of my next move.

With confidence, I emerge from behind the stone steps and walk out onto the street, swiftly crossing the road and turning down the passageway beside the coffee shop. She doesn't know what I look like; I've not shared an image of myself, and neither has Kate or Sarah, so I'm pretty comfortable that we could walk past each other, and she wouldn't register who I am. I need to check out the rear of the coffee shop on the off-chance Jody used this as an exit, and if not, I'll use this to change my position again. The passageway is quite dim, and I move quickly, heading towards the light at the end. My footsteps echo slightly from the stone walls and slab roof, and the temperature has dropped a few degrees in this gloom. As I emerge at the end and walk out into the light, I squint slightly at the brightness and then see her, Jody, standing there… waiting for me.

# 57

## Kate – Paul's Offices

Oscar is walking directly behind a woman who fits his description of Jody. They both look dishevelled, her hair messed up, his ruffled beyond its usual groomed flicks. Oscar is sporting a bloody lower lip, and Jody has the makings of a swollen eye and cheek to the left-hand side of her face. Oscar prods her in the back slightly with a simple instruction: 'Go on, get inside.'

I pull the door fully open, and she passes by me, stepping into the marble-tiled interior, followed closely by Oscar, holding what looks like a short metal rod in his right hand, seemingly with more length tucked up the sleeve of his jacket, he's using it to nudge her along. As he passes me, I quietly ask if he's OK.

'Yes, I'm fine; she obviously doesn't like to play nice, this one. Be careful near her.'

Closing the door, I lock it again using the mortice lock, remove the key, drop it into my pocket, and then turn to follow them. Oscar asks me which way to go, and I direct them down the corridor to the second door on the right.

'Go on, you heard her; move it,' and he prods her again with the end of the iron bar.

'Fuck off, will you!' she retorts, only to receive another prod from Oscar.

'Enough of that; it was you that brought this thing to the meeting, not me,' he replies. 'Now get in there so we can talk.'

Jody turns the door handle and opens the door wide, walking into the meeting room, followed closely by Oscar and me. Sarah is standing at the end of the large table, looking at us; she looks surprised and nervous, turning her hands over slowly in front of her. Oscar directs Jody around the table, away from the door, and instructs her to sit at the table. I close the door, and all is quiet for a few seconds.

'And this lady, and I use that term loosely, is Jody, our half-sister,' Oscar announces as if needed.

'Bastard!' Jody snarls at Oscar.

'You'll need to be sharper than that to catch me out,' he replies, 'there was plenty of opportunity and time to take up martial arts in boarding school, especially when daddy dear was in the military and expecting me to follow in the family footsteps. Now, shall we all be civil and have a sensible conversation?'

'Well, that's why you got me here, isn't it, to ask me why I did it?' she replies to him, not beating about the bush.

Sarah breathes in deeply, audibly shocked by Jody's comment and admission.

Oscar remains standing beside Jody, just to her right, keeping the iron bar away from her in his right hand, no doubt in case she turns violent. He looks down at her, 'So, you admit killing him then?'

'Pointless trying to deny it, don't you think? You saw me do it.'

It's clear these two would use and are ready to use, that iron bar on each other if the opportunity necessitated, so I try to defuse the situation, remaining calm and collected.

'Jody, look at me. I'm Kate, this is Sarah, and you've already met Oscar. We're your half-siblings, you are our sister.'

'And? Is that supposed to mean something to me?'

Sarah puts her right hand over her mouth and mumbles something; this is not what she expected or wanted it to be like.

'What's that, speak up?' Jody snarls again, but this time looking to her left at Sarah. 'You're obviously the weak one, the runt of the litter.'

Oscar swings his left hand around from behind Jody and slaps her across the back of her head, making her head dip forward and almost hit the tabletop, following with, 'That's my sister you're talking to; you need to show some respect.'

The slap alone shocks me; he didn't hesitate or show any hint of restraint, and his words were curt and direct. This is a side I've not seen in Oscar.

Jody raises her head, and I see her biting her bottom lip, casting a sideways look at Oscar, making a low hissing sound, clearly showing contempt toward him.

Releasing her lip, 'So, you're the brawn,' she says to him, then turns to me, 'Leaving you to be the brains, I guess.'

I look at Oscar, and he shrugs his shoulders and raises his eyebrows slightly as if we are dealing with an errant teenager who shows no sign of respect or discipline.

What the hell have I got us all into here?

I sit opposite Jody, lean forward slightly, and look directly at her. 'Jody, why did you kill that man?'

'What's it got to do with you?'

'Look, we were all for turning you into the police last night, but we thought, well, there may have been a reason you followed him and attacked him. You are our newly found half-sister, and we felt that, well, you should have the opportunity to give us your side of the story first before involving the police. Why did you kill him?'

She just tuts and stares at me.

'Did he hurt you, Jody?'

'Uh, did he hurt me? If he hurt her,' flicking her head in Sarah's direction, 'like he did me, would you let him get away with it?'

'No, but I don't think we would kill him. What did he do to you? Why did you kill him?'

'You might think that now, sitting here in these fancy rooms, with your perfect, happy little lives, but there is something in every one of us that would make us want to do it, make each of us want to kill that one person. You might not know what it is or what will bring it on, but we've all got it in us; it's just a matter of finding what your buttons are and what needs to be pressed to take you to the edge. Trust me, I know; I've seen it, lived it, and I've done it.'

The smile on her face is terrifying when coupled with her words, her eyes almost searing into me. She is delusional, psychotic even; we should have just reported her to the police last night.

Oscar sighs and repeats my question to her, 'Why did you kill him?'

'Because he had it coming to him!' She snaps back at Oscar.

'So, he did hurt you then?' I ask.

'Yes, he hurt me, so I hurt him. He was a liar, a cheat, a fake. He was no father to me; he was a bastard mongrel who didn't deserve to carry on living.'

'What did he do to you?' I ask, and as I say it, her words repeat in my head. 'No, wait, what do you mean, he was no father to you?'

'Exactly that. I wouldn't want to call him my father. After all these years, he still wouldn't admit to what he had done.'

'Your… father? What, your stepfather, you mean?'

'No, my real father, my biological father.'

As she says the words, the impact hits all three of us at once, stunning me and obviously Oscar as I see his reaction, but it's Sarah who speaks the quickest. 'Your biological father? You mean *our biological father?*'

'Yeah, I suppose so. That's why we're all here, isn't it? I killed our father.'

Sarah screams and launches for Jody, clawing at the chairs between them. Jody rises to meet her advance, but Oscar is quick. The blow he strikes her with is fast and aggressive, hitting her right arm just below her elbow, causing her hand to slip off the table, removing the support she had her weight on as she stands, twisting to meet Sarah. She tumbles forward onto the chairs to her left just as Sarah reaches her and starts to pummel the back of her head and neck with clenched fists. The rage on Sarah's face is nothing short of blood lust and vengeance.

Oscar tries to pull Sarah away from Jody, and I run around the table to assist him. I grab her right arm and pull it away, trying to pull her backwards from Jody, but she is way too overpowering for me. Oscar grabs her other arm and moves around behind Jody, who is now crumpled between two chairs, laughing with a sickening contempt.

As we pull Sarah away, Jody stumbles over one of the chair legs and crashes to the floor beside me. Oscar reaches down and grabs Jody by the back of her hair with his left hand, lifting her, and as she starts to rise, he swipes the bar across the top of her right shoulder. Jody's scream is of a wounded animal caught in a trap of no escape. He swings again, this time catching her on the right hip, and she screams out again, falling to the floor. She crawls, dragging her leg behind her towards the corner of the room, cowering, looking back at Oscar, dominating a hawk-like stance above her.

'Stop it! Stop it!' I shout as I reach down for Sarah. 'Enough!'

'This is how you treat a wild animal,' he replies as he raises his right arm high again.

'Oscar! No! STOP!'

He freezes at the top of his swing, the iron bar fully extended like a baseball bat. If he hits her now, he'll kill her.

'Oscar! Back away! She's not worth it.'

And, as if I had flicked a switch, he lowers his arm and steps back away from her. 'No, you're right, she's not worth it.'

I have Sarah in a tight grip, my arms locked around the top of hers, pulling her into me. She is sobbing heavily. 'She killed him, she killed him. I'll never get to talk to him now. Why? Why would she do that?'

'I don't know, Sarah, but we must stop this now; we have to call the police and get them here.'

'But I want to know why first,' Oscar says. He kicks the bottom of Jody's foot and asks her, 'Why?'

Jody, still cowering, holding her arm with the other, replies quietly, 'Because he got my mother pregnant, then abandoned her and me.'

'That's it? That's why you killed him?'

'And some, it's a long story,' is all she replies with, wincing in pain.

I look over to her, 'What is his name?'

'Huh, you'll have to wait to find out, I'm not saying anything else, so fuck off, the lot of you.' She spits, and in reaction, Oscar kicks her right foot hard, jolting up through her injured hip so that she cries out with the pain; she snarls back at him.

Oscar removes his trouser belt with his left hand, keeping the iron bar poised in his right hand at the ready. He holds out his belt to me. 'Kate, tie her arms together behind her back with this; we need to restrain her.'

I reach across to him and take it. Releasing Sarah, I approach Jody as she starts to swear at me. Oscar kicks the bottom of her foot hard once more, and she again reels from the pain it causes her.

Oscar forces Jody to roll on her stomach, telling her to put her arms behind her back. She visibly struggles to move her right arm behind her back; Oscar bends and pulls it around her as she screams out again. I'm terrified of approaching her, frightened she might react and turn on me. He sees my hesitation.

'Go ahead, Kate, tie her arms behind her.' He looks down at Jody, 'If you so much as squirm, this bar will meet with your head… understand this, there'll be no hesitation on my part. I don't care what happens to you now; you got that?'

She doesn't speak.

'Have you got that?' he shouts at her.

'Yes!' she snarls back at him.

He looks at me and nods to go ahead, 'Tight, Kate, please.' His expression is firm, with an aura of brutal confidence about him that I've not experienced from him before.

I feed the belt around her upper arms, pushing the tail through the buckle, pulling it through hard so it is tight, before inserting the tang through the leather strap. Her arms are pinned behind her, and lying on her stomach will make it difficult for her to move now.

Oscar looks over to us, beckoning us across the room away from Jody and, at the same time, extracting his mobile phone from his trouser pocket. He speaks calmly and quietly.

'OK. I am going to call the police in a minute, but we need to get our stories straight, or we'll all be in deep water. This is how I see it playing out; we all met here tonight to talk about our search for our biological father, etcetera. I'll likely be captured on CCTV somewhere walking with her, so they'll pick that up and it'll fit. We get inside, and we talk; she gets more and more anxious and unsettled before flipping out and losing control. She said she had killed him and threatens us with the bar. Sarah, you screamed as she tried to attack you, and I intervened and fought her; Sarah, you also hit Jody; it'll explain bruises on the pair of you. I got a hold of the bar and hit her in self-defence to subdue her, no lethal strikes, only body blows. If the three of us stick with that story, we should be OK. They'll have their murderer complete with a similar murder weapon, if not the real one, and hopefully add charges of attempted murder for her attack on us, or at least assault or something. You both got it? A simple story that we all stick to. Yes?'

It kind of makes sense; we do need a story that ties her into killing our biological father and then her being here with us. I start to run aspects and logic through my head. 'But what about you following her down to the canal? The police may have a witness that saw you there.'

'I didn't see anyone else. Besides, there was no mention of them wanting a certain witness to come forward in this morning's news. It's a gamble, I know, but it's one that we're going to have to take. I can't now say I saw her do it, as I should have reported it there and then.'

'I know, but…'

He raises his right index finger to his lips, 'I have to phone now; someone may have heard the screaming. We can't wait anymore.'

He presses the keypad three times and speaks, 'Yes. Police... and an ambulance. We've just been attacked, and we have the woman restrained here in the office. Yes. Yes, she's injured. Oscar Courtauld. We're in the offices at 12 Oxford Row, Regency Street. The front door is locked, but we'll open it when the officers arrive. Yes. No. Yes, I'll keep the line open.' He moves the phone away from his mouth, slowly shaking his head from side to side, putting his index finger to his lips, 'It's OK, the police are on their way.'

To add to our story, I reply, 'Oh, thank god.'

Sarah pulls out a chair from the table and sits, lowering her head into her hands, her dreams shattered in one fell swoop.

Oscar moves closer to Jody again to keep an eye on her, and I sit beside Sarah, putting a comforting arm around her shoulders. She lowers her hands and leans into my shoulder as I embrace her. Oscar sees us and smiles sweetly at me. He has the caring attention one would hope for from a brother, coupled with the confidence and strength to protect us. This is the first time I've really felt close to Sarah and Oscar, and the irony of the situation is that this is what Jody could have had but she threw it all away with her anger.

Within a couple of minutes, we hear approaching sirens and then racing engines, followed by squealing tyres as vehicles come to a stop outside.

Oscar turns to look at me, ‘Kate, will you open the door and let them in, please?’

‘Yes.’

Leaving the meeting room, heading towards the front door, they beat me to it, banging loudly on the locked wooden barrier.

‘Police!’ Open Up!’

# 58

## Jody – Beech Road Police Station

This cell reminds me of some of the rooms I was locked in during my youth, bare walls, a plastic-covered mattress, a simple blanket, and a stainless steel sink and toilet. Listen to me, my youth; I'm only twenty-four years old; I feel like I've lived a whole life already. I've no idea why Oscar decided to follow me down to the canal; what made him think he had to follow me, but that doesn't matter anymore, as I got what I wanted; they're both dead now, by my hand. I am satisfied I've closed that chapter of my life for good.

I still can't believe he would go to his grave, not acknowledging what he did to my mother, still denying his role in my miserable life. But in that split second, just before I hit him again, he looked puzzled, like he had recalled what he'd done. Was he about to repent and ask for forgiveness? It wouldn't have mattered either way; he was going to die then, regardless.

It was stupid of me to kill him there, though, in a public open place; that's what's done me in; I should have followed him home and done it behind closed doors. Oscar will not have seen me from outside his house, and if I'd left from the rear after I killed him, he wouldn't have seen me leave. Now I think more about this in the quiet of this box, his mate, Paul, photographed me in the car park the other night, so I could have been linked to his death anyway and still picked up by the police. So, either way, it would have ended up with me in here. I never thought beyond killing him, to my escape, my future; I suppose that's because I never thought I had any real future, and my only ambition was to repay them both for the suffering they imposed on me.

Oscar surprised me, though; I didn't think he had it in him, and I didn't give him the caution and respect I should have. I had him down as a gentle type, well educated, wimpish even, but no, he had it in him to kill, and if it wasn't for Kate, he may well have done. His weakness seems to be Sarah, for as soon as she was in danger, he protected her with the energy and resolve of a big brother.

I wonder what sweet Sarah will think of me now and of sweet Oscar. She was getting a bit too clingy for my liking anyway, wanting to get to know me; huh, smothering me more like. I was right about finding that button to press inside everyone; Sarah wanted to kill me; I could feel it in her rage and the blows she rained on me. All those years, she held onto a dream to find him, and I took it away from her in an instant; her being so close yet so far must be frustrating, haha. Yeah, she wanted to kill me for robbing her of that; I have no doubt about that.

Kate. Now, she was focused, almost calm through it all, impressive. I sense that she wasn't that interested in finding her biological father, probably due to her loving and provided-for upbringing; she didn't have a gap in her life, she didn't suffer from his actions; he was just a stranger to her, so she had no emotional investment in him; at least I think so. She could just be one of the calmest people I've come across in a long time.

Anyway, fuck 'em. He got what he deserved, and I spared them all of his falsehoods and lies. They never knew him like I did, so it's no big loss for them. If anything, I've done them a service, I've spared them the pain and torment they didn't know they were walking into.

I half heard them getting their stories straight for the police, and I'm going to let them have that; there's no way I'm helping the police put someone else in prison. Can they carry it off when the investigation starts? We'll see, but that part is up to them; if it collapses, it'll be because of Sarah.

I'm not even going to deny it was me that killed him, Graeme Oglesby; I'm proud of what I've done, finding both my so-called parents when they thought they were invisible, untouchable, allowing me to exact my justice on them. Yep, I'll admit it, for I know what I am; I'm a product of the system, so why change. Life was shit outside anyway; at least inside, I know I can earn some respect; nah, I will get respect; no one will dare cross me again. And, to that, Oscar has taught me another valuable life lesson, take nothing and no one for granted.

# 59

## Oscar – Video Call

'I was in the police station until the small hours, making my statement, and they formally arrested her this morning; I'm glad she is off the streets. The officers wouldn't tell me the identity of the victim; his family have been informed, but they're holding his identity back until his next of kin have formally identified his body. I suppose we'll find out his name in due course.'

'Jeez, Oscar, you poor thing,' Kate says to me whilst Sarah seems lost for words. 'What happens next?'

'The judiciary will process her now. Apparently, during her interview, she made a full confession when they confronted her with the iron bar, saying it had blood traces on it. The police said she'll be held on remand, given her propensity for violence and the seriousness of the crime, and, of course, her confession. Apparently, she has also confessed to killing her biological mother for the same twisted reasons she killed him.'

'She killed her mother also? Oh my God.'

'I know, unbelievable, isn't it? The senior detective who took my statement asked me about her and sticking with our story, I told him she was our half-sister, explaining that we had been on this journey to find our half-siblings and biological father and that her DNA was matched with ours.'

'Do the police think you're involved with his murder?'

'No, not at all. They didn't say much, but I overheard a couple of the detectives saying that she has a past, that she is known to the authorities, and that she has been in trouble before. I showed them the messages in NeuvaGen, which indicated when we first learned of her and how we were tied by matched DNA. The police accepted this, but they will want to speak with the two of you to obtain your formal statements.'

'So, your instincts were right; there was something about her that didn't quite add up.'

'Yes, I suppose so,' I reply to Kate and then look at Sarah sitting half upright in the hospital beside Kate; Sarah remains quiet, just listening to us; I'm not sure if she is taking any of it in. 'Kate, can we have a chat?' raising my eyebrows slightly, hoping she interprets the intent of it.

'Er, yes, one second.' She lowers the phone slightly and talks to Sarah, who doesn't respond in any meaningful way. The video is jumping around as Kate stands and turns back to Sarah, but I see and hear enough to piece together Kate is making sure Sarah is comfortable, informing her that she'll return in a few minutes.

Outside the hospital room, Kate turns off the video and puts the phone to her ear.

'What is it?'

'I'm worried about Sarah; how is she?'

'The doctors say she is in shock, her catatonic state being the result of the events last night. They are expecting her to fully recover though, but she will need some time and maybe specialist help.'

'If she needs anything, any expert private care or help, anything at all, I'll pay for it all.'

'That's kind of you, and I said the same, but the doctors assured me she is in the right place, with an excellent and capable team available to help her. What about you, are you OK?'

'Yes, I am, I suppose. It's not often I get to tangle with a murderer.'

'So, where are you going now? Will the police let you go back home?'

'They've asked me if I can stay local for a couple of days, so I'll return to my hotel if they have the space.'

'Nonsense, you can come stay at ours. Paul is away at the moment, and I'd welcome the company.'

'No, I'm fine, Kate, honestly. Knowing she is locked up puts me at ease, although I don't think I'll ever get over what I saw. When I close my eyes, I get flashes of it; it's the first time I've seen someone die in front of me.'

'Murdered, more like. It's awful, I can't believe we are actually related to her. I'm stunned by it all; I am. It's just… so unbelievable. Why would she connect with us and then go and do something like this? I can't comprehend why she did what she did. We were all just starting out on this journey, finding new family links. No, I want you to come to ours, I insist; I'm worried about you.'

'Honestly, I'll be OK; I'll just go back to my hotel and extend my reservation for another few days. You'd best return to Sarah, sit with her, and look after her. Call me as soon as anything changes, promise?'

'I will, of course. Look after yourself, Oscar, for us.'

'I will.'

Ending the call, I lower the phone from my ear, take a deep breath, and let it out slowly. It's starting to rain lightly; I pocket my phone and raise my jacket collar before stepping out from under the entrance canopy of the police station and heading off towards my hotel.

I can never forgive Jody for what she has done to Sarah, regardless of why she thought she had to kill him. She should have let Sarah, and Kate and I, at least, meet him before killing him. Her reasons must be pretty compelling to take such drastic action on both her parents. Both of them; it's unbelievable.

# 60

## Kate – At Hospital

I wish he would come and stay with me; Paul will understand. Oh my god, in all the confusion and being here, I forgot about Paul; he tried to call me last night and left a voice message. I scroll to the recent call menu and see that there are now three voice messages waiting for me. I hope everything is alright with him.

Sitting on one of the plastic chairs lined up along the corridor wall, I hit enter and wait for the message to play.

> "*Kate, it's me. I have some terrible news. Graeme is dead; they found his body in the canal, and the police are treating it as suspicious; he may have been murdered, and his body pushed into the water. I wanted to let you know before you heard it cold on the news. Graeme's brother called Lauren, and Lauren called me. I'm on my way back on the train; I should get in around eight-thirty. Call me as soon as you get this.*"

The automated voice on the phone asks if I would like to play the recording again, delete it, or store it, but I can't process any of it. As I sit dumbfounded, the automatic voice reminds me again of the options.

Paul's message goes around in my head. *Graeme is dead.* His body was found in the canal. He was murdered. He's the one that was on the news. He's the one Jody murdered.

She killed Graeme. Then, what… Graeme is our biological father? Nooo! It can't be true. Can it? Graeme? Paul's best friend?

A nurse walking by stops in front of me and says something I don't quite register. She touches me on my shoulder, and I lift my face to her; I see her lips moving, saying something, but…

I lower the phone to my lap and look down, slowly moving my left index finger to the red screen button to end the call.

'Are you OK?' she asks, lowering herself to her haunches, putting herself on the same level as me. 'You don't look so good'.

I know I am just staring at her, almost through her, not speaking or engaging, but the implications of this news are just so incredible. All this time I have known Paul and been out for drinks with him and his best friend Graeme, I've never contemplated the possibility that Graeme could be my biological father, our biological father. Why would I? It was only recently that I found out Dad wasn't my biological father, leaving the field wide open to unknown anonymous candidates; why would I even think it could have been Graeme?

'Do you need some help?'

'Er, no… thank you, I don't think so. It's just that... I've had some bad news.'

To the nurse, that's probably something she hears often in this place. She has a calm look on her face, coupled with a soft, comforting voice. She reaches to hold my hand in hers, 'Can I get you anything? Would you like me to call someone for you?'

'No. I'll be OK… thank you. My husband is on his way home; he works away a lot, you see.'

'Would you like me to sit with you until he arrives?'

'No. It's fine, honestly, I'll be OK, he's on a train; no, he'll be home now. It… it was a message to tell me his best friend has died, someone who I cared for also.'

'Oh, I'm sorry. Would you like a cup of tea or a glass of water?'

'My husband will be home soon; I need to go to him.'

'You said he should already be home?' She pauses, looking at me. 'I don't think you should be driving; I can arrange a taxi for you if you like?'

'Yes, please, that's kind of you. I just need to go back to my friend on the ward and tell her I'm heading home. She'll worry if I'm not there.'

'OK, I'll come back to you in a few minutes. Go see your friend, then sit back down here, OK?'

'Yes. Yes, thank you.'

The nurse stands and turns to walk away to call for a taxi, and I sense her looking over her shoulder occasionally as she heads off down the corridor. I can't tell Sarah about this, not yet anyway; it could tip her fully over the edge. Our biological father, Paul's best friend, was in front of me all this time; I could easily have put us all together if I had known. It doesn't make sense; Graeme was so nice; why would Jody want to kill him? Surely, he couldn't have hurt her, not the Graeme I know.

I must see Paul, but what will he think when I tell him? He'll already be in a bad place, and this revelation will add to it. If I hadn't done the test, Graeme may still be alive today. No, I can't think that; Jody could have still found him anyway; she didn't need me.

I suppose it'll all come out soon enough; it'll be fodder for the press, Jody admitting she killed him because he was her biological father, our biological father. If I'd picked up Paul's message last night… I don't know what I'd have done. I loved Graeme as a friend too, and having Jody in front of me, at that moment, immobilised, I could have easily…

Returning to the ward, I stand just inside, looking at Sarah from a few metres away. She is still staring at some distant place, not moving an inch since I left her. I can't face her now, not knowing this, I wouldn't know what to say to her, and I'm frightened I could cause her more damage. The coward in me speaks, takes over, and convinces me that I should leave.

# 61

## Kate – At Home

As I lift the key up to my front door, Paul opens it from the inside, leaving me with my key pointing at him, poised in mid-motion, as though I am going to thrust it at him.

'Kate?'

Hearing his voice brings me to my senses, and I falter, my legs failing beneath me. He steps forward quickly and catches me.

'Here, come on, let's get you inside. Where have you been? I've been worried about you, especially with this killer on the loose. Why didn't you return my calls?'

He half carries me over the door threshold into the hallway, and we shuffle into the living room, where he lowers me onto the settee. 'You don't look so good; I'll get you a glass of water. Take your jacket off, and I'll be back in a second.'

As instructed, I slip my jacket off without further thought, letting it fall behind me, and I drop backwards onto the settee, letting my head rest on the cushion behind me. Paul returns with a glass and tries to put it in my hands before giving in, placing it on the small table, and sitting in one of the armchairs opposite me. I sense him looking at me and wonder how he must be feeling, losing his best friend yet having to worry about me, at the same time having this medical worry hanging over him. He doesn't know the whole story yet, so he must be wondering why I'm the one who looks so shell-shocked. I must do this; I have to tell him the whole story.

I sit upright and look at him. He looks tired, almost gaunt, like he hasn't slept, or he had too many drinks last night, and it's still too early for him, or both, I suppose. I don't think I've seen him in such a state before.

'I'm sorry, Paul, sorry about Graeme.'

'I know. You loved him too; he was a great guy.'

'Yes, yes, I did.' I feel a calm coming over me now; it's strange, as I don't know why. I suppose it could be because it's all coming to a close now, and we can get back on with our lives and plan and live our future together. 'Have the police said anything further about his death?'

'Paul's brother called me about fifteen minutes ago; they have someone in custody, arrested her last night; a woman. She's been charged this morning with murder. Apparently, she confessed to killing him and pushing him into the canal.'

'Oh... a woman. Did they say why she did it?'

'No, not yet. But apparently, they said she knew him; this is not some random attack.'

'Oh.'

'Now I've said it out loud, I've just remembered, I did see Graeme having a heated exchange with a woman in the car park at the cricket club last weekend; he said it was mistaken identity or something, said she was confused, probably unstable. It could be her, couldn't it? I mean, a nutter that's attacked him for some reason. Damn. I forgot all about that; I took a video of them arguing; I should tell the police; this could be important.'

I watch him fishing out his mobile phone and unlock it, scrolling to look for the video he has.

'Paul, I have something to tell you.'

'Yes, yes, one sec, let me just…'

'Paul, stop, please; what I'm about to say is important; you need to hear this now, from me, before you find out from others.'

He stops and looks at me. 'What is it, Kate?' he shuffles forward in the armchair, 'Where were you last night? You weren't with another…'

'No. No. It's not that.'

I'm unsure where to start; do I give him the whole story or just the finale? Surely, the end will be more than enough when he fully appreciates it.

'Kate?'

Did he know about Graeme, that he was my biological father? Is this why he was a little weird when I told him about the test kit a few weeks ago?

'Kate, what is it?'

No, surely not; if he knew, he would have said something to me; we agreed we would have no secrets from each other.

'Kate? What is going on?' now with an elevated voice and an inquisitorial expression emblazoned across his face.

I sit up and look across at him. I'll start with the end.

'Graeme was my biological father. It was Jody that killed him.'

His surprise is evident; he didn't know. His posture visibly tightens, and he looks back at me like a rabbit caught in a car's headlights.

'What… what are you talking about?' What…?'

'Look, this is going to sound weird and somewhat surreal, but it's all true. Graeme was my biological father and father to Oscar, Sarah and Jody.

'What the fuck are you talking about, Kate, and who the hell is Jody?'

'Jody is our other half-sibling. Jody murdered Graeme for what he had done to her.'

'How, how can that possibly be true? The police haven't released the identity of the person they've arrested yet.'

Shit. They haven't yet.

'I know it sounds incredible, but it's true. Graeme is my father; he donated to the clinic all those years ago. I take it you didn't know then?'

'What, that Graeme was your father? No, of course, I didn't know. No, he can't be, you're wrong. I don't get it; why would you think Graeme is your father?'

'His DNA test results.'

# 62

## Paul – At Home

'His DNA test results.'

Her words hit me like a hammer. How did…? I know he wasn't her father because I am; I'm the man who donated all those years ago; I'm her father.

'What are you talking about?' My left leg immediately starts bouncing again on my toes, my nervous habit displaying my inner anxiety. I catch myself and stand up. 'What DNA test results?'

She sighs and stands up, walking across the rug to me. I turn away, and instantly, she stops. I can't hug her; I can't touch her. Shit, this is all getting out of hand.

'What's wrong, Paul?'

DNA test results. How the hell did Jody get her hands on his DNA test results? Not his, mine. Fuck. She thinks he is her father; why would she think that? Of course, I used his name for my sample. Me. Oh fuck, I caused this. Did Kate give this Jody his name from my test results? That woman murdered my best mate because she thought he was me, the real donor; no wonder Graeme didn't know what the hell was going on when she approached him. My god, what have I done?

'Paul? I'm sorry, I know it's a shock. I'm sorry. I'm so sorry I got into this whole DNA thing with Ally. If we hadn't done the test and I found out Dad wasn't really my dad, and I hadn't shared my results to find out about my half-siblings and then gone along with this whole search for our biological father, maybe none of this would have happened. We wouldn't have shared the DNA results, and maybe Jody wouldn't have found out about Graeme. Oh my god, Paul, I'm sorry, really, I am. I'm so sorry.'

She steps up behind me and puts her arms over my shoulders and around my neck, pulling at me, almost choking me, sobbing into my back.

'Paul, please forgive me, I'm sorry.'

Her grip is irritating, and I don't want her touching me; she can't be near me.

'Paul, look at me, please.'

I grip her wrists around my neck and prise them apart, casting them aside and taking a large step forward, away from her; I shout at her. 'Get off me, woman! For god's sake, get off me!'

'Paul!'

'Leave me alone, won't you!'

'No! We need each other; everything is going wrong, and it's times like these when we should be stronger together.'

'Stop blathering on, will you? I'm trying to think.'

'Think about what? Me? Us? What? I didn't know it would turn out like this.'

'No, neither did I!'

'How could you? If Graeme never told you what he'd done, then how could you know it could end up like this? So, you didn't know everything about him then; he had his secrets, I suppose. Some best friend he turned out to be!'

'For god's sake, Kate, he wasn't your father!'

'Yes, he was!'

'No, he wasn't, I know he wasn't.'

'He's dead, Paul; stop defending him. Just accept he wasn't perfect. He did something bad to Jody and her mother, and she came looking for him.'

'Stop it! He's not your father!'

'Yes, he was! That's why she killed him!'

'No. No! He's not your father. I am! She killed the wrong man!'

The instant silence betrays my confession. Oh fuck. I turn to look at her, seeing she is staring at me through tear-filled eyes, her reddened face betraying the sudden turmoil of emotions I've created within her. I walk past her as she stands motionless and drop back into the armchair, masking my face with my hands. My breathing is short and deep, and my leg is bouncing again with a will of its own.

She's quiet. I can't even hear her breathing; she's not even sniffling anymore, but I can feel her processing the enormity of what I've just confessed to. My words are sinking in; she's absorbing what I've just said. I take a deep breath, release, and then another, trying to calm myself, preparing for the next onslaught. This is going to be hard; I thought losing my best friend was bad enough, but betraying the love of my life and then her finding out, and like this… I don't know what to say next. I don't know what to do; there's no way I can mend this.

There's no way back now.

# 63

## Kate – At Home

What did he just say? She killed the wrong man? That he is my father, not Graeme. As I stop and look at him, the realisation of what he's just said hits us both equally. He's blurred through my eyes, and as I start to wipe away the tears, watching as he looks away from me, he walks past me as though I'm nobody. With no shred of love or empathy evident, he drops into the chair and covers his face.

Has he finally snapped? The pressure of work, the illness, the loss of his best friend. Even considering all this, I don't understand why he would say that he is my father, to me, his wife.

Looking down at him, it's as though he's just confessed to the crime of the century, and his world is about to implode. 'Paul. Why would you say that?'

Nothing. His head buried in his hands, his heavy breathing… what is going on here? I reach out to him, and as I touch his hand, he bats mine away, turning his head from me.

'Paul! Why would you say that?' my now raised voice turning the scene on its head. But he still doesn't reply. 'Paul! For god's sake!'

'Stop it, will you? Stop it!'

'Oh yes, right, you want me to stop it, do you? You are the one who, out of nowhere, that's just said you are my father. That is so warped, Paul. Do you have any idea what this sounds like? Feels like? Look, I know he was your best friend, but I am your wife; I'm here for you, to support you. Why would you even think that saying you are my father is even acceptable?'

As I ask him the question, the conversation a few weeks ago with Ally about what Lauren and Ruth had discussed, starts ringing small alarm bells in my head. I thought she was just being vindicative and vexatious to the point I just dismissed it as a pair of bitter women, but… is there something in what he's saying?

'Paul. What is going on?'

He's still looking away, saying nothing. I reach across to him and slap him across the side of his head as I shout, 'PAUL! Talk to me!'

He spins in the chair and stands, squaring up to me. The fury in his face scares the life out of me. His clenched fists and that look in his eyes remind me of what I recently saw in Oscar, another side to him, to them both, that I've never seen before, and it frightens me. I wince and pull away slightly, expecting him to swing at me.

'For god's sake, Kate, I'm not going to hit you. What do you take me for?'

'I'm… I'm not sure; I don't know you anymore.'

He spins around and heads towards the bay window, placing his outspread hands on the windowsill and lowering his head in a penitent pose, looking for some kind of salvation. Neither of us moves; the rise and fall of his torso as his breathing slows is reassuring, but this whole situation is leaving me wondering what the hell has been going on with him. He's been weird since I told him about Dad not being my father, my real father, and then all that business with Lauren and Ruth… was it vindictive, vexatious tormenting of me for marrying him, or was there some truth in it?

Can it be true?

'Paul, you just said you are my father. Did you mean that? Please tell me you didn't.'

He doesn't reply.

'PAUL!'

He remains with his head bowed. I pick up a cushion and throw it at him, hitting him in his back, 'PAUL! Don't ignore me!'

He spins quickly, pulling himself upright and facing me down as he shouts back at me.

'YES! YES! YES! I AM YOUR FATHER!'

A horrible silence drops over us once again, but this time, I can't let the silence get any airtime. 'You? You are my father? My biological father? No, you can't be… you're my husband.'

'Yes,' as he lets the air escape from his chest. 'I know I'm your husband, but I'm also your father.'

The room begins to close in on me, my head starts to spin, and my legs are unsteady again. I reach out for the backrest of the armchair but miss it and start to fall, except this time, he doesn't step forward to catch me. I tumble forward into the armchair, rolling off it to land on the rug near his feet. He ignores me, takes a large step over me and sits back down on the settee.

'Here, take this.' As I raise my head to look at him, he's holding out the glass of water, shaking it slightly from side to side, almost as if he is trying to make the water rattle in the glass.

I ignore him and push myself up, moving my weight from my left hip up onto my knees and lifting myself into the armchair. He places the glass back down on the table.

The gravity of his confession is immense, the thought of him on me, touching me, laying with me… I want to be sick. I wretch, but nothing comes up. He knew! He knew!

A rage is building in me now, a feeling of being duped, of being cheated, used, of feeling dirty. How could he have known but still slept with me?

'It's out now, Kate, now you know the truth too. I've been living with this knowledge, but I couldn't do anything; I couldn't face you; that's why I have been hiding in London, staying away from you. I didn't want to hurt you, I promise. This is the last thing I wanted to happen.'

I try to speak, but my mouth isn't moving. My father. He thought it could be true but never said anything to me. How long has this been going on?

'Did… you know before we got married?'

'Kate?'

'DID YOU KNOW?'

'No.'

'So, when did you find out?'

'The results from the DNA test I did a few weeks ago.'

'And? I don't get it. Your DNA wasn't matched with mine; we were all matched with Graeme.' Then it dawns on me, the realisation he must have used Graeme somehow in all of this, and that's how Graeme's identity as our biological father came to light when he shared his match information. 'But you said there was nothing of any interest and dismissed it all as a waste of time. So, if you are my biological father, then how come Graeme's matched DNA shows him as our biological father?'

He turns away from me and walks back towards the bay window.

'Paul, I asked you a question.'

'Graeme did a test at the same time I did.'

'Wait a second. Even if Graeme did a test, then his results wouldn't match with mine; yours would.' I'm not sure what he's trying to say here; Graeme's results would be Graeme's results. 'Paul?'

'Look, I needed to know if I was or wasn't your father, but obviously, I didn't want you to know I had this concern, but I had to find out the truth, if I was your biological father or not, so, I err... switched samples with Graeme, so my results would come across as his. If it turned out that I was your father, then we'd split up without you or others ever knowing the real reason.'

'Wait, you mean to say you manipulated all this? Was your best mate Graeme in on this? Did you two hatch this plan together?'

'No. Graeme didn't know; I did it without him knowing.'

His head is down again, and his back is to me. 'What? You stole a sample from him?'

'Well, er, kind of.'

'Paul, look at me when we're talking; this is so fucking serious.'

He turns but stands still, looking at me, not offering any further explanation.

'What did you do, Paul?'

Is this really happening? How has all this got messed up?

I ask him again, 'Paul, what did you do?'

'I… I… oh, fuck it. I spun him a line that there was a complaint made against him at the cricket club, an allegation that he had been using drugs, and the club board wanted a quiet test done, you know, low profile to keep it all secret like. Their precious club and reputation and all that.'

'And he bought it? He went along with it?'

'Why wouldn't he? He trusted me; we were best mates. So, he provided me with a sample, and I swapped it out with mine, fixed the postal addresses and sent them off.'

As he says the words, he starts to blub, and I can see he is about to break down.

'Exactly, Paul, he trusted YOU. And you did this to him. You caused him to be mistakenly identified as our biological father, and then Jody found out who he was and what… *killed him by mistake?*'

'You can't hold that against me; no one could have known you would find another sister, one that is a nutcase with murder plans. Besides, if Jody had known it was me, it's me she would have murdered.'

'Precisely, and your point is? Your actions, Paul, take account of your actions. You could have spoken to me about your concerns when you first had them, and we could have gone through this together; that's what trust and marriage is all about. If you had been honest and acted with integrity, then Graeme would still be alive, and Jody wouldn't be in a police cell for his murder.'

'Well, how could I have discussed this with you? Think about it. And then what, when you found out, and others may have found out, then what…?'

'So, why did Jody want to kill her biological father? She was very angry and acidic towards him… and for him, I mean you; what did you do to her?'

He lowers his head and looks away.

'Well, what did you do? And who was her mother? I've heard that Jody killed her as well.'

'I didn't know she would come looking for me. If I had any idea she would, I would not have done the test in the first place.'

'But why did she come looking? What the hell did you do?'

He doesn't reply immediately; he's thinking of what to say next. Can I trust the next thing from this man's mouth?

'Paul?'

'Look, it was stupid, we were young. I had an affair with her mother,' quietly replying, lowering his head even further.

'What? When? If you have any decency left in you, tell me the truth now, Paul; at least show some backbone and integrity.'

'I was working away from home in London; Lauren and I hadn't been married for long.'

'Jeez, Paul, who the fuck are you?' My deep sigh and astonishment seem to give him some new impetus. He looks up at me.

'Her mother was a young woman, we had a short affair, she got pregnant, and I… I ran, I left them.'

'So, why did Jody not know your name and come looking for you earlier?'

He turns to walk away from me, but I grab his arm and swing him back around.

'Because I gave her a false name and told her I worked at a fake company. There was no way she could track me down; her mother couldn't give her anything to use.'

He deceives so easily; this whole trust thing is starting to ring alarm bells with me. Then, the pieces begin to fall into place.

'Hang on a second. You don't have an illness or a medical condition, do you? You started all that genital nonsense when you suspected something like this may be the outcome, didn't you? You lied to me. You let me think you had a serious condition.'

He looks away from me again, tutting loudly. 'I had to wait until I had the results, I had to do something, something to prevent us from sleeping together until I knew the truth.'

'Well, I suppose in some perverse way that's the only half-decent thing you've done, but I was worried about you, about us. I really thought you had something seriously wrong with you. I've been stressing out about it for weeks, waiting for you to tell me exactly what was wrong with you. Have you any idea what you put me through?'

My anger is growing inside now. I can feel the rage building within me and a fury rising. He lied to me, deceived me, used his best friend in another deception, and then sat on the information which ended up with his best friend being murdered.

'I couldn't sleep with you until I knew; you see that, don't you? We were newly married, and you would be expecting a sexual relationship.'

'Is that the measure of your integrity?'

'I don't think you have the safe ground on integrity, do you? Where was your integrity when we first kissed? I was married, had two grown children, and had a happy life, but you… no, you were the one who made a move on me.'

'Don't start playing tit-for-tat games with me on this, Paul; you will lose; I can guarantee that. You were the older, wiser, and more experienced person; you didn't have to reciprocate; you could have pushed me away.'

'No, Kate, now I come to think of it, it was you; it was all about what you wanted.'

'NO! No, it wasn't! I'm not having that.' I take a step towards him, drawing back my right arm, raising my hand to slap him, but as I swing forward, he catches my arm at the wrist, gripping it tightly and pulling me in towards him. As I close on him, I lash out with my left hand and slap him fully across his right cheek. He pushes me away, and I stumble backwards, the heel of my shoe catching on the rug, making me stumble and lose my footing. I scream out as I try to arrest my fall, but there's nothing to save me, and I fall to the floor, my back hitting the hard floor and my head whipping backwards, smacking against the floor. The rug softens the impact slightly, but I know instantly it's going to hurt.

He steps forward and bends down to me, reaching out, 'Oh my God, I'm sorry, Kate. I didn't mean for you to fall. Here, take my hand.'

I look up at him, and a feeling of instant despise washes over me. I slap his hand away, 'Go away, get off me! Don't you dare touch me!'

'Kate! Please!'

'Get out! GO! Leave me like you left her. You're a user. A liar. I hate you!'

He stops. Looking down at me on the floor, I can see I've hurt him or his pride. He is motionless, bent over me, thinking, but it's the tears that come from him that surprise me. He stands upright and coldly says, 'If anyone is leaving this house, it's you. I own it. Close the door on your way out. Go back to your beloved parents; I'm sure they'll take you in and tell you how horrible I am and what a mistake it was to marry me. I tried to do what I thought was best, but we're done now. There's nothing more to say except goodbye.'

He turns and walks out of the living room, heading into the kitchen.

He's right. It's over.

As I stand, I hold the back of my head and can already feel a lump forming, which is sore to the touch.

I walk slowly to the kitchen door and see him, his back to me again, head down, arms spread out on the kitchen worktop, the same penitent pose as earlier.

'I'm going. I'll get over this, but I don't think you will. You killed your best friend just as much as Jody did. Live with that knowledge and own it. Have the divorce papers addressed to my parent's home, and naturally, I'll sign them without contesting.' I twist the wedding ring from my left hand and throw it towards the sink. It ricochets off the mixer tap and clatters along the worktop.

'And I won't be needing that anymore.'

As I turn to leave, I hear him sobbing to himself.

# 64

## Julia – At Home

Kate is a mess; she arrived just before lunch and broke down, telling us everything. I can't believe Paul is her biological father, that he was the donor at the clinic all those years ago. She explained the stunt he pulled to get his DNA tested and then matched, using his friend Graeme in his sleight-of-hand trick to get to the truth secretly.

I put Kate to bed in her old room an hour ago, and with the aid of a little sleeping draft in her tea, I stayed with her, comforting her until she slipped into a deep sleep.

Ironically, in afterthought, I thought more about what Kate had told us, and it was quite clever really. If Paul turned out to be her father, then they would split, and the real reason would only be known to him, so no shame would befall them or the wider family; and if he wasn't her father, then they would simply continue in their marriage where they left off, and Kate would have been none the wiser. Paul feigning a medical condition provided him with a plausible reason to not sleep with Kate while he awaited the outcome of the test results; it would have been so wrong of him to continue sexual relations with Kate, knowing there was a possibility of him being her father; at least he did the right thing there.

But it all went wrong when he got the result he didn't want, and then Kate's half-sister Jody appeared on the scene. I met Graeme at the wedding; he was a nice, charming, polite man with a beautiful family, making it all the more shocking that he was murdered by Jody for the reasons Jody told Kate. Especially now in the knowledge, Graeme was an innocent, an unaware pawn in this whole thing, and Jody's intention was to kill her real biological father, Paul.

Paul should have trusted Kate. His deceptions and lies were believable, and Kate and others fell for it all; unfortunately, that belied the inner man, his ability to deceive those closest to him. I suppose the signs were there from the beginning; he was a married man having an extramarital affair. I have never seen Kate hurting like this before; a big part of the hurt is her realising she has been duped by this man; it's undermined her own confidence in reading and trusting people.

He can't be allowed to get away with hurting my daughter like this; I won't let him. Duncan doesn't have it in his character to face up to Paul; he doesn't like blatant confrontation, and his approach to difficult matters is to handle them with tact. My Duncan is calm, controlled and willing to wait for the right moment before striking; he's a planner. He's undeniably reliable, trustworthy and loving. What more could a woman ask for in her man.

But Paul, no, he is so different. I am annoyed with myself now for supporting the marriage and convincing Duncan that everything will be good. Duncan must have sensed something was wrong about Paul, as he never wanted them to marry, but I was so sure Paul was, in the main, a decent man who had fallen in love with our daughter and was prepared to make a future together with her.

How wrong I was.

Duncan would never put this back on me; he is too good-natured to say, “I told you so”. No, he will bide his time with Paul, but he knows how much Kate means to me, to us both, and he will not let Paul go unpunished.

Naturally, they’ll get a divorce now. I wonder if the police will get to the truth and press charges against Paul; after all, it was his deception that led to Graeme being incorrectly identified and then murdered. I’ll have to ask Duncan if there could be any charges against Paul; the one thing we don’t want now, which Kate needs protecting from, is the media stoking up a scandal.

# 65

## Paul – At Home

She is right; Graeme died because of me; it's all my fault. But how could I have known Kate's half-sibling had murder in mind, that she was searching for her biological father for revenge? How could anyone have known?

Graeme was my best mate; his wife, Susan, is completely broken, and his children have lost their father… in such a brutal way… for nothing; he was innocent of everything.

I can't believe Jody killed him. There is nothing that actually links Jody and Graeme; their two paths crossing was all down to me, and I don't think it will take the police long to put it all together.

Pouring another large, neat whisky, I gulp it down in one, smacking the glass back down on the table, only to recharge it again. The whisky is taking effect, and through the sobbing and bleary, tear-filled eyes, I drink down my fourth large glass.

I did this. I caused all this to happen. Me. It all started back at the end of the nineties, donating sperm for cash; then having that stupid fucking fling with that girl, then deciding to run away from her and her pregnancy when she told me of what we had created; me leaving her all alone. But I was recently married then, and I couldn't have done anything else; I had to leave and never mention it again, or I would have lost Lauren.

Yes, I could have done something. 'You arrogant prick', speaking it out for no others to hear, chastising myself; I could have kept it in my trousers, been a decent man, and not slept with a seventeen-year-old girl; I should have known better. I had everything I dreamed of, but I wanted more.

Lifting the glass and shaking my head from side to side, saying to myself, 'Christ, what an utter bastard I've been.'

I empty my glass again in one swallow and refill it. Placing the bottle on the table, I stand unsteady, wander over to the sideboard, pull open the drawer and take out a writing pad and pen. Leaving the drawer open, I return to the table and drop back down on the wooden dining chair to vacantly look down at the pad, staring, waiting for some words to come to me.

Nothing.

I roll the pen slowly between my thumb and finger, but I can't think of any words that will fully describe the shock and total remorse I have for all my actions.

Lauren was the love of my life until I met Kate.

Kate.

We had an instant bond from the first day we met each other. How the hell was I to know that bond was one of father and daughter; who would, who could? How could anyone know without doing a DNA test first?

I shouldn't have done that test, and certainly, I shouldn't have used Graeme as I did. We could have carried on; I could have lived in self-denial, not knowing the truth, but when I rang that bell, it could not be unrung. When I knew the truth, I had to stop us, cancel us, separate us. In my head, the quickest and cleanest way was to have a fictitious affair, with me choosing the other woman again. My self-imposed abstinence from Kate would have supported this fiction. No one else would have suspected anything, and my secret could have remained solely with me. It's not like having an affair is new territory for me, is it? I'd have been a villain no doubt in everyone's mind, but this would have been the only way to keep Kate protected from such devasting news. I know it would have hurt her badly and deeply, but having an affair would have been less damaging than the reality of sleeping with her biological father. In my mind, having an affair would have been more palatable and relatable given my past. But my god, how it's all backfired and the devastating impact on Graeme and his family is all down to me.

I did it all, all for her; there was no other way.

I lift the glass and swallow it all down again. The effects of the whisky are taking hold at last. I sniff loudly and pull the pad a little closer to me, then empty the remainder of the bottle into the glass, pushing the empty bottle across the table.

Why the fuck am I using a glass? Followed by what a stupid thought to have at a time like this.

Picking up the pen and clicking it, I hover over the page, blinking and wiping tears from my eyes. But the only thing I can think of writing is, "I am sorry."

The initial tears turn heavier, and I start to sob gently, which turns into a full-on wailing. I bang my head against the notepad on the tabletop to control myself, trying to knock some sense into me.

I cough and sniff loudly.

Then decide, enough; it's time.

I swallow the last of the whisky, then throw the glass across the kitchen to smash on the far wall, fragments and shards peppering the area where her wedding ring came to rest.

Reaching over to the other dining chair, I pick up Duncan's loaded shotgun and snap the barrel closed, the mechanical click priming the weapon. Spinning the stock towards the floor and taking a firm grip on the two barrels in my left hand, I put them under my chin. Sniffing loudly and trying to focus my movements, I wipe my right hand down both my cheeks.

Reaching down, twisting slightly, I place my right thumb through the trigger guard, letting my thumb rest on the trigger, then wrap my fingers around the top of the grip to the stock, firmly steadying the weapon in place, and close my eyes.

My breathing is heavy, but I want it to stop. I've had enough. I start breathing faster, trying to find the courage to send the signal to my thumb to close on the trigger. That one last decision I need to take to make all this go away: one more decision by me.

Breathing faster. Deeper. Faster. Deeper.

Gritting my teeth together, screwing my eyes up tight, and sounding out a guttural 'URGGGHH', I stiffen my thumb, pushing down firmly on the trigger.

# 66

## Kate – Beech Road Police Station

I'm not sure why the police want to see me again so quickly; I thought we covered everything yesterday. The phone call from the detective was short, polite, but firm; I am needed back in the police station to confirm a couple of matters in relation to Paul's death, which may, apparently, require me to update my earlier statement.

Paul's suicide was just that, suicide. He was in our home, the doors were locked, he'd left a note, and his body was discovered by chance by the visiting window cleaner, and it was the police who informed me. I'm not sure what more I can add to my earlier statement.

I'm back in the police station within the hour and taken to one of those impersonal interview rooms deep within the building. We passed through a couple of doors when the police officer guiding me had to insert a PIN number to walk through. The room is bland; on one wall, there is a large mirror, which instantly makes me think of those mirrors you see in TV shows, with a couple of people standing on the other side watching and listening.

The simple wooden table, with four chairs, two on either side, is orientated perpendicular to the large mirror, which reinforces my thoughts on the viewing capability of others. Built into the wall, at the head of the table, is a recording unit; the room is light and at about nineteen degrees centigrade; it has nothing of any personality, just official bland and functional.

Within a couple of minutes, the door opens. DS Jackson enters the room with DC Khan, and they both pull out chairs and sit across the table from me. DC Jackson opens the conversation as DC Khan places a notepad on the tabletop and pulls a pen from his pocket.

'Thank you for coming again at short notice, Mrs Hunter, to help us further our inquiries.'

'Anything to assist, although I don't think there is much more I can add to my earlier statement. Has something happened?'

'How do you mean?' asks DS Jackson.

'Well, DC Khan's call, forgive me for saying, was a little more than a polite request to drop in sometime, so I presume you have come across some new information that you think I can assist with or clarify.'

'Perceptive, Mrs Hunter. Yes, we have some new information and want to ask you some further questions about your husband's death.'

'I would rather you said former husband; you are aware we had recently separated and were about to start divorce proceedings?'

'Yes, we are, but you hadn't started them and were technically still husband and wife, but it is with regards to the separation that we want to clarify a couple of things. Following your husband's death, you stand to inherit, as his wife, quite well from his passing; is that fair to say?'

'Er, yes, I suppose so. Paul was always one to plan ahead for unknown events; I know he had made his last will and testament, and I know within it, he had bequeathed certain things to his two children, Ben and Ruth, and left something for his former wife, Lauren. He wanted me to know.'

DC Khan speaks up, 'Does it bother you that he left something for his former wife in his will?'

'No, why should it?'

'We're not sure, although it is a little unusual in our experience. And, of course, you would potentially inherit a substantial sum following Paul's death from his business interests and insurance.'

'Yes, probably. Like I said, he planned for future events; I don't know what or how much, but Paul did make provisions.'

'Could you tell us when Paul's Will will be opened and read?'

'It's scheduled for tomorrow; he may have left some funeral directions for consideration. What has this got to do with new information?'

Are they playing the insurance and money line for a motive of some kind?

'We are looking at Paul's suicide from a slightly different angle, wondering whether or not it was actually a suicide. Have you any thoughts on that?'

Where are they going with this? Paul shot himself. Paul had many reasons to commit suicide, but they are only aware of some of them; they don't know that Paul is, was, my biological father; no one does except me, Mum and Dad, and I agreed with Mum and Dad we would try to keep a lid on this secret and bury it deep.

So, I need to go along with their questioning, 'What thoughts? That someone else shot him?'

'Possibly,' replies DS Jackson. 'There was a short suicide note, admittedly, the shortest I've ever read, although there is no hint in his emails, messages, or conversations that we can see where he indicated the possibility of him taking his own life.'

'And why is that surprise? He was struggling with our marriage, losing touch with his children, and pressures at work, and to top it off, we were separating and heading for a divorce as Paul had said he had been unfaithful to me. I've even been informed that the Pathologist has confirmed suicide, something about a typical bruising pattern found to the back of Paul's thumb caused by the shotgun recoil. Come on, after everything you are aware of, you don't see he had a reason to take his own life. Really?'

'Who told you about the pathologist's observations?' Jackson asks, looking directly at me.

'One of your officers.' I can see this narks Jackson.

DC Khan speaks, 'Did Paul own a shotgun?'

I turn to him and reply, 'No.'

Khan continues, 'Do you know of anyone Paul knew who may own a shotgun?'

'Possibly.' It's about the gun, and he knows I know who has one. I can't say who, though; I can't put Dad in the middle of their investigation.

'Possibly? Well, is that a yes or no?' DS Jackson pushing me for an answer.

Turning back to Jackson, 'Er, well then, yes.'

'Who?' asks Jackson. My pause is too long for him, and he continues, 'Mrs Hunter, does your father own a shotgun?'

I'm not answering his question; I just look at him, neither of us removing our fixed eyes or daring to blink.

DC Khan breaks the stalemate, 'We know he does; in fact, your father has two shotguns registered in his name; is that correct, Mrs Hunter?'

I use this interruption to break my stare at Jackson, shifting my gaze back to Khan.

'Then why the silly question if you already know?'

But he doesn't answer this; he asks another question, 'Do you know where your father keeps his shotguns?'

'Yes, of course. He keeps them at home in a locked gun cabinet. Why?'

'And they are both in that cabinet at this time?'

'Yes, as far as I'm aware.'

'Do you know where your father keeps his keys for the cabinet?'

'No. Should I?'

DS Jackson interjects, 'OK, we need you to stay here for a few moments while we consult with colleagues.'

Both officers stand and leave the room, closing the door behind them. I can hear them outside the door talking, but it's mumbled, preventing me from making out any of their words. I hear them walking away down the corridor, the voices getting quieter with distance. This gives me an opportunity. I reach into my bag and pull out my mobile phone, open the case, go straight to contacts and favourites, and hit the icon for Dad; I lift it to my ear. The phone beeps three times and then stops, and looking at the screen, it indicates there is no signal to a network. Damn it; I'm in a concrete room within a large building; I can't reach anyone.

Without warning, the door opens, and I snap the phone down to my lap. A large, uniformed officer fills the door frame, 'Would you care for a cup of tea, Miss? The DS and DC will be back in about ten minutes; they have some more questions for you.'

'Er, well then, yes, please, tea with milk, no sugar.'

'No problem, I'll be back in a tick,' withdrawing and closing the door again.

I need to warn Dad the police are asking about his shotguns. I stand and walk quietly to the door and listen. The corridor outside seems quiet, and I open the door slowly, carefully listening for any sound. Why am I tip-toeing around here? I've not been arrested, charged, or even accused of a crime. I pull the door fully open and step out into the corridor, looking both ways. There is the general hum of office work coming from somewhere, but no one is to be seen. Turning right and retracing my steps, I reach the end of the corridor, and as I turn left, the police officer approaches with a cup of tea in hand.

'Sorry, Miss, you can't wander around unaccompanied.'

'Oh, er, sorry, I was looking for the lady's loo.'

'Ah yes, OK, one minute, let me put this cuppa down in the interview room, and I'll escort you,' raising the cup of tea slightly. 'One moment, please.'

He walks past me, enters the room and quickly returns. 'Now, Miss, if you'll follow me, please.'

We go through another PIN-coded door, and he indicates that the female toilet is the second on the left.

I rush in, closing the door behind me and pulling out my phone, checking the three cubicles that are empty as I walk deeper into the room. Relieved they are, I look down at my phone screen but notice there is still no signal. Damn it. I wander around the room, looking to pick up the faintest signal, but there is nothing, so I pocket my phone again. All I can do now is play along with the questioning, then call Dad as soon as I get out of the station. I flush one of the toilets and then wash my hands in the sink, making use of the loud hand dryer unit for my pretence.

Leaving the room, the officer is waiting for me, and he escorts me back to the interview room, leaving me with my cup of tea. I take a sip, it's not the best, but it's drinkable.

Watching the minutes tick by on the clock on the wall, a quarter of an hour passes, and then, nearing half an hour, I stand up again, annoyed by being left here on my own without further updates or contact. Walking out of the room, I decide this time to turn left in the hope of finding another human or an exit. I walk past several numbered interview rooms, all of which appear empty, before coming up against another PIN-controlled door. I try the handle, but a PIN code is needed. I'm getting more frustrated and irate; I could be forgotten about down here.

Looking through the glass vision panel of the door, I notice a female police officer enter the corridor on the other side of the door, and using the bottom of my mobile, I bang hard on the glass to catch her attention. She turns and looks at me, and I wave, indicating that she should open the door. She holds up her left index finger, indicating to wait as she reaches for her radio mike clipped to her shoulder tab and speaks. I suppose she doesn't know me from the next person, and to her, I could be a criminal or an arrested person trying to escape the police station.

After a few seconds, she turns and heads in my direction. Thank God.

Hearing the slight beeps of the PIN being entered, she releases the door lock and pushes it toward me. 'Good afternoon; are you lost?' she asks me.

'No, just annoyed. I've been sat in an interview room for over half an hour now, waiting for someone to come back.'

'Are you here to make a statement?

'Well, yes and no. I was being asked some further questions about my husband's suicide, and DS Jackson and DC Khan left to check something with a colleague, and I've been sat alone, waiting ever since.'

'I'm sorry. Let me try to raise DS Jackson now.'

She clicks her mike button again and asks for DS Jackson's whereabouts. 'Sorry, it'll just be a minute.'

I let out a deep sigh, showing my displeasure. She continues talking while she awaits a return, 'I'm surprised they've put you down here in these interview rooms; we rarely use them these days. There is no phone signal down here, and we rely on mobile comms quite a bit; luckily, these units keep us in contact through local boosters,' tapping her radio piece.

Have they done this for a reason? Get me to call in here under false pretences while they go and arrest Dad? Surely not.

'Can I leave now?' I ask the officer. 'I have appointments to keep, and if your colleagues are tied up, I can come back another time. I'm happy to help with inquiries, but I can't be of any help if there is no one here to be helpful with.'

'Just a second. I'll try to raise the DS or DC Khan.' She speaks into her mike again, and a few seconds later, there is a semi-incoherent reply. She quickly turns down the volume control as she steps back, away from me, moving down the corridor, trying to keep the communications from my ears.

'Hello.' I call out, indicating my frustration. 'Can I leave, please?'

She raises that index finger again while listening to the comms.

I'm getting even more frustrated; now that I've found a human, I'm still stuck in here.

I walk through the door and head towards her. She looks up and sees me, then loudly says into the mike,

'Yes, will do.' Turning to block my path, she smiles, 'Apologies, DS Jackson and DC Khan have been called away on some urgent business. I can escort you out of the station, and DC Khan will be in touch later today.'

'That's it?' my annoyance obvious, 'What a waste of my time. OK, please show me out.'

'Follow me, please,' and we head off through another series of locked doors. As we get to the front reception area, she turns to me, 'Here we go,' indicating the exit.

I look at her smiling at me, and I feel a pang of regret for having a go at her when all she has done is try to help me. 'Look, I'm sorry I was short with you back there, I just wanted to know what was happening.'

'There's no need to apologise; enjoy the rest of your day.' She turns and heads back into the bowels of the station from where I have just escaped.

Outside the building, I pull out my phone, and seeing the full-strength signal, I call Dad. It rings out until the voice message starts to speak.

# 67

## Julia – At Home

From the bedroom window, I watch two cars coming down the lane and come to a stop outside our house. The two front doors of the first car open in unison, and I recognise the two plain-clothes police officers from the earlier interviews. The marked police car stops a few yards behind them, and three fully uniformed and armed officers step out; in an almost trance, I watch them. I know why they are here.

The Detective Sergeant is giving instructions to the three armed officers that I can't quite make out, and two of them are the first to walk down our front path, the third walking down the side path to the rear of our house. I need to get downstairs quickly before things get out of hand. Crossing the bedroom, I hear Duncan calling for me, followed almost instantaneously by loud banging on the front door, with calls of 'Armed Police! Open the door!'

Duncan is shouting from the foot of the stairs, 'Julia! Don't panic! Don't do anything foolish! It's the police, and they're armed with guns!'

How has it come to this?

As I leave the bedroom and step onto the upstairs landing, I hear Duncan replying to the police officers, 'I'm coming! I am not armed! I am not armed! I'm opening the front door now! OK?'

I'm halfway down the stairs when Duncan opens the front door, and one of the armed officers is standing partially behind the door opening, aiming what looks like a machine gun directly at Duncan. I catch my breath and shout, 'Please! Stop!'

The officer ignores me and remains focused on Duncan. 'Do not move! Put your hands above your head where we can see them! Do it now!'

Duncan complies, slowly raising his hands above his head. Just as he does, his mobile phone starts to ring in his pocket and through instinct, he moves to answer it, lowering his right hand.

'DO NOT MOVE!' shouts the officer.

'Oh, no, sorry,' as he raises his hand again. Leaving the phone to ring in his pocket.

'Now, slowly walk outside towards me! No sudden moves!' The officer shouts his instructions even though there are only a few yards between them.

'Duncan!' My shout is lost in the intensity of what is happening on the doorstep.

A second armed officer looks up to me on the stairs. He shouts at me, 'Stand still! Do not move!' and he aims a large gun at me, too.

'Duncan! What is happening? Why are the police here?' He doesn't reply for obvious reasons; he has at least one weapon pointed at him and has eye contact with its holder.

Duncan slowly walks forward, heading outside and stepping down onto the garden path. The second officer lowers his weapon and moves to Duncan, quickly pulling Duncan's right arm down behind him and clicking on handcuffs, swiftly followed by his left arm. Duncan's phone, at last, stops ringing.

The second-armed officer lifts up his weapon again and points it at me, shouting to me to do the same, to slowly walk outside with my hands in full view. As I step outside, I see the two plain-clothes detectives watching from the end of the driveway. DS Jackson calls out to the second officer, 'It's OK, calm down. The cuffs are not necessary for Mrs Leyden; stand down.'

The second officer looks at me as though he is weighing me up, assessing if I am safe or not. After a few seconds, without a word, he lowers his weapon slightly and takes a step backwards.

DS Jackson speaks again, 'Thank you. Now, let's all just take a moment, shall we? This will be a shock to you, I know.' He turns to one of the armed officers, 'Go ahead,' indicating he is to go into the house and clear it.

After what seems an age but is really a few minutes, he calls out, 'All clear.'

'Shall we all step back inside so we can talk?' says DC Jackson.

This was an instruction rather than a question. The second-armed officer lowers his weapon, hanging on a sling by his side, places his hand under the pit of Duncan's arm and guides him back into the house, turning left into the living room. I look at the DS, and showing no emotion, he nods his head, beckoning, 'Shall we join your husband, Mrs Leyden?'

I turn and follow them into the living room. Duncan is already sitting rather awkwardly on the settee as the DS indicates I am to sit in an adjacent armchair.

'Now,' the DS starts, 'Mr Leyden, I presume you know why we are here and why we need to bring along armed officers?'

'I have a fair idea, yes,' Duncan replies, looking directly at the DS.

'Firstly, the formalities. Duncan Leyden, I am arresting you for the murder of Paul Hunter on the tenth of October, contrary to common law. You do not have to say anything. But it may harm your defence if you do not mention when questioned something which you later rely on in court. Anything you do say may be given in evidence. Do you understand?'

'Yes.'

The short reply from Duncan shocks me, he doesn't even ask why.

'Duncan, what's going on?' I ask him.

'It's OK dear, this is just something we must go through. The police are just doing their job.'

The DS speaks before I can reply, 'Mr Leyden, you are aware that Mr Hunter was found deceased, the result of a shotgun discharge to his head?'

'Yes.'

'Can you tell me, do you own a shotgun?'

'Yes, I own two, but you already know this, or you wouldn't be here.'

The DS nods slightly. 'Please, can you direct my officers to your secure gun cabinet?'

'Yes, but I'll save you the trouble; my gun cabinet is through there, but one of my shotguns is missing,' nodding his head towards the door to the kitchen. 'It's in the Boot Room just off the kitchen.'

An armed officer walks away swiftly, heading to the Boot Room.

'Do you know the whereabouts of your missing shotgun, Mr Leyden?'

'Yes, I can hazard a guess that it's probably in your police station, bagged as evidence.'

I look at Duncan and notice how calm and confident he is with his replies.

'Mr Leyden, do you want to say anything to me regarding the death of your son-in-law, Mr Paul Hunter?'

Duncan looks at me, smiling, and whispering, 'It'll be OK,' turning back to the DS and adding, 'Yes… it was me, I provided him with my gun and talked him into shooting himself.'

The room falls silent. The police officers look at each other, surprised by the blunt confession, before looking back at Duncan. I can't believe what Duncan is saying. The DC leans into the DS and speaks softly, 'We need to stop this now; he has rights, Sarge. He needs to be interviewed properly at the station.'

The DS is sitting motionless, almost as if he has been stunned, showing no expression. 'Sarge?' the DC asks.

'Erm, yes. Yes, you're right, Khan. Please, take Mr Leyden out to the car.'

The DC steps forward, but Duncan interrupts him mid-step, 'DS Jackson. Can I possibly ask for a few moments alone with my wife, please? We've been married for nearly forty years, and I owe her an explanation. Thereafter, I'll come along quietly and provide you with all the answers you need.'

The DS looks at Duncan, then at me. 'You know I can't do that.'

Duncan directs his words again to the DS without looking at me, 'Even though you have your man, he's confessed, and he's handcuffed; please, Detective Sergeant, if not for me, then do this for my wife.'

DS Jackson tuts loudly, then breathes out deeply, 'OK. Two minutes. But the cuffs remain on.'

'Yes, agreed, thank you,' Duncan replies.

'Come on, you lot, outside.' As they leave the living room, DS Jackson looks back at us both, 'Two minutes from when I close this door.' He steps outside into the hallway, closing the door behind him, and our limited time alone begins.

Duncan stands, and I run across to him, throwing my arms around his shoulders and pulling him in tight. He lowers his head and whispers softly into my right ear.

'Shh, I know it was you. I know you killed Paul.'

I release him and step back slightly to look at him. 'What?'

'I knew within a few moments of the police informing us of Paul's death. Kate was devastated; she clearly didn't want that outcome for Paul. You were there for Kate without a flicker, consoling Kate like any good mother would, strong, stoic, and caring, but there was something in the news of his death that didn't shock you; it didn't faze you; it was almost like it wasn't a surprise to you. Then, when the officer mentioned to me that Paul had used a shotgun, an awful realisation came over me that Paul had used one of my guns. I don't know why, a sixth sense, I suppose, so I made my excuses, needing some air; as I went out back, I had a look in my gun cabinet in the Boot Room, and one of my shotguns was missing, but the cabinet was still locked. Only you and I know where my keys are kept for my gun cabinet and that my ammunition is kept in a different secure locker box out in the garage. Paul knew about my two shotguns, but he didn't know where I kept the keys or where I stored the separate cartridges; I never shared that information with either Paul or Kate; only we knew, and my love… I know I didn't kill him. It was suicide, wasn't it, just assisted by you?'

I look at him, and tears are filling my eyes. I struggle to find the words to reply, but the sand in our timer is quickly settling. I swallow hard, 'It was suicide, but yes, with some assistance. So, you knew and never said anything? And now you're confessing to a role in it you never had. Why? Why would you do that?'

'I knew the police would be back; the gun is registered in my name; they came armed as they know I have another registered gun. As for the why? Simple, because Kate needs you now more than ever, and you've always needed Kate.'

'No, Duncan. Look, I'll admit it, it was all me, but in the end, it was a suicide; he was the one that pulled the trigger on himself, I… I… I just convinced him it was the right thing to do and provided him with the means to do it. Between us, in our relationship, I know it has always been me; it was me that wanted my own baby, and I pressured you into doing what we did; it was me that didn't want you telling Kate about not being her biological father, it was me convincing you that Kate marrying an older man would all work out fine. So, when all this awful mess happened, I decided it would be me that would clean it all up.' I start to cry from the sheer relief of saying this to him. He takes a step forward, his chest heaving heavily in front of me as he sighs deeply.

'Julia, you are the love of my life; you always have been and always will be. This is something I need to do for Kate and for us. I want to do this; this is my decision.'

Openly crying now, I throw my arms around his shoulders and hold him as tight as I possibly can, trying to squeeze him out of the extended nightmare we are in, out of the mess that I created, the mess that I started all those years ago. Through my sobbing, I whisper to him, 'No, Duncan, no. I did this, and I need to own it. It's my price to pay.' I try to hug him even tighter, 'You are a wonderful man, but I cannot let you do this for me.'

I hold him and wish the handcuffs could be released just so he can hold me again.

DS Jackson, out in the hall, is speaking loudly, indicating he is about to re-enter the living room, and as I look over to the door, I see the door handle being turned down slowly, and the door cracks open.

Duncan lowers his head again down to my ear, ‘Promise me you will look after yourself and our daughter.’

His use of the word our hits me hard, and I whisper back to him, ‘Our daughter.’

He lowers his head to my ear, ‘We both know she is ours; she always has been and always will be; I’m doing this thing for the both of you. You need Kate more than you need me, and the good lord knows she needs her mother now more than ever before. I can accept that, and that’s what I want. This is my decision this time, not yours. Accept this for me. I love you, Julia.’

The voice of authority behind Duncan cuts through my sobbing, ‘It’s time to leave, Mr Leyden.’

# 68

## Kate – Dobson Park

'OK, Mum, I'll get home as quickly as possible. Please wait for me.' I close my mobile phone as I sit down on the park bench and look out over the pond.

It was inevitable; the police were always going to check the gun's serial number against gun registration and then come calling on Dad.

Mum didn't sound too good, and right now, I know she will be packing her handbag and getting her coat ready to head down to the police station and wait for Dad.

Dad's arrest isn't that much of a surprise, given it was his gun that Paul used.

I know Dad; he wouldn't have been involved in Paul's death; that would be so alien to him to even think like that; never mind, act it out. Knowing Dad as I do, he's willing to take the fall for Mum. Mum knew where Dad kept the keys to the gun cabinet and cartridge locker, allowing her to unlock them both before heading over to see Paul, intending to make him pay for what he has done to me, to them, and to poor Graeme and his family.

In all of this, Ben and Ruth have lost their father. I'm not sure how they are taking his death, but there was a clear degree of animosity there from what Paul did to Lauren and to them. Paul choosing me over Lauren was a significant upheaval in their three lives, creating tension and strain. Lauren will probably take Paul's passing far easier, especially after their acrimonious divorce, and then the surprise of him still bequeathing her a decent inheritance. Ruth will be upset, and no doubt her head and emotions will be all over the place; she will need her mum more than ever now. I think Ben, however, will be the most upset of the three; he wanted to retain a father-son relationship with Paul, and I know Paul wanted that more than anything; well, not more than having me, of course.

Oscar and Sarah have also been denied the opportunity to meet their biological father. Well, truth be known, they never knew him; he was and will remain, a stranger to them. I don't suppose they will want to boast now about their biological father being implicit in deception that directly led to the death of at least two people, one, an innocent in all this, being murdered by their half-sister, and Paul, taking his own life because of that murder. It won't make for good family history reading for the generations that follow. They may want to stay in touch with me, but then, it's probably best we just drift apart again. Their biological father died because of me, and that won't be easy for them to accept or forget.

Me.

It was me. Mum will know it was me who gave Dad's gun to Paul and that I talked him into doing it. She knows she didn't do it, even though she wanted Paul to pay for what he had done. And, she knows Dad, like I do, and that he didn't do it either. So, she is protecting her only child, her daughter. Dad is prepared to do this for Mum, and if he is, then why wouldn't I let him do it for her and indirectly do it for me? He is, and always will be, a gentleman, honourable, and a strong man of principle, and I love him for that. With some luck, he may get a sympathetic jury when it all comes out in court; let's hope there is some justice left in the world.

I knew where Dad kept his keys; I've known for a long time but never said. Sensibly using latex gloves, I'll have left no trace of me on the gun or the cartridge, but if I did, I'm sure a good lawyer will argue it as circumstantial, the result of my previous handling of the gun, leaving historical trace indications or inadvertent cross-contamination; after all, it is my dad's gun.

Mum and I have a true bond, true ties of genes and nature. If she is letting Dad do this, then she is indicating that her maternal bond means more to her than her marital bond, and why shouldn't it? We are, after all, true family, and blood is thicker than water and all that. Dad is the man she married, but I am the daughter she gave birth to, nurtured, and cherished.

No man should dare come between a mother and her daughter, and if he did, well…

I had best go see Mum and support her through this; although I'll never admit to her it was me, and that way, she can hold onto the belief, the fiction, that Dad is taking the rap for her, his sacrifice allowing the two of us to carry on together.

As I stand up quickly, I startle a mother duck and her solitary juvenile that are feeding at the pond edge; she takes to the water with her juvenile following behind, paddling away serenely as though my startling them is nothing more but a momentary distraction before they continue with their everyday lives.

All is as it should be.

# 69

## Kate – Beech Road Police Station

I wasn't expecting another call from DC Khan anytime soon, so when he called this morning asking me to return to the police station to discuss a new development, my first thoughts turned to Dad's shotgun and if, somehow, they had found out it was me, but I couldn't reconcile that in my head; Dad thinks it was Mum, Mum probably knows it was me, but neither would give up on what they believed, each holding a secret close to them for their own reasons. Since DC Khan's call, I have wondered what this new development could be.

On arriving at the station, I was only waiting a few minutes before being directed to an upstairs office; the nameplate on the door indicated the occupant as Chief Superintendent Fisk. On entering, a man in full police uniform sitting behind the desk rises to greet me, and as I step into the room, I register more people are already waiting for me.

'Good afternoon, Mrs Hunter, I am Chief Superintendent Fisk, and these are my colleagues,' indicating to each person in turn, 'Detective Inspector Armitt, Detective Sergeant Jackson, who I believe you already know, and this is Linda Thompson, from our Victim Support Team.' As he introduces Linda, she steps forward, holding out her right hand with a smile and an inviting warmth about her; we shake hands, and she indicates for me to take one of the empty seats in front of the Chief Superintendent's desk. As I sit, the others take a seat, except for the DS, who remains standing to the left of the room.

The Chief Superintendent sits, squaring up a report folder in front of him on his almost empty desk. Looking first at Linda to my left and then at the Detective Inspector to my right, the Chief Superintendent looks squarely at me and continues, 'As you are aware, we have a very unusual situation surrounding the murder of Graeme Oglesby by your half-sibling Miss Jody McTee, followed by the unfortunate related suicide of you husband, Mr Paul Hunter, and then the subsequent arrest of your father,' opening the file, he slips on a pair of half-moon reading glasses looking for his name, '…Mr Duncan Leyden, in relation to firearms offences, pending a further decision on a course of action by the Crown Prosecution Service. All very unfortunate, as I am sure you'll agree.'

As he is saying this, I can't help thinking this is like a formal summarised version for a press interview, probably what this man is used to, and all I can say is 'Yes.' I am still unsure why I'm here and don't want to say anything I shouldn't.

He continues, 'I am unable to provide much detail currently, naturally, as these are ongoing inquiries, but during formal interview, Miss McTee provided some information that we needed to verify to corroborate as part of her statement.'

He pauses as though waiting for me to speak, but I just hold my tongue. He clears his throat slightly and continues.

'I believe you are aware that Jody McTee has intimated that Mr Oglesby was her biological father, and thus, by extension, he was yours also.'

'Yes.'

'Well,' Fisk removing his reading glasses but holding them between his right index finger and thumb, gently waving them as he speaks, 'Miss McTee has confessed to killing Mr Oglesby after we confronted her with traces of Mr Oglesby's blood found on the iron bar that she brought to the meeting in your husband's offices, the bar she was using to attack you and your half-siblings with.'

'Oh my god, really?' and for effect, I turn to Linda to show my surprise at hearing this information. But then Fisk continues.

'It seems that Miss McTee is a very troubled individual; she has also confessed to taking the life of her biological mother some time ago in a care home, whilst working there under a false identity. Following some further enquiries, my officers consider there is some merit in her admission.'

The first part of his news is not a surprise to me, but the second part is; making my emotions and manner all the more believable now. I didn't expect her to confess to the police of her murdering her mother.

'No. Really? Why on earth would she kill her parents?'

'As I mentioned, Miss McTee has some issues and is carrying much trauma from her younger life that, in her mind, justified her taking the lives of both her parents.'

'But she told us that her mother passed of natural causes, and that was what prompted her to find out about her biological father. Unbelievable; just terrible.'

Linda speaks, 'Are you alright, Mrs Hunter? Would you maybe care for a glass of water or a cup of tea?' I turn my head to look at her, 'No thank you,' but there is something in her expression that tells me she knows more than she is letting on; it's her empathy, her soft, kind tone that gives it away; that they all know more than I do, thinking I'm the last one to find out.

Fisk continues, 'We needed to verify this admission, and that was the reason that DS Jackson here, and his team, asked you and your other half-siblings to provide a DNA sample to corroborate her assertion that Graeme Oglesby was your biological father.'

Again, he pauses, but I do not react or say anything, which seems to irritate him a little. He takes this opportunity to return his reading glasses to the bridge of his nose and turn some pages within the report folder. I'm not sure what I'm supposed to do here; his pause is unsettling; what have they found out?

No one speaks, awaiting the next move.

All I can think of is, 'OK, and I presume then that you confirmed my DNA matches with Jody's and my other half-siblings, Oscar and Sarah?'

'Yes, that is the case, all four of you are related biologically as half-siblings from the same paternal line.'

'Well, we knew that from the results and our matches on the NeuvaGen website; I had already shared this information with DS Jackson in my earlier statement.'

'Yes, thank you, we are aware of that, but we needed to verify it independently,' pausing again. I see him look at Linda and then back to his report, almost as if giving her a preliminary sign that he is about to move into something more sensitive.

Again, clearing his throat with a further cough, 'However, some additional information came to light that required us to carry out further investigation. Naturally, we had to take your husband's DNA for identification purposes, given the severity of his injuries.'

'Oh, right, yes, I suppose so. And?'

Then, it dawns on me that this is how they eventually pieced together that Paul is my biological father. After all this time and trying to keep a lid on this secret, it's finally coming out into the open. Keeping this a secret was always going to be difficult, and whilst hoping it would stay buried, it was only ever really living on borrowed time. I've known Graeme isn't our biological father since Paul told me, meaning that Jody got it wrong, and I feel a little more confident to take part in this conversation now that I know where it's going, but in doing so, I'll need to show surprise when they break the news about Paul. So this is why Linda is present; she is here to support me when I am informed that Paul is my father. Here goes…

Fisk replies, 'After obtaining all the DNA results, we compared your shared DNA with Mr Oglesby's DNA and…' he pauses again to review the notes in his report, and I notice DS Jackson show a flicker of frustration at his senior officer, lifting his eyes and shaking his head ever so slightly.

'And we can confirm that Mr Oglesby is your shared biological father.'

'But, no, that can't be right, Graeme's DNA was matched with ours by the specialists at NeuvaGen. Graeme is our biological father.'

'Yes, Mrs Hunter, that is what I said; Graeme Oglesby was your biological father. I'm sorry, did I confuse you? I didn't mean to; it can be somewhat confusing following all this medical science material.'

Anticipating he was going to say Paul was my father and being prepared to react to this shocking revelation, I hadn't realised what he'd actually said. He can't be right, and I'm worried that my surprise is weirdly counter to him saying Graeme is confirmed as my biological father. No, no, this can't be right; Paul was adamant with me; Paul was my father; he told me what he had done, and had the DNA proof; he even admitted sleeping with Jody's mother and abandoning her.

Linda, turning to me, speaks again, 'The information Chief Superintendent Fisk has is correct. I know all this is upsetting for you, and the shock of hearing such facts so coldly can sometimes play tricks on a person's understanding of what is happening.'

'But…' is all I can say for the time being, I'm speechless. Linda is holding my shaking hand now.

Fisk speaks again. 'There is some further information I need to share with you, Mrs Hunter, which is, well, erm, quite sensitive. It's regarding your husband's DNA test results.'

If Graeme was my father, then why is Paul's DNA of any interest now? I'm already supposed to know about Graeme, so I need to be careful how much surprise I show when they give me information. Fisk, confirming that Paul's DNA has been looked into and is not linked with me, has me confused now, but I need to go along with what they are telling me, and I reply, trying to indicate I'm catching up.

'But Paul had already done a DNA sample and said there was nothing of interest. He even showed me the results from NeuvaGen.'

'Yes, well, it seems that Mr Hunter obtained a sample of his own saliva and a sample of Mr Oglesby's. However, before submitting them for testing with NeuvaGen, Mr Hunter swapped them so that Mr Hunter's sample was registered against his apartment address in London but under Mr Oglesby's name, while Mr Oglesby's sample was registered at your married home address here but under Mr Hunter's name. This took a little thought and some careful planning by Mr Hunter, and we got to wondering why he would do this.'

I know the reason, well I thought I did, but do they? 'Why on earth would Paul do that? Oh my god! Are you saying that Paul could be my biological father?'

'No, Mrs Hunter, no. What we're saying is that Paul Hunter thought he may have been your biological father, but we can categorically state that he is not. It seems that the test results and the addresses the results were returned to somehow got crossed; NeuvaGen seems to think this is more likely to have been by Mr Hunter, mislabelling the samples at the outset.'

I jolt and look at him with eyes wide open, then turn to Linda. 'Really?'

'Yes, I'm afraid so,' she replies.

Fisk continues, 'A handwriting expert has compared the two forms accompanying the two samples sent to NeuvaGen, and both are in Mr Hunter's hand. From Mr Hunter's actions, we deduce that he may have suspected or been aware of the possibility that he could have been your biological father, and he wanted a clandestine way of finding out. Mr Oglesby's widow, er…' looking at the file once more, 'Susan, has provided a statement that Paul Hunter took saliva samples from Mr Oglesby in relation to an allegation of drug use made to their cricket club, a complaint that the cricket club were apparently not aware of.'

'What? No. I didn't know he'd done that.'

Fisk picks up again, 'Is this why you separated and were heading for a divorce? It could well be the reason why your husband took his own life, him thinking he was your father.'

'No! We were about to divorce because he told me he was having an affair; he decided he wanted her more than me. He had lied about a medical problem to prevent us from having sexual relations because he was having sex with her. I've said all this to your officers.'

'Quite; however, we now believe Paul Hunter feigned the medical condition as soon as he believed he was your biological father after he mistakenly mixed up the samples and thus the results; we have checked with his doctor, and Paul had no such health condition or any ongoing medical issues. Thus, believing he was your father, we think that his only course of action was to create an imaginary affair so that the two of you separated, and then you both filed for divorce. Would that make sense to you, Mrs Hunter?'

I lower my head into my rising palms and start to breathe and exhale quickly. This is all shattering news to me, and I'm not coping with it; how could they piece all this together? It's not what I expected to hear. Linda shuffles her chair closer to me and puts her arm around my shoulder, whispering something quietly to me, attempting to comfort me in some caring way.

# 70

## Kate – Beech Road Police Station

Linda can see I am struggling with this conversation, but it's not for the reason she thinks. My thoughts are whirling around in my head like a tornado. If Graeme was my biological father, no, he is my biological father, then Paul and I could have continued as we were; we wouldn't have been genetically related. But then, this also means that Graeme was the man who got Jody's mother pregnant. How could that have happened? Paul admitted he was seeing Jody's mother, that he believed he had gotten her pregnant and then decided to break it all up, to abandon her and the baby. Registering that was wrong on so many levels, I can, however, appreciate that he was young and he made a mistake. Could I have lived with that knowledge if we'd found out together that he was Jody's father? Well, maybe, I don't know. But this means Graeme was also seeing her, sleeping with her at the same time as Paul; is that possible? I know Paul and Graeme were inseparable, but I can't believe Paul wouldn't have considered this possibility if he had known Graeme was sleeping with her at the same time. No, when Paul started off with his subterfuge, Jody wasn't on the scene, and he wouldn't have anticipated that Jody would have submitted a DNA sample and then posted her test results in the hope that she would find her father to then exact her revenge.

Jody said her mother had told her that her pregnancy was the result of a one-night stand; was that a reference to Graeme? Was he the one-night stand? Or was she using that one-night stand line with Jody to hide what Paul did, mask it, and make it more palatable somehow? Or did her mother genuinely believe Graeme was the real father but desperately wanted it to be Paul?

'Are you OK, Kate?' Linda asks.

'To be honest, I'm not sure; I don't know.'

'Would you like to take a short break before we continue?'

'Continue?'

'Yes, we have some further information to share with you,' Fisk adds.

I turn from Linda to Fisk, and he gently nods to me. What more can there be?

'Well then, yes, I suppose we should continue; if there is more to this, then I need to hear it.'

Fisk looks at me, then at D.I. Armitt and D.S. Jackson. 'Gentlemen, could we have the room please?'

'Sir?' Jackson queries and I see him turn to Armitt, who nods at him and then tips his head towards the door, indicating they are to leave the room. 'But Sir?' Jackson protests in the submissive realisation he is out-ranked in the room. But why does he want to stay?

I look back to Fisk and then Linda, 'What is going on?'

Linda takes a deep breath. 'We have something further to tell you, something which is very personal and will come as a shock to you.'

The door closes behind the two men leaving the room, and I can hear Jackson complaining to Armitt as they walk away. Fisk stands and walks from behind his desk, occupying Armitt's now vacant seat. He looks past me to Linda first and then back to me.

'Mrs Hunter, when entering your DNA profile into our police system to run the DNA checks against your half-siblings and Mr Oglesby, a red flag appeared on our screen.'

'A red flag? What red flag? What does that mean?'

Fisk raises his eyebrows slightly toward Linda.

He continues, 'It seems when Mr Hunter and Mr Oglesby were both working in the London area, they both frequented, sorry, that's not quite the right word, they both visited fertility clinics to leave sperm donations for cash payment. It was quite a common practice then, given the assured promise of anonymity.'

'Yes, I recall Paul saying something about that.'

'Well, as you can imagine, those donations were used in subsequent fertility treatments.'

'Yes, I am aware of that also; that is how my half-siblings and I were conceived, well, save for Jody, it seems. We were the result of treatments with couples who were struggling to conceive children of their own.'

I see Fisk flick a quick look at Linda, and I continue.

'I know about my past, my origins. My mother and father have told me about the clinic; I knew Dad was not my biological father, hence our searching for our donor.'

'Yes, quite. Exactly when did your parents inform you of this?'

'Not that long ago. Ironically, it was as a result of the DNA test I did with NeuvaGen and then being matched with Sarah and Oscar that brought this to light; if we had a common father, then I thought Dad had been unfaithful or something, so I confronted him about it.

Mum and Dad were open with me when I asked them, so I know why my mother and father used the clinic, and I'm OK with that.'

'Yes, your parents have told us that they only recently informed you of this.'

'My parents? You mean you have interviewed them both?'

'Well, yes. We interview any person that may have a bearing on an investigation.'

'And?'

'Well, your mother has been helping us further with our enquiries.'

'What? Is my mum also under investigation? Has she also been arrested with Dad?'

Linda takes hold of my hand, and we look at each other. 'Kate, yes, your mother has been arrested.'

'What? Why?' The fear of their two stories not holding up to questioning and scrutiny, with one or both of them turning on me, has me worried that the police have finally realised it was me who took the shotgun to Paul and that I talked him into using it on himself. This is going to get quite serious for me now, especially as Paul was not my father.

It's Fisk's turn to speak. 'Kate, as a result of the red flag hit on our systems and from further inquiries, we have arrested both your parents. We have something important to share with you.'

So, this isn't about the shotgun. 'What? Why have you arrested my mum?'

'As you know, Duncan Leyden is not your biological father.'

'Yes, I know, but what has that got to do with arresting my mum?'

'Well, Mrs Hunter…it seems that Julia Leyden is also not biologically related to you. Julia Leyden is not your biological mother.'

Did he just say what I thought he said? Mum isn't my mum. I spin my head to look at Linda, her face portraying some kind of sympathetic expression or sorrowful look; I can't interpret what she's trying to exude.

'What? What did he say, Linda? What does he mean?'

'Just that I'm afraid; Mrs Julia Leyden is not your mother.'

'Nonsense, of course my mum is my mum; Mum and Dad told me.'

'No, I'm sorry, Kate. Your real name is… Emily Collins.'

# 71

## Emily (Kate) – Bimpson Remand Centre

It took me a long time to gather myself after finding out the truth of who I am and even longer to pluck up the courage to come and meet Dad to confront him. Dad? Why do I still think of him that way? I must start referring to him as Duncan; he's even further away from being Dad now than ever, and I can not think of him in that light again.

The facts were put down in front of me; copies of police reports and newspaper articles, the extent of the police investigation, the searches that were carried out looking for clues to my disappearance, the excavations looking for my body, the reward that was put up by my grandparents, and then the recriminations, allegations and accusations levelled at my real parents that followed what has now been confirmed as my abduction.

Now I am 'found', the world can see that my real parents, well my biological mother and her husband, were innocent of everything they were accused of and that the unbearable shame and pressure wrought on them was unfounded; well, the accusations of infanticide anyway; there remains the question of culpability for not taking proper care of me, leaving me alone to be taken in the first place without a trace of my disappearance; but losing a child was punishment enough in the eyes of the law.

So, I agreed to come here today to talk with him, Duncan. I need to know everything before I get on the plane to be reunited with my real mother.

This small room is simple and basic, just what you'd expect in a place such as this. I was unsure at first when I was told he wanted to meet me, to tell me what happened, to allow him to 'explain'. Explain; really? As though my abduction was just some everyday occurrence that simply happened, but as he is only willing to tell me, it left me no choice; I had to come here to hear it from him.

Naturally, the police wanted me to do this, but the specialists I've been talking with provided mixed opinions; some said it would be good for me to know everything for my healing process, while others said it could trigger unknown issues buried deeply within me that I'm not yet aware of.

But I have my opinion. It's my life; I want to know, and I want to own it again.

The door opens, and he walks in, wearing a plain grey tracksuit, looking older, tired, and visibly much thinner than the last time I saw him.

'Hello, Kate.'

'No. It's Emily. Kate never existed; Kate is a fiction.'

'I'm sorry, but Kate does exist.'

'You're sorry for what? My name, my abduction, all the events that followed. What? What is it you are sorry for?'

'Yes. All of it, I suppose, well, most of it.'

He sits on the chair opposite me, looking at me without any tangible shred of remorse evident.

'Well, I didn't come here for an apology; I came here to listen to what you have to say, nothing more, nothing less, then we'll never see each other again.'

'What I have to say is important, Kate.'

'OK, well, I need to leave soon, so what do you want to tell me?'

'I, we, want you to know we both love you dearly and that we never intended for you to find out the way you did.'

'I bet you didn't. You stole a baby from a pram and took a child from her mother; of course, you never intended for me to find out.'

'No, we did, just not like this. We have explained everything in writing, in a sealed letter held with our solicitors to be given to you at the Will reading of whichever of us passed last. We always wanted you to know the truth; how we used the Letona Pro clinic to try, but we couldn't conceive, and of our meeting them at the clinic and our concern that they weren't good enough to be parents, and so we had to step in to give you what they couldn't.'

'Nonsense.'

'No, it's true. I will send instructions to my solicitor to release the letter to you to prove we always intended to let you know the truth.'

'Well, if you always intended me to find out, why all the lies about the clinic, about you being the supportive man to her after accepting you couldn't father a child, and her wanting to have her own baby? You had an opportunity then to explain it all when I confronted you about my DNA results. But no, you already had another deception established, a script prepared in case I stumbled on something related to parentage. I bet you had different stories planned for whatever unfolded.'

'No, Kate. We couldn't tell you then. You must accept that if you became aware then you would have reported us to the police, and we would have been arrested; then the three of us forcibly separated for a very long time. You do see that, don't you? We had to remain and continue as a family.'

'And what of my real parents? By the time I would have found out the truth, they would, more than likely, have already passed away. Did you think of that? Did you consider that I would have been robbed of the opportunity to reunite with them?'

'The thought occurred to us, but you were the most precious thing in our lives, and we had to put the three of us first.'

'No, what you did was to put you two first. I can't believe we are having this conversation.' I can't get him to see the wholly selfish and wrong attitude they adopted; it's like trying to cut through steel with a wooden knife; I'm not making any impression on him at all.

'Were you not loved Kate? Did you want or need anything that was denied to you? We were the perfect parents to you. We doted on you; we gave you everything you asked for or needed, far more than you would have received if you had stayed with them.'

'If I'd have stayed with them? You don't see it, do you? They were my parents. This was not a life choice I made; don't try to make it out to be anything other than you and her abducting me.'

'Please don't refer to your mother as "her"; she is your mother, Mum, and she loves you.'

'No! No! I'm not having that.' I check myself; I must try to remain as calm as possible; I want to get something out of this other than rage and anger. Hearing him say these words without any genuine remorse or regret is mind-blowing. The specialist reports forwarded to me concluded they both harbour sociopathic tendencies and antisocial personality disorders, but both have the distinct rarity of supporting each other and the ability to act out for mutual gain. It's been explained to me that she does love me in her own way; they both do, but their love or their belief does not make their actions in any way acceptable or excusable. I need that letter from him; I presume it will be so much more powerful and persuasive than a confession if ever it will be needed in court.

'So, that's it? All you wanted to tell me was that you were going to come clean one day, absolving yourselves from the grave.'

'I wouldn't put it quite like that, Kate. No, I wanted you to know you were always loved, still loved, and always will be.'

My deep sigh is an outward sign of my frustration and desire to put all this behind me. He keeps calling me Kate; he must know it grates on me.

He leans across the table, moving closer to me, indicating I should do the same, but I don't want to; I don't want to be any closer to him than I am right now. But he keeps indicating for me to move in toward him, nodding his head slightly, saying something so quiet I can't pick it up, so I lean forward until we are merely inches apart.

Whispering, barely audible, he continues, 'I know it was you, Kate. I know you took my shotgun and gave it to Paul, and I understand why you did it.'

This startles me, but I can't react as I know this is being recorded on CCTV. She, Julia, must have told him.

'This is our little secret, Kate. We won't let the police know about what you did.'

'Why would you do that? Knowing that neither of you did it, why would you say you did it?' I whisper back to him.

'At first, I thought it was Mum, I wanted to protect her and you and stop the police looking deeper into the three of us. But then, we spoke briefly before she was arrested and well, as I keep saying, it's because we love you; we still want the best for you. We're going to prison anyway now, so why not keep this secret and do this for you?'

So, they both know the truth. Will they hold this over me or try to play games with me? This is unsettling, but what can I do about it? Nothing. Then again, I have the upper hand here; if they do try to leverage something for themselves using this information, I'll just deny it; after all, which of us is going to be more believable? I pull back from him, observing the small, smug smile on his face. I'll let him have that if that's what it takes to remain a secret.

'Look. I have to leave now; I have a plane to catch in a few hours. You will send me that letter; I want to believe you.' Just saying it makes me feel sick deep down.

'Of course I will; you can trust me, you know. Are you going on a holiday?'

'No.'

'Or, maybe running away?'

'No. In fact, I'm flying to America to meet my mother, my real mother. She hasn't long left with us.' Instantly, I'm annoyed with myself; I didn't have to tell him that; why did I just share that with him?

'Oh, I'm so sorry to hear she's unwell.'

I don't know how to respond to this; I am truly lost for words. It's like his politeness is trying to coat over their barbaric actions of the past twenty-odd years. His detachment from reality is unbelievable. This is the man I called Dad, a man I admired, loved and held dear. Worried the rising nausea is going to engulf me, I stand, pushing the chair back slightly, and hear the door behind me unlocking from the other side. As I turn to leave, he says something quietly, but I don't look back, I won't look back. I'm done now. I never want to see him again.

# 72

## Kate – En Route to Heathrow

Locking up what is now my house and leaving the keys with a neighbour didn't stir any emotions in me; it's just a collection of bricks and timber and no longer a home anymore. The taxi taking me to Heathrow pulls away, and I don't have the urge to look back at the house or street or anything; my focus is on looking forward.

I didn't think I could do that, talk Paul into taking his own life, but as I spoke to him, it became obvious that this was the only way out for him and for me when he thought he was my biological father. I'm sure now that I couldn't have lived with him anyway after finding out about what he had done to Jody's mother, especially after finding out how he cheated his lifelong best friend, Graeme, to the point it led to his murder, but what became the biggest issue for me was how easy he found it to deceive me and how gullible I was in blindly trusting what he said to me. He made a fool out of me, made my love for him a lever he could use to mask what he was really doing in the background.

Now I look back at him and his life and the choices he made, it feels to me that he must have had narcissistic tendencies or traits; it was all about him, and he didn't seem to care how he got what he wanted, so long as he got it. He had no consideration for what hurt or damage he was inflicting on others, especially those close to him, those who loved him, and whom he supposedly loved back.

I knew he had bequeathed something to Lauren in his Will, and I honestly thought it was a token of the love that he had for her in the past, but now I think the reality is it was probably because he knew he wouldn't need the money anymore and he wanted everyone to talk of him in a good way, even after he was gone; to keep the myth of Paul being an angel going.

I can't call them Mum and Dad anymore; it even takes an effort to refer to them as Julia and Duncan. Taking Duncan's shotgun was easy enough, but I should have thought it through a little better; in hindsight, the police were always going to connect the gun to Duncan, which could lead them to me. Me; the person who wanted Paul dead and provided him with the means and the mindset to do it. But then again, would a narcissist take their own life? I suppose they might if they were about to be uncovered and exposed for all the world to see, as it's the last bit of control they would have. But then again, they would probably revel at being in the spotlight and having their fifteen minutes of fame during their public exposure. Anyway, it's all done now, and I can look forward to my future, so long as Julia and Duncan keep to their beliefs and their twisted loyalty to their shared love for each other and for me, a love I can no longer reciprocate. However, I know I will have to play them carefully for fear of their rejection of me and informing the police of what I really did. "Three can keep a secret, if two of them are dead" rings true, but there's little opportunity of realising this position, especially when the two in question are locked up at His Majesty's pleasure and I have no way of getting to them. All I can do is rely on their loyalty and discretion to each other and to me, that they will not betray it and tell the police what really happened.

I received the confession letter from Duncan's solicitors as he described; it was in an old, faded envelope, dated twenty years ago, addressed to me in Duncan's handwriting and marked "Confidential - addressee only", sealed with one of those old wax sealing stamps. I've not opened it yet; I've decided to keep it safe and secure and only bring its existence to light if the court case is not going the way it should, as using it against them could indicate my loathing for them and possibly trigger them into confessing their lies and telling what I did. This is a piece of secret information I'm going to keep to myself as a future insurance policy.

Following Paul's death, the police naturally became involved. The police needed to use Paul's DNA for identification purposes; then, coupled with Jody making her claims about Graeme being our biological father and the police double checking all our DNA, it led to me finding out who I am and to the real truth of what had happened all those years ago.

Now I have Paul's business interests, his house, and most of his savings and investments to look forward to when all the official paperwork is resolved; I'm going to be very comfortable from a financial perspective and totally free of the bonds of marriage. This comfort will allow me to do whatever I want, whenever I want, and, importantly, with whomever I want. The months following our wedding were turbulent at times, confusing, and ultimately revelatory, and out of it all, I have the complete freedom I never thought I actually wanted, but now that I have it, I'm loving it. The lover, the wife and now widow status have all been worth it.

‘Off for a holiday, are we?’ the driver asks in a strong Birmingham accent.

‘No, a business trip to the States,’ I reply, pulling out my mobile phone and hoping he’ll notice I’m not in a talkative mood.

# 73

## Epilogue

## Kate – Flight to Texas

Leaving Heathrow and climbing to cruising altitude, we break through thick, white clouds and level off, the aircraft turning to chase down the setting sun. I'm glad of the peace and quiet this nearly eleven-hour flight will give me and the opportunity, without interruption or distraction, to think and plan what I'm going to say to my mother. My real mother.

She's been informed that I'm on my way to her. Apparently, on hearing the news I'd been found alive, she fainted, and then, on coming around, she was not sure she wanted to meet me given her condition. We've not spoken yet, but we will soon; I've been communicating through an intermediary, a professional, helping my mother come to terms with this event after everything she has been through; the shock to her on hearing I was still alive would have been immense.

Over the years, the file on my disappearance was never really closed, but there were plenty who thought I was already dead, murdered, my body disposed of, never to be found. Since the news broke, the media coverage has been frenzied and chaotic, and this shiny, pressurised plane has provided me with temporary respite from all that attention. The subterfuge we planned so that none of the press would follow me to the airport, that they wouldn't know I was leaving the country, was necessary, if for nothing else, to protect my sanity. I've been front page and TV news since my identity was leaked, and on hearing I was travelling to see my mother, it would have all been stoked up again. But I'm not naïve; I expect it will all start again when I land in Houston or not long after; the intermediary has already indicated the growing interest in the US and of the news agencies trying to get to speak with my mother.

This is the first time I've travelled business class; I thought I owed it to myself to spend some of Paul's bequeathed fortune on me. And why not? I did think about flying first class, but the cost for just this journey of eleven hours, I didn't think, merited the price increase from business class. Business class is still a big upgrade for me from regular economy class, and I'll get the chance to sleep some of the way in a pod bed with a degree of privacy.

Everything in my life has changed over the last few weeks; I never thought I'd be flying to the US to meet a complete stranger who is my actual mother.

So, this me time during the flight allows me the opportunity to write down my thoughts, consider what I want to say to her, what I don't, and which questions to ask, including the big one. That is a question I'm still unsure I want to hear the answer to, or even if she'll tell me.

Her life must have been awful. From archive searches in the local library and on the internet, the news articles were all pretty damning on her and her husband. Their neighbours, locals and others from around the country and overseas soon started to channel their frustrations and anger on them, accusing them of killing me and disposing of me in some way. The police thoroughly investigated my disappearance and looked very closely at my parents. After months of interviews, searches, and investigations, they could find no shred of evidence to indicate I'd been poorly treated by my mother and her husband, but that wasn't good enough for the baying masses. Maybe things would have turned out differently if some of that time and resource had been channelled on looking for an abductor.

I'll never get to meet him, my dad; he died just over nine years ago now. His death, the result of a frenzied attack with a kitchen knife in his own home just outside Crockett in Houston County, shocked everyone.

The psychological evaluations carried out on my mother after his death placed great emphasis on my abduction and the stress and strain my parents were living with, not just from the fear of their new neighbours ever finding out and hounding them but also the everyday tension between the two of them. He blamed her for leaving me in my pram in the rear garden while she chatted at the front door with a friend, and although it was a joint decision to start afresh in a new country, he never put any effort or invested any time with her in their new start.

She tried. She wanted another baby, but he wasn't interested. Apparently, he portrayed an image of a loving, supporting husband, helpful with neighbours, supportive of local events and all those good things that make for a community spirit, but behind the scenes, he was horrible to her. What I cannot understand is why. I wasn't his offspring; he wasn't my natural father; that, as it turns out, was Graeme via one of the clinics he made donations with. So why did he treat her so badly? Was it the pain and humiliation, the aggression, the allegations and torment he, they, faced after I was abducted? Or was it the thought of going back to another fertility clinic and her conceiving another man's baby again?

So, will I have the nerve to ask her the big question? Why did she kill him?

What triggered her to brutally slay him at home? Will she reveal all her secrets to me?

Waiting for me at George Bush Intercontinental Airport will be the intermediary, accompanied by an interested party who wants a conversation with me with a view to writing a book about the events of my life. An accomplished author, he is experienced in writing about true life events, having suffered significant trauma himself in recent years. He's English, moving out to the States a couple of years ago, initially during the making of the movie of his autobiography and thereafter looking into other projects; and now he is interested in my story. I've read his book, "Loved and Loathed; A Life Lived", and I can see the benefit that the release from unburdening himself of the truths and lies that surrounded him provided and how his decision to document it in a book and then a movie, allowed him to make that significant leap forward in his own life; the want to have a future and live again, one that he is in control of.

He's helped several people since coming to terms with their own events, and he's received some serious recognition and acclaim for his work; he sounds like a very interesting person, and I'm looking forward to meeting him and spending some time together.

What I'm not looking forward to is meeting my mother on death row.

Your Secret

# ALSO BY MARK HURST

# The Lies

**When Samantha and David decide to have a night out separately with their friends, events overtake them, and the lies lead them down a path of destruction.**

To everyone else, it looked like Samantha and David had the perfect life. From meeting at university and falling in love to starting a successful business together, they made a great team. However, as everybody knows, appearances can be deceptive…

That one night out changed everything between them and things would never be the same again; not unless they could face up to their own truths and correct the wrongs.

Neither thought they could become the people they became and do the things they did. But that's just what happens when two people wronged become consumed by a need for the truth, for justice, and ultimately, for the price to be paid.

If either of them had let it go, it could have all been so different – but neither of them could.

***The fast paced and gripping debut novel that will keep you turning the pages as you try to answer the question yourself – would you have let it go?***

# Lies Never Die

**In the sequel to 'The Lies', Samantha and Blade continue playing the game of truth versus lie, reality against perception.**

Dame Samantha Walsh, now a world icon, a person of respect, wealth and charity, flawless and untouchable in equal measure, continues to grow her empire on her terms. Her enormous wealth and reach bring about power and control never before contemplated, opening up new interests and outcomes for her, both inside and outside legal and moral boundaries.

Blade, recently released from prison, needing to re-integrate with society, has his path to follow to find the truth. He needs work, he needs income, and what better way to fund finding the truth than by taking paid work doing what he is good at, what he was trained to do?

The race is on to find out the truth of what happened to their loved ones. Who will find out first, who will win?

***Fast paced and gripping, 'Lies Never Die' is the sequel to the bestselling debut book 'The Lies' from crime and psychological thriller author Mark Hurst.***

# My Partner's Friend

***Should you trust the people closest to you?***

A well-deserved weekend away in the English countryside, a time to catch up with friends and have fun. Martin and his wife Tanya, meet up with friends Melissa and her husband Craig, in a luxury barn conversion outside the small village of Brambleside, in the tranquil Lake District in the north of England.

Four close friends, each with very different professional careers, enjoy their collective time together, reconnecting after Martin's recovery from a recent illness. Within forty-eight hours, two are dead, one is unconscious in the hospital, and the fourth is charged with double murder and attempted murder.

***With unexpected twists and revelations, who can be trusted? Is everything as it seems?***
***Would you trust your partner more than your friend?***

To accompany "Your Secret"; these stories converging to bring two destinies together…

## ***A note from the author***

*Thank you for reading my book, I hope you found it entertaining. If you would like to pass a comment to me, please do so via email to mark@markhurstauthor.com and I will reply.*

*You may have already downloaded my FREE shorter story "The Last Woman", but if not, it is still available, please visit my web site at www.woodedhillbooks.com and click on the download link.*

## ***About the author***

*Born and raised in Bolton, UK, a true Lancastrian and a child of the sixties, Mark finally decided to pursue his passion for storytelling after a long and eventful career in a completely different industry, that sometimes involved more fiction than fact!*

*Mark entered construction at the age of eighteen and has been involved with hundreds of large civil engineering projects for the last 40 years as a Civil Engineer and Surveyor, Estimator and Commercial Director, working in various far-flung locations such as Hong Kong, Scandinavia and Wigan.*

*Mark has a passion for reading legal, crime and psychological thrillers and enjoys firsthand accounts of military and espionage events. When he's not reading and writing, he can be found watching the History Channel.*

*Married with two grown children and four grandchildren, his son Daniel convinced him it was time to start committing some of his own stories to print ... and there are a few. Drawing on his own life experiences, Mark weaves them into his stories but with a twist ... it all could have happened.*

***Why Wooded Hill Books?***

*The origin of the surname Hurst – ancient Anglo-Saxon topographic name for someone who lived near a wooded hill or thicket.*

PLEASE KEEP IN TOUCH

***Facebook.com/markhurstauthor***

**www.woodedhillbooks.com**

Front cover design by 100Covers

***Wooded Hill Books Limited***

Printed in Great Britain
by Amazon

55837958R00187